"Do you like it here at Manresa House?"

He watched her lips as they parted. She had beautiful lips, lips that begged to be kissed.

Swiftly he drew back. Kissing the governess was the quickest way to send her running, even if he did detect a spark of something that looked like desire in her eyes when she glanced at him. By her account Miss Salinger had been raised to follow the rules of society, and those rules were very clear.

"Yes, Lord Westcroft, I enjoy my work very much." It was a measured answer, crafted not to give too much away.

"Good."

Silence fell between them. Matthew knew he should excuse himself, return to his neglected accounts and maps, but he wanted to stretch this moment just a little longer.

"Join me for a drink," he said, midway between a request and an order.

"I'm not sure..."

"One drink, Miss Salinger. What could be the harm in that?"

She swallowed, her eyes darting up to meet his, and he knew in that moment she could read his darkest thoughts. Slowly she nodded, and Matthew knew if he was a gentleman he would withdraw the offer, make it easier for them both to walk away. Instead he offered her his arm, waiting as she hesitated for only a second before slipping her hand into the crook of his elbow and moving to his side.

Author Note

I've always been drawn to books where the characters are pushed off course from the lives they are supposed to have, needing to adapt and modify their behavior and expectations. It was this very broad theme that I had in mind when first plotting *The Brooding Earl's Proposition*. I wanted to take a society lady and put her into a scenario where she has lost every material possession and has to rely on her intellect and education to get by. Selina is the remarkable heroine who was born from this, a woman who knows her own mind despite being forced from the life she was brought up in.

There were not many respectable avenues open to young women of good birth who found themselves in hard times during the Regency period. Becoming a governess was certainly one of the better options, but can you imagine living a life suspended halfway between the family and the servants, not quite fitting in with either? It may have been respectable but it would often have been lonely, too. This idea of loneliness was the second spark I needed for *The Brooding Earl's Proposition* to become fully formed. What better gift for a lonely governess than a gentleman who knows barely anyone else in the country?

I hope you enjoy *The Brooding Earl's Proposition* and the windy North York moors.

LAURA MARTIN

The Brooding Earl's Proposition

HARLEQUIN
HISTORICAL

HARLEQUIN®
HISTORICAL™

Recycling programs for this product may not exist in your area.

ISBN-13: 978-1-335-50536-1

The Brooding Earl's Proposition

This edition published by arrangement with Harlequin Books S.A.

For questions and comments about the quality of this book, please contact us at CustomerService@Harlequin.com.

Harlequin Enterprises ULC
22 Adelaide St. West, 40th Floor
Toronto, Ontario M5H 4E3, Canada
www.Harlequin.com

Printed in U.S.A.

Laura Martin writes historical romances with an adventurous undercurrent. When not writing, she spends her time working as a doctor in Cambridgeshire, UK, where she lives with her husband. In her spare moments Laura loves to lose herself in a book and has been known to read from cover to cover in a single day when the story is particularly gripping. She also loves to travel—especially to visit historical sites and far-flung shores.

Books by Laura Martin

Harlequin Historical

The Pirate Hunter
Secrets Behind Locked Doors
Under a Desert Moon
A Ring for the Pregnant Debutante
An Unlikely Debutante
An Earl to Save Her Reputation
The Viscount's Runaway Wife
The Brooding Earl's Proposition

Scandalous Australian Bachelors

Courting the Forbidden Debutante
Reunited with His Long-Lost Cinderella
Her Rags-to-Riches Christmas

The Governess Tales

Governess to the Sheikh

Visit the Author Profile page
at Harlequin.com for more titles.

For everyone who has ever read one
of my books, you are the reason I get to
live my dream every single day.

Chapter One

'Five minutes down the drive,' Selina muttered to herself, grimacing as her boots splashed into another puddle. The coachman had refused to take her any closer, instead throwing the cloth bag that contained all her worldly possessions down from the coach and pointing with a crooked finger through the rusted iron gates.

It had been twenty minutes so far, twenty minutes of battling against the wind that whipped at her skirts, twenty minutes of cool drizzle soaking through her cloak. Twenty minutes to really start to regret the decision to travel so far north, to take up a position where she knew no one and where it seemed the weather was unforgiving and the locals unfriendly and suspicious.

As she rounded another bend the house came into view. It was large, with a central section and two sweeping wings jutting out from either side. The façade was of grey stone, weathered and beaten, and looked as though it was in need of some care and attention. Ivy grew up one side, covering the walls and creeping on to the windows.

'Home…' Selina murmured, feeling a sinking dread in her stomach. It didn't look like a home, not one she wanted to live in.

She paused, knowing she had to go forward, but not able to take another step. Perhaps she could go back to London, go back to the agency and see if there were any other suitable positions. Somewhere a little more inviting, somewhere a little less isolated. Her fingers closed around her small purse of coins. Going back to London wasn't an option; all the meagre amount she'd managed to save over the past year had been spent on her coach fare up to north Yorkshire and a new dress in the hope of making a good impression on her employer.

Lord Westcroft. A man she hadn't been able to find much out about no matter how many people she asked.

The rain was getting heavier, the droplets pattering on the hood of her cloak and dripping off the edges. She could delay no longer. It was time to meet the family she would be living with for the next few years.

Selina took a step forward, pulling at her boots that had become a little stuck in the mud where she'd stood still for a few moments. The movement unbalanced her and Selina felt her boots begin to slip. She thrust her arms out, frantically waving them in the hope of regaining her equilibrium, but even before she began to fall she knew it was too late. Her heart lurched in her chest as she felt her feet slip out from underneath her and her body plummeted to the ground.

She landed in the biggest puddle in sight. Bottom first, skirts almost fully submerged. For a second Selina just sat there, unable to believe the coldness of the rainwater that soaked through her skirt. Unable to believe how fast this horrible day had got even worse.

With a shudder she stood, looking down in disbelief at the muddy mess of her clothes. Bedraggled as she was she looked more like a beggar woman than a respectable governess come to take up her position in the house of a peer of the realm.

'Head high, back straight, shoulders down,' Selina said to herself. It was how her late mother had always told her to deport herself. How to look people in the eye, even if they insisted on haughtily looking down at you.

With as much confidence as she could summon she stepped towards the front door, the feeling of being watched making her pause as her hand reached for the heavy iron door knocker. She glanced up, just quickly enough to see two sad faces disappearing from an upstairs window. They'd looked pale, almost ghostly, and Selina wondered if the two little girls she had been employed to look after ever saw the sunshine. With a grimace she eyed the thick clouds above her head. Perhaps this far north they didn't get much sunshine.

Before she could talk herself out of it Selina lifted the heavy iron door knocker and let it fall twice, wincing as the door rattled with the force of the metal. A heavy silence followed, broken only by the splashing of the rain in the puddles behind her.

'What do you want?' a surly old woman asked as she opened the door little more than a crack and peered through. She eyed Selina up and down and shook her head. 'No beggars allowed.'

'I'm not...' Selina's protest was drowned out by the creak of wood as the door was shut firmly in her face. Feeling the first fire of indignation in her stomach, Selina lifted the knocker again, dropping it again and again in quick succession, knowing no servant would ignore such a commotion that could disturb their master.

'Off with you,' the old woman demanded as she opened the door again, reaching out a thin hand to push Selina down the steps.

'What is all this noise?' The deep voice came from somewhere in the darkness beyond the doorway, irritated and impatient.

'I've told her to be gone,' the servant said. 'I've told her no beggars are welcome here.'

Selina opened her mouth to protest, to tell them her true identity, but the swift movement in front of her made her pause. Standing on the threshold, his large figure blocking most of the doorway, was a man she assumed must be Lord Westcroft. He was tall, well built with broad, strong shoulders. His expression was a mixture of irritation and shrewd assessment, but it was his eyes that held her attention. They flicked over her, assessing the mud-splattered dress and windswept visage before coming to meet her own eyes, the attention making Selina feel uncomfortable.

'Give her some food from the kitchen,' he said, his tone authoritative, before turning away.

He'd nearly disappeared back into the darkness before Selina found her voice. 'Lord Westcroft,' she called, her cultured tone causing him to pause where he was.

'Stop bothering the master,' the servant said brusquely. 'Come round to the kitchen door.'

Once again the door started to close in her face, but this time Selina was ready. She stuck her booted foot in the gap just in time, wincing as the heavy oak hit her instep, but determined not to be dismissed again.

'Lord Westcroft,' she said more firmly, 'I'm cold and wet and tired. I understood from the agency that you were *desperate* for a governess, so if you don't want me to turn right around and take the next coach back to London I suggest you invite me in. And point me in the direction of the nearest fire.'

* * *

Matthew felt fear seize him. The woman in front of him didn't look like a governess, with her filthy clothes and windswept hair, but she certainly sounded like one. Her tone was the right combination of commanding and disapproving, and he felt himself stand up just a little straighter as he turned back round. His instinct was to rush towards her, to pull her into the house and tell her in no uncertain terms that she wasn't going anywhere.

He held himself back. Even only a newly titled man knew not to beg, especially in front of the servants.

'Miss Salinger?' he asked, recalling the name in the letter from the agency. A name he'd given heartfelt thanks for after two long months of searching for a governess for the unhappy girls in his care.

'A pleasure to meet you, Lord Westcroft,' the petite woman in front of him said, sounding anything but pleased. He looked at her properly, looking past the mud, and realised that underneath the layer of grime she must have picked up on the journey here her clothes were of fine quality and fitted well. Her skin was clear and bright and her hair, where it peeked out from underneath the hood of her cloak, was windswept but shiny and healthy. He wondered how he could ever have mistaken her for a beggar woman.

'Come through to my study,' he said, motioning down the dingy hallway. 'The fire is roaring and the room warm.'

'Thank you.'

She followed him, her movements stiff, her skirts leaving a wet trail on the floor behind her.

'Governesses looking like beggars, how am I supposed to tell the difference,' he heard Mrs Fellows, the housekeeper he'd inherited along with everything else in this house, mutter.

'Come in, get warm,' Matthew said, watching as Miss Salinger stepped towards the ornate fireplace, seeing the tension begin to seep from her shoulders. For a moment in the hall he'd thought she might carry out her threat, that she might turn around and head straight back to London. He wouldn't really blame her after the welcome she'd received, or after seeing the imposing façade of Manresa House. It wasn't the most inviting of houses or locations, isolated as it was on the edge of the moor.

'I am sorry about my appearance,' Miss Salinger said eventually. 'The coachman refused to bring me past the gates and the driveway was treacherous.' She grimaced as she raised a hand to her head, touching the wispy strands of hair that framed her face. She turned to face him and gave a little half-smile. 'I fell in a puddle.'

As her eyes came up to meet his he felt a jolt pass through his body, a feeling he hadn't experienced for a very long time. Quickly he suppressed it, suppressed the urge to glance over her pretty features and the soft curves of her body. He wouldn't even contemplate jeopardising her role here with an inappropriate look.

'I hope your journey was not too arduous,' he said, wondering how long he needed to make polite conversation before he could usher the new governess up to the nursery and officially hand over the responsibility of his two nieces. It had been a responsibility that had weighed heavily on him these last two months and he could not wait to return to being accountable for no one but himself.

Miss Salinger looked at him, her dark eyes probing his, a hint of a smile on her lips. It was almost as if she could discern his impatience, carefully hidden though it was.

'You are a *very* long way from London,' she said.

'It is your first time in north Yorkshire?'

'Yes.' She shivered, glancing past him and out of the window. 'I'm woefully poorly travelled.'

'You hail from London?'

'Cambridge. Forgive me, Lord Westcroft, it seems as though you have somewhere else you wish to be.'

He frowned, not at the directness of her words, but at how she'd detected his eagerness to usher her upstairs.

'The children are keen to meet you,' he lied smoothly.

At the mention of her new charges he saw something soften in her and a spark light in her eyes.

'Tell me about them,' she said, shrugging off her cloak and looping it over her arm. Underneath the dripping garment she was dressed in a sober grey dress. Something entirely suitable for a governess. It was practical with its dark material and long sleeves, and designed to be as unattractive as possible, but it couldn't entirely hide Miss Salinger's narrow waist or the curve of her hips.

'Priscilla is nine, a quiet, watchful young girl who enjoys reading and music. Theodosia is seven…' He paused, wondering how to sum up his younger niece's character diplomatically. 'She's lively and curious about the world and enjoys being outside.'

'They sound delightful. Have they had much schooling before?'

'A little.' In truth he didn't know. Before his brother's death almost a year ago now he hadn't even been aware he had nieces. The rift in the family had meant communication had been limited to only what was absolutely necessary and his brother hadn't seen the birth of Priscilla and Theodosia as important information. For his part Matthew had enjoyed the freedom, the lack of responsibility.

Not any more, he thought grimly. There was no running away now. He was the Earl, he was guardian to his nieces, he had responsibility for the estate and all the people who lived on it.

'Let me take you to meet them, then Mrs Fellows will show you your room,' he said, reaching forward and taking the still-dripping cloak from Miss Salinger's arms. As he did so his hand brushed against hers, the softness of her skin a contrast to his still-calloused hands. She pulled away quickly, her eyes flashing up to meet his, a wariness about her that made him take a step back. 'This way.'

He deposited the cloak in the hall, leading Miss Salinger up the sweeping staircase to the first floor and then up a smaller, much less grand staircase to the second floor where the nursery was situated. She walked a couple of steps behind him, her hands held demurely together, her eyes moving to take everything in. There was a quiet energy about her, an energy this house sorely needed.

He paused outside the nursery, steeling himself for what scene he might find inside.

'Go away,' a flat voice called out as he pushed open the door.

The nursery was tidy, eerily so, and the two girls sitting side by side on the window seat were both looking out the steamy windows at the rain.

'Girls, this is Miss Salinger, your new governess.'

Theodosia began to turn round, interest on her face, but a quick tug on the arm from her sister stopped the movement. Matthew felt a bubble of irritation welling up. He knew the girls were grieving, knew it would take them a long time to feel anything approaching happiness again, but rudeness was still unacceptable.

'Girls,' he chided. 'Come and greet your new governess.'

Slowly both girls got to their feet, Priscilla flashing him a dark look before tossing her blonde hair back over her shoulders and looking defiantly at the mud-spattered governess.

'Good afternoon,' Miss Salinger said. 'It is a pleasure to meet you both, Lady Priscilla, Lady Theodosia.'

'Did you walk here?' Priscilla asked haughtily. 'In this rain?'

'Only from the end of the drive,' Miss Salinger said, her calm demeanour making Matthew want to step back out of the room and hand things over to her immediately.

'That was foolish.'

'It was necessary,' the governess said with a shrug. 'And a little mud never hurt anyone.'

Priscilla wrinkled up her nose, but Matthew caught her younger sister trying to stifle a smile.

'I look forward to getting to know you girls,' Miss Salinger said. 'Tomorrow we can decide what you would like to learn.'

'We can choose?' Theodosia stepped forward with shining eyes. 'I want to learn archery—all the bravest fighters can shoot a bow.'

'I'm not sure archery is quite what Miss Salinger meant.'

Theodosia pouted, but out of the corner of his eye he saw the governess wink at the little girl. Matthew felt himself relax. *He* might not be able to manage his two nieces, but it seemed that Miss Salinger was more than up to the job. It would allow him to recede into the background, to spend the next few weeks sorting out the house and the estate. Then, when the girls had settled with Miss Salinger he would be able to escape back to India, back to the life where he belonged.

Chapter Two

Selina pulled the comb through her hair with a satisfied sigh. Her initial welcome at Manresa House might have left much to be desired, but when she'd been shown to her room the housekeeper had already set the maids to filling up a large bathtub with steaming water ready for Selina to wash the mud from her skin and hair before dinner.

Quickly she pinned back the still-damp locks and checked her appearance in the small mirror. She looked pale, tired from the travelling, and the face that stared back at her was thinner than the one she imagined, the one she remembered.

Pulling herself from the melancholic thoughts of how her life used to be, she stood, smoothed down her dress and headed downstairs for dinner. Tonight she would be dining with Lord Westcroft, a chance to discuss the girls' education and find out a little more about them. Every other night no doubt she would take her meals in the nursery with the children.

Selina had learned to walk quietly this past year, always conscious that she was in someone else's house, never wanting to draw attention to herself. As she made her way to the drawing room she paused just outside the door. Lord Westcroft was already there, standing at one of the large mahogany tables, bent over something that was laid out on it. She watched him for a moment, taking in his absolute concentration, the small frown between his eyebrows as he traced a finger over the paper.

Suddenly he looked up, his eyes coming to meet hers immediately. Selina felt the heat begin to rise in her cheeks at having been caught staring, but forced a smile on to her face. She saw his eyes flicker over her and brought a hand up instinctively to her throat, a gesture of protection she'd become used to needing this past year. Not all her employers had kept the distance they should have.

'Miss Salinger,' he said, his expression unreadable.

'Good evening,' Selina said, dipping into a low curtsy. She walked into the room, catching sight of the document he'd been so engrossed in. It was a large and well-drawn map, with different colours denoting different continents and looped, ornate writing depicting the oceans. Open next to it on the table was a smaller, tattered book of maps and he seemed to be comparing the two. 'I hope I'm not disturbing you.'

'I have time for dinner,' he said, his tone brisk. It was clear that he saw the next hour as a duty, a time to hand over responsibility for his wards, but then he would be keen to return to whatever work he saw as more important.

Selina adjusted her stance. Direct and to the point she could do. They both obviously wanted the same thing: to ensure the welfare of the two grieving little girls upstairs. If Lord Westcroft did not have time for small talk, then she would use the time over dinner to find out as much about her charges as possible and perhaps a little about the man responsible for them.

'Shall we?' He offered her his arm.

Selina hesitated, unused to being shown such respect. In her last position as governess to the son of Lord and Lady Gilchrist she had been treated as a servant, always pushed into the shadows, never spoken to directly.

Carefully she placed her hand on his forearm and let him lead her into the dining room. It was grand, but decaying like the rest of the house, a gloomy room barely lit by the candles dotted around the edges. Selina felt herself stiffen as Lord Westcroft's arm brushed against her as he drew out her chair, but a quick glance at his face showed her the action wasn't deliberate.

As soon as they'd sat down a footman appeared carrying two plates, setting them down carefully so as not to spill the thin soup that lay inside.

'I should tell you a little about Priscilla and Theodosia's background,' Lord Westcroft said as he lifted his spoon. It was straight to the point and Selina felt a little ripple of irritation. The man could not be more eager to be rid of her. Quickly she suppressed it, reminding herself this was what she wanted, a courteous but formal relationship with her employer.

'Please.'

'I do not profess to know the girls well,' he said stiffly. 'Their mother died two years ago. Their father, my late brother, died nine months ago. I was in India at the time and the journey back to England took several months, so I have only been in residence with the children for just shy of nine weeks.'

Long enough to get to know two children if he had wanted to.

'They have been through a lot,' Selina said, thinking of the defiant little girls, one in particular, sharp and suspicious. It was only to be expected after losing both parents in such a short time.

'Indeed. They are grieving, but they need boundaries. I'm afraid before I arrived back in England they were looked after by an elderly female relative who let them run wild. They have not coped well now that they are expected to behave like young ladies rather than animals.'

'Children,' Selina corrected quietly.

'Excuse me?'

'Well, they're children, not young ladies. They will become young ladies all too soon, but at the moment they are children.'

Lord Westcroft looked at her long and hard for half a minute before giving a dismissive wave of his hand.

'Even children have to have certain levels of expected behaviour.'

Selina inclined her head. It was true, children thrived when there were boundaries, routines. As long as those boundaries and routines were accompanied by love and praise and positivity.

'How would you like me to address them? Should I use their title all the time, or just their names?'

'They're children. I think their names will suffice,' he said with a little nod of his head. 'You will instruct the children in mathematics, history and music.'

She waited, but no more was forthcoming.

'How about art? And literature? The natural world?'

Lord Westcroft looked at her with a steely expression on his face. 'I do not care how you occupy the girls for the entire day, as long as they come out of it with a decent basic education.'

'An education for what?' Selina asked mildly.

'What do you mean?'

'Well, what I teach them depends on what you hope

their futures will look like. If you merely wish the girls to catch the eye of the most eligible gentlemen in the district, then they will need to focus on music, dancing and managing household accounts. If you wish them to have a different future, then the other subjects will become more important.'

Silence stretched out between them and Selina knew she had gone too far. It was only her first day and she risked being thrown out, sent back to London in disgrace. She'd just wanted to provoke the steely Lord Westcroft, to probe into the hard façade. To get him to see that the little girls upstairs weren't the inconvenience he so obviously thought they were, that they were living, breathing humans with dreams and ambitions of their own.

'Let's start with mathematics, history and music,' he said eventually. 'Once they have mastered those subjects they can be free to pursue other areas of interest.' It was a measured reply, calm and diplomatic, and Selina felt a flicker of respect for the man in front of her. He'd risen to her challenge and deflected it.

The next course was brought in by the footman, succulent slices of chicken with an assortment of vegetables.

'I shall see the girls every Sunday afternoon in my study for a report on their progress.'

'Once a week?'

'Yes. On a Sunday.'

'Surely you will want to see them more than that? To interact with them, to get to know them.'

'They are children, Miss Salinger. And they have you.'

'But I'm just a governess, someone paid to look after them. You're family.'

Lord Westcroft put down his fork, letting the silence stretch out between them.

'Before the letter arrived notifying me of my brother's

death I had no idea Priscilla and Theodosia existed,' he said quietly. 'They do not know me. We might be relatives by blood, but we have no shared experiences, nothing to bond us.'

'But—' Selina started, but Lord Westcroft held up an authoritative hand to stop her.

'I will see them once a week on a Sunday, to ensure they are learning what they should and their welfare is being taken care of. The rest of the time they are in your hands, Miss Salinger.'

His tone was so stony, his words so final that Selina didn't try to object again. She wondered at the rift that must have torn this family apart to have resulted in Lord Westcroft not even being told of his nieces' existence.

'I shall do as you wish, Lord Westcroft,' Selina said quietly. That and so much more.

Silently Matthew padded across the hallway. On his feet he was wearing only his socks, having long ago divested himself of his shoes in a bid to get more comfortable. The house was quiet, eerily so, with just the occasional creaking of the wooden windows to add to the effect. Outside somewhere an owl hooted, a dark shadow streaming past the window as it flew through the night.

Matthew felt unsettled. He'd felt unsettled for the past nine weeks. It was being back here, at Manresa House, the one place he'd vowed never to return to. Every room had a memory he would rather forget, every nook and cranny threatened to transport him back to a time when he was a vulnerable young lad. If he had his wish, he would have the building knocked to the ground, destroying the stone it was made from and the memories it held inside.

'It's only a building,' he reminded himself, muttering

under his breath. He couldn't destroy the house, no matter how much he wanted to. It was a place of familiarity for Priscilla and Theodosia, a place filled with memories for his two nieces. Hopefully happier memories than his own. He wouldn't take their home from them as well as everything else.

Silently he opened the door to the library, feeling the tension seep out of him as he always did when he entered this vault of a room. It had been his own special place as a child, with neither his parents nor his older brother caring to peruse the thousands of books housed on the shelves, his sanctuary. He stepped inside, feeling the smile form on his lips as his eyes danced across the familiar titles on the heavy leather spines. Sleep might be difficult to come by, but at least he would not grow bored.

Matthew reached out and slipped a book from the shelves, gripping it tightly just as he heard a quiet cough from directly behind him. For a second his heart squeezed in his chest, every muscle in his body clenched and primed for action. It took another second for the rational part of his brain to calm his instincts and stop him from spinning round and lashing out. Here he was safe. It was highly unlikely he was about to be pounced upon by a man-eating tiger or attacked by a deadly snake.

Slowly he turned, fixing his expression into a mild frown.

'Please forgive me, Lord Westcroft,' Miss Salinger said, her cheeks flushing. 'I didn't mean to startle you. I thought everyone else in the house asleep and hoped you wouldn't mind me borrowing a book to read.'

Of course it was the governess. She'd been in residence for a grand total of seven hours and already she was becoming a thorn in his side.

Unfair, he silently chastised himself.

'Do you often walk around strange houses in the dead of night without a candle?' he asked, his voice low.

'N-no,' she stuttered.

He felt a perverse pleasure at her discomfort and allowed himself to watch as her lips searched for her next words. They were full lips, rosy even in the darkness, lips no doubt many men had fantasised about over the years.

'I was taught never to bring a lit flame into a library,' she said.

'Who taught you that, Miss Salinger?' It was a rule he observed himself, but he doubted his new governess grew up in a household grand enough to have a library.

'My father.'

When she did not elaborate he nodded slowly. 'Sensible man. Did he have any views on the best time of day to visit a library?'

'There is sufficient moonlight to see by,' Miss Salinger said, raising her chin a notch.

As she spoke the moon emerged from behind the thick clouds and shone in through the windows. As well as illuminating the books it reflected off the white of Miss Salinger's nightgown that peeked out from under the loosely tied dressing gown.

Matthew couldn't help but look. He was a man. A flawed man. A man who would never take advantage of a woman in his employ, but who couldn't entirely avert his eyes when the moonlight made the cotton of a woman's nightgown appear almost sheer over her body. He could only see a sliver of nightgown, but it was enough.

He swallowed. Blinked. She was an attractive young woman, tall with a body full of soft curves. This evening her hair was loose, dark locks cascading over her shoulders, framing a pretty face.

'Indeed there is,' he murmured.

She shifted slightly, making the nightgown ripple against her skin, hinting at the curves underneath.

Matthew closed his eyes, counted to five. He had been too long without a woman.

'Did you find what you were looking for?' As he spoke he moved to one side so he wouldn't be looking directly at her.

'Not yet. I was just browsing your titles. It really is a fine library.'

He murmured agreement, his eyes seeking out her lips again as she spoke. They were remarkably pink. Remarkably kissable.

As soon as the thought sprang into his mind he dismissed it firmly. Miss Salinger was far too important to even consider a dalliance. He couldn't risk anything that might scare her off. Nine weeks he'd waited for a governess, nine weeks of emotional torture as the two little girls upstairs withdrew further into themselves.

'Perhaps I can help you find something,' he suggested, deciding his best course of action would be to hurry Miss Salinger on her way back to her bedroom. Far out of his line of sight. 'What were you hoping to find?'

'A classic, perhaps. The *Iliad* or the *Odyssey*.'

A woman of fine taste in literature. Not that he should be surprised that a governess was well read.

'Here…' he reached up to the shelves a little to his left and plucked two books from their places '…the *Iliad* and the *Odyssey*. You can decide later which you wish to read first.'

'Thank you,' Miss Salinger said with a smile. Her fingers brushed his as he handed the books over, soft skin against his callused hands, and he had to fight the urge to pull away quickly, pretending instead not to notice the contact.

'Goodnight, Miss Salinger,' he said, stepping back so she could make her way to the door. As she walked away he found his eyes trailing her, noting the sway of her body beneath the shapeless, sensible dressing gown.

'Give me strength,' he murmured to himself.

'Excuse me?'

'Sleep well.'

With a final smile thrown in his direction she was gone, leaving him to his decidedly unchivalrous thoughts.

Chapter Three

'A little rain never hurt anyone,' Selina said, her tone calm but firm as she ushered the two young girls from the nursery, gripping their coats tightly in one hand.

'It killed everyone who wasn't on Noah's Ark,' Priscilla said, flashing her a dark look.

'I hardly think we can compare this light drizzle to a biblical flood.'

Four hours, that was how long they'd been cooped up in the schoolroom, Selina trying her very hardest to follow Lord Westcroft's instructions and teach the girls mathematics and history. It had been a disaster. For months they had been allowed to run free, to live their days without structure or discipline. She had been foolish to think she could instil it back in them in one day.

'Coats on,' she said, taking her cloak from a hook by the door. One of the maids had worked some magic on it, cleaning off the worst of the mud after her fall on the drive the day before.

'If we catch a fever, our uncle will not be pleased,' Priscilla muttered. At nine years old she was the more difficult of the two sisters. She was quiet but resentful, objecting to everything Selina did for no good reason.

Selina knew it would take time, time to show the young
girl she could be trusted, that she wasn't going to disappear, that she was eager to help shape Priscilla's future.
Theodosia was more cheerful and accepting, although
seemed to have limitless energy and a rather short attention span.

Selina peered out of the front door, smiling brightly
as she regarded the sky.

'Look, even the drizzle has stopped. I think I can even
see a patch of blue sky.'

Priscilla looked at the grey clouds dubiously, but said
no more.

'Will you teach us to ride?' Theodosia asked. 'Mama
never let us and Father was far too busy to arrange it. I'd
love to have a horse of my own.' Something caught her
eye and the direction of her thoughts spiralled off at a
tangent. 'Archery...you promised you would teach us to
shoot a bow and arrow. Can we? Will you teach us now?
Please say yes.'

Priscilla snorted. 'She's a *governess*, Thea, not a sol-
dier.'

'But she promised.'

'People promise things all the time.'

Selina watched as the little girl bit her lip, digesting
this harsh lesson from her sister.

'Did your father have a bow and arrows, Theodosia?'
Selina focused her attention on the younger of the sisters for a moment.

'Yes. They're in the back of the stables. He has one of
those big target things as well.' A note of hope crept into
her voice. 'Does that mean you'll teach us?'

'A promise is a promise,' Selina said.

Theodosia slipped her little hand into Selina's and
squeezed it softly. She was only there for an instant, but

Selina knew it was a start, the first building block of the relationship she would have to forge with these two grieving young girls.

'It's dirty,' Priscilla observed as Selina hauled the target out of the corner of the stables. 'And there are spider's webs all over it.'

'A little bit of dirt never hurt anyone.'

'Try telling that to all the people who died of the bubonic plague,' Priscilla muttered.

'That was rats. *This* is mud.'

Ignoring her screaming muscles, Selina hauled the heavy target out on to the lawn at the back of the house. She set it down, tweaking its position until she was happy, then returned to the stables for the bow and quiver of arrows. Theodosia danced around her feet, excitedly chattering, but Priscilla remained where she was, watching the proceedings with the haughty disdain of a nine-year-old.

'The bow is heavy,' Selina said, weighing the weapon in her hands. 'It is made for someone much bigger than you, so don't be disappointed if you can't get much movement.'

'I'm strong,' Theodosia said. 'I eat all my vegetables.'

Priscilla snorted, earning her a black look from her younger sister.

'I eat *most* of my vegetables,' she corrected herself.

'I'll let you into a secret,' Selina whispered. 'I never eat my carrots and I can't stand cabbage.'

Theodosia giggled.

'Have you ever tried archery before?'

'No, but I'm sure I'll be very good at it.'

'Have you, Miss Salinger?' Priscilla challenged her.

'It's a strange skill for a governess. And if you don't know how to shoot a bow then you shouldn't be teaching us.'

Silently Selina weighed the bow, plucking the string to feel the tension. She selected an arrow, checking the point and the tail, balancing it in her fingers before positioning it against the bowstring. Taking her time, she adjusted her stance, raised the bow and released the arrow, sending it in a perfect line towards the target. It sank into the material with a satisfying *thunk*, not quite in the centre of the bullseye, but not far off.

The two girls looked at her with a mixture of awe and disbelief.

'Do it again,' Theodosia whispered.

Selina selected another arrow, repeated all the preparatory steps before sending it flying through the air to the target. Another hit, another excited squeal from Theodosia.

'Where did you learn to do that?' Priscilla asked.

'My father taught me.'

'I told you,' Theodosia rounded on her sister. 'I told you she would teach us.'

'Come here.' Selina watched as Theodosia crowded close, but Priscilla hung back, even though there was a spark of curiosity in her eyes. The older girl didn't want to be intrigued, didn't want to be engaged.

There's no rush, Selina told herself. It could take weeks to build up the necessary trust, weeks that would be well spent. For now she had to just keep Priscilla interested, keep her from closing off entirely, and hopefully she would slowly start to allow herself to have fun.

'When you hold a bow the most important thing is safety,' Selina said, motioning to the arrows by their feet. 'These are deadly weapons, and you need to treat them with respect at all times.'

* * *

Matthew turned the page on the report he was reading, about to delve into the latest accounts for the cargo ships that had recently docked in London. As his eyes skimmed across the first line a squeal of delight from outside made him pause. Nine weeks he'd been in charge of his two nieces and in that time he'd not heard them laugh, let alone squeal with happiness.

Resolutely he turned back to the report, but this time he only managed the first three words before another exclamation of awe came to his ears. Intrigued, he stood, crossing to the window. He expected to see the girls and Miss Salinger engaged in a game of some sort. Perhaps something that involved chasing or hiding. Hardly the most educational of pastimes, but he understood the need for fresh air and exercise to break up the school day.

As he looked out the window he nearly choked on the air he was breathing. Standing on the lawn was Miss Salinger, her arms wrapped around little Theodosia as she showed her how to hold a bow. He watched as the young girl drew back the bowstring, frowning with the difficulty of the task, and loosed an arrow. To her credit it did sail through the air, flying a few feet before embedding itself into the ground a fair distance away from the target.

For a moment his eyes focused on the figure of Miss Salinger, lingering just a little too long, before he stood and hurried out of his study. Someone had to stop them. Archery was dangerous, not to be trifled with by amateurs and certainly not to be taught to children by someone who didn't know what they were doing.

Half-marching, half-running, he made it across the lawn in less than a minute, coming up behind the impromptu archery lesson.

'Breathe in and draw the bow,' Miss Salinger was

saying to Theodosia, helping the young girl to pull back the bowstring. 'Breathe out, focus on the target and then release.'

'Stop,' he shouted, seeing his niece's quivering hand as she strained to keep the bowstring taut. He was sure she would drop her aim and shoot herself in the foot.

At his shout Theodosia jumped, half-turning and pulling Miss Salinger off balance at the same time. Matthew saw the governess's eyes widen in horror as she started slipping, losing her grip on the bow. The arrow flew loose, travelling in an arc in his direction. Matthew tried to jump back, but was too slow, and with a bellow of pain he saw the arrow embed itself in his boot.

For a moment no one moved. Then everyone moved at once. Miss Salinger set the bow down carefully, a good few paces from the arrows. Then she moved forward. Matthew assumed she was coming to his aid and was surprised to see her crouch down in front of Theodosia.

'Lord Westcroft is fine,' she said, wiping the young girl's hair from her face. 'It was an accident, nothing more, and his fault, not yours.'

His fault?

He saw his little niece nod, her face pale, and was surprised when Miss Salinger brought the young girl in for an embrace.

'Come to your sister, Priscilla,' Miss Salinger said softly. 'Take her hand while I see to Lord Westcroft.'

Only once she was convinced the children were safe did she move towards him.

'Thank you for your swift attention,' he murmured.

'Sarcasm doesn't become you,' she said breezily, as if she hadn't just shot him in the foot. He was sure she should be a little more contrite, a little more obsequious.

'You just shot me in the foot.'

'The arrow barely had any force behind it.'

'You still shot me in the foot.'

'And I'm sure it hasn't even penetrated your foot.'

He looked at her with disbelief.

'Luck and nothing more,' he ground out.

'I'm sure you've had much worse done to you in the past.'

'That is not the point.' He couldn't quite believe he was getting a lesson in stoicism from an English governess.

'You shouldn't have shouted,' she said resolutely. 'Come, girls, let us get your guardian inside.'

'Shouldn't we pull the arrow out?' Theodosia was peering over Miss Salinger's shoulder with interest.

The governess bit her lip, looking down at the foot-long arrow sticking out of his boot.

'Has it gone through the leather? Do you feel pain?'

'Only a little.'

'I worry if I pull it out here then it might begin to bleed in your boot,' she said, her voice softening. He saw the concern in her eyes and realised her brisk manner before had been mostly to put the girls at ease.

'If you give me your arm, I can lean on you back to the house. We can pull it out there,' Matthew said.

He expected her to offer the slender arm that was currently hidden under the thick folds of her cloak. Instead she slipped her whole body under his arm, straightening up so he could rest his weight on her shoulders. It was an intimate position, even with the thick layers that separated them, and Matthew could feel the heat of her body. Something began to stir inside him, something long suppressed and primal.

'You lead the way, girls,' Miss Salinger said, motioning for them to go first.

As he walked he felt the sharp point of the arrow

grinding against something in his foot. He clenched his jaw, picking up the pace in a bid to get back to the house quicker. They entered through the front door, held open by a surprised Mrs Fellows, her face settling back into a disapproving frown when she saw no one was seriously injured.

'Into my study,' Matthew instructed, and their little party made their way into the oppressive room that functioned as a private study. Miss Salinger helped him ease down into one of the armchairs and immediately sank down to her knees in front of him.

'We will need clean hot water and something to bind the wound,' she instructed Mrs Fellows who had followed them into the room.

The old housekeeper shuffled out, muttering something unintelligible under her breath.

'Perhaps you could run down to the kitchens, girls,' Miss Salinger said over her shoulder. 'Lord Westcroft will want something sweet after we've seen to his injury. Ask Cook to prepare something.'

'You think of everything, don't you?' he said quietly as the two girls reluctantly left the room. Although he was still miffed about the arrow in his foot, he found his main emotion was awe at how she was handling Priscilla and Theodosia in a situation where there could quite easily have been hysterics.

'Shall I just pull it out?' she asked, looking up at him from under her long, dark eyelashes. He knew it wasn't *meant* to be sensual, that she wasn't trying to be seductive, but the look sent the blood pounding round his body.

He nodded, gripping the arms of the chair. She pulled, putting her whole body behind the action, and Matthew felt the tip of the arrow shift in his foot, but after that there was no more movement.

She bit her lip again, a gesture that was fast becoming familiar, as was his reaction to the innocent but provocative expression.

'Allow me,' he said, finding the proximity of his governess more difficult to deal with than the pain in his foot.

Gripping the arrow, he pulled, feeling it slide from his foot and through the leather of his boot.

'Well done,' Miss Salinger said, as if she were congratulating a ten-year-old on her letters. 'Now I'll take off your boot and we can see the damage.'

Gently his fingers tugged at the leather, slipping off the boot and the sock underneath. Matthew glanced down, seeing the trickle of blood from the thankfully small wound. He flexed his toes, feeling a sharp stab of pain, but there seemed to be no impairment to his movements.

'I'm sorry I...' Miss Salinger muttered.

Matthew turned his attention to her, saw the pallor on her cheeks, the slightly glazed look in her eyes, and sprang from his chair just in time to catch her before she collapsed to the floor.

She was heavy in his arms, her body completely limp, and it took him a few seconds to lower her gently to the floor.

'What have you done to Miss Salinger?' Theodosia shouted as she reappeared at the door. The little girl launched herself at him, fists raised, in a show of temper Matthew hadn't realised she possessed.

'She's fainted. She's fainted,' he repeated, waiting for the words to sink in. Theodosia slumped back, still looking at him with a frown.

'Arrows shot at the master, governesses swooning all over the place. What is this house coming to?' Mrs Fellows muttered as she came back into the room, clutching a little bottle in her hand. She brushed Matthew aside and wave the bottle under Miss Salinger's nose.

He watched as, like magic, the governess's eyes fluttered open.

'Oh, I'm so sorry,' she said, a hand flying to her mouth as she tried to sit up.

'Stay there,' he instructed her. The sharp tone of his voice was enough to draw dark looks from all the other occupants of the room. 'You don't want to faint again.'

Despite his words Miss Salinger wriggled up on to her bottom, closing her eyes momentarily as she adjusted to her new position. Theodosia stepped forward, looking as if she were about to throw herself protectively on top of her new governess.

'Everyone out,' he ordered. 'Mrs Fellows, take the girls up to the nursery.'

'But…' Theodosia protested.

'No arguments. Upstairs. Now.'

A shuffling of feet followed and after a minute he was left alone with Miss Salinger.

'I'm sorry for fainting,' she said, looking embarrassed. 'I've never been very good with the sight of blood.'

She looked young sitting on the floor and he realised she couldn't be much more than twenty despite her air of authority with the children.

Silently he stood, hobbling over to where Mrs Fellows had set down the water and strips of cloth for a bandage. Carefully he cleaned the wound in his foot. It was just over half an inch deep, but seemed to have missed all the important areas. Only once it was properly dressed did he turn back to Miss Salinger.

She was struggling to her feet and for a moment he

thought she was about to swoon again. He darted back across the room, catching her arm.

'Thank you,' she said softly and, for the first time, looked him properly in the eye, holding his gaze for a long few seconds. Her eyes were dark green, wide and earnest, eyes a man could get lost in.

He had the urge to pull her closer to him, to cover those full lips with his own, to press her body to his. For a moment he thought he saw her sway towards him, thought her lips parted ever so slightly, but then she straightened and stepped back, her cheeks flushing and her eyes casting down to the floor.

'I am sorry,' she said. 'For shooting you.'

He wanted to murmur that no real damage had been done, that accidents happen, to pull her back into his arms, but that way ruination lay. She was a governess, his employee, someone he should safeguard not seduce.

'You should never have put the children in danger,' he said abruptly.

Miss Salinger looked up at him in surprise and it took her a few seconds to catch up with this change in his manner.

'Before you came out we were perfectly safe,' she said quietly and calmly. 'Any fool knows not to creep up on someone with a loaded weapon and then shout out just as they are about to loose an arrow.'

'Priscilla and Theodosia should be learning mathematics, history and music, not how to kill someone with a deadly weapon.' He realised how stuffy he sounded, but felt his defences slamming down and couldn't help himself.

'They are *children*. They cannot be expected to work every waking moment of the day. They need fresh air, fun, something to fill their lives with joy.' She paused, taking a deep breath. 'Please excuse me, my lord, I need to get back to my charges.' She swept from the room, turning back only when she was safely beyond the door. 'Perhaps you could find time in your schedule to reassure Theodosia that you are not angry with her. That *she* did nothing wrong.'

Before he could answer she had disappeared into the darkness of the hallway, leaving him feeling unsettled.

Chapter Four

Selina turned back to the chalk board, ensuring neither of the girls could see her expression, and screwed her face into a silent scream. Four days she'd been at Manresa House. Four days of Priscilla's sad, defiant little face watching her every move as if willing her to give up and go away. She needed a new technique, something to entice the little girl out of her protective shell, something to make her engage and let go of some of the anger she carried with her.

With a flourish she wiped the names of the Tudor Kings and Queens from the board. Today they would try something a little different.

'What is history?' she asked.

The two little girls looked at her with mild surprise in their eyes.

'Learning all the Kings and Queens and battles,' Theodosia volunteered.

'Boring things that happened to people a long time ago,' Priscilla said, looking at Selina defiantly. She knew the nine-year-old was testing her, she'd been doing it all week, trying to provoke her into shouting or losing her temper, probably so Priscilla could be satisfied in her dislike of her governess.

'It does sometimes seem that way, doesn't it?' Selina said, pulling out a chair and sitting down in front of them. 'Battles and marriages and alliances. All between people who are long dead and who lived very different lives from those we live today.'

'Why do we learn it, then?' Priscilla challenged her.

'I've always thought to learn lessons from the people who went before us. A great military commander could study the battles that were won and lost and work out which tactics to avoid and which to employ. Kings and Queens could look back at their ancestors and see which policies worked, which decisions were unpopular.'

'And for us normal people?' Priscilla said, a challenging tone to her voice. 'I'm hardly going to be Queen of England or a military commander.'

Selina smiled—the young girl had asked the question she hoped she would.

'That is why for our next project I want you to write something about your own history. Choose a memory, happy or sad, and write about it.'

Both girls looked at her blankly and Selina sighed inwardly. She'd tried this once before, with the little boy she had looked after before taking this position. He had been stifled in his education, too, all creativity and free thought knocked out of him by a dull and limited curriculum.

'Priscilla, think of your favourite person in history, someone you admire…'

For a long moment she thought her pupil wasn't going to answer her.

'Queen Elizabeth.'

'Very good. When Queen Elizabeth was young, before

she was crowned, before she ever thought she might be Queen, do you think she thought her life would be pored over by historians, eager for every little detail?'

Selina saw a light dawning in Priscilla's eyes.

'No one can know where their life will lead them,' she said, thinking briefly of her own surprises that had brought her to this classroom in Yorkshire. 'One day you might be so successful that people want to read about *your* history.' She let the girls have a moment to think about her words, then instructed them to get out their paper to begin writing.

'I'm going to write about when Papa fell into the lake trying to rescue Colin,' Theodosia said with a grin.

'Colin?'

'Our dog. He was so naughty and always running away.'

'*That* sounds like a wonderful story to write about. Priscilla?'

The older girl was looking down at her paper, chewing her lip.

'You don't have to tell me,' she said quietly. 'Just write.'

Head high, back straight, shoulders down, Selina told herself as she hesitated outside Lord Westcroft's study door. It wasn't a Sunday, the agreed day that she would update him on the girls' progress and bring them in to see him for a short spell after dinner.

'Ridiculous rule,' she muttered to herself. She didn't think Lord Westcroft was a bad person despite his occasional brusque outbursts and she thought she had seen flashes of affection in his eyes when he'd been close to his nieces, but it was clear he had absolutely no idea how to be around young children.

She rapped on the door, waiting for the curt command to enter before she slipped inside.

The study was dark, despite it being only late afternoon, and there were candles burning at points around the room. Lord Westcroft was sitting behind his desk, regarding her with poorly concealed irritation.

'Miss Salinger,' he greeted her, rising as she stepped into the room. He motioned to a chair, the good manners that would have been drummed into him in childhood winning out over his obvious desire to usher her out of the study as fast as possible.

Selina sat, making herself comfortable. What she had to say, what she had to show him, might take a while.

'Is there a problem?' As he spoke his dark brows came together in a frown.

'In a way.' Selina hesitated, gripping the sheets of paper tighter in her hand. She reminded herself it wasn't a betrayal, that Lord Westcroft was Priscilla's guardian and as such needed to know when something affected her welfare, even if that something was the girl's own memories. 'I asked the children to write a little excerpt of their own history, to choose something that they thought was interesting or important to them and imagine they were writing for an audience of the future interested in their lives.' She paused, her fingers dancing over the sheets of paper in her lap nervously.

'Go on,' Lord Westcroft prompted. He did not seem overly intrigued, but at least he hadn't chased her from the room.

'Theodosia wrote an amusing little anecdote about her father falling into the lake as he tried to rescue their dog.'

Selina saw a twitch of a smile on Lord Westcroft's face, but he got it under control quickly, his expression returning to one of impatient attention.

'Priscilla wrote about something a little more disturbing…' Selina gripped the papers in her lap and after a moment's hesitation she held them out. 'Perhaps it is better that you read it.'

With a frown Lord Westcroft took the proffered sheets and laid them on his desk. As he read Selina looked around the room. It really was oppressive, with dark panelling covering the walls and thick curtains blocking out much of the light that filtered through the windows. Her eyes flicked back to Lord Westcroft, watching his face, waiting for him to reach the part where Priscilla talked about her mother's death. And what had come after.

He read in silence, only setting the papers down when he reached the very end, letting out a long breath and regarding the words for a moment longer before looking up.

'It could be fiction,' he said, although his tone suggested he didn't really think that was the case.

'Do you know how her mother died?'

'No. I was in India. I hadn't heard from my brother for a number of years. I didn't even know she had passed away until the letter summoning me back here, telling me of my inheritance and guardianship.'

'It must have been a shock.'

'Quite.'

He was regarding her with his dark eyes, the intensity of his gaze making her feel uncomfortable.

'Did you ask Priscilla about it?'

'No. They handed them over just before their dinner. I came straight to you once I'd read it.'

Selina could see the thoughts running through Lord Westcroft's mind. She knew a part of him would wish she would just deal with this by herself without troubling him, but she refused to let him get away that easily. He was their guardian, their one constant. Governesses could come and go, but he would be the one thing in their lives that they should be able to rely on.

'Someone should talk to her about it,' he said.

'I wondered…' Selina said, trailing off. It was a bold suggestion and had the possibility of going very wrong quite easily.

'Go on.'

'I think she is testing us, testing me. She could have chosen anything to write about, but she revealed the details of her mother's suicide and the trauma of how she was forced into a grave outside the churchyard, marked as a sinner for ever.'

'How is that a test?'

'Priscilla has convinced herself that I am the enemy…' She paused. 'Perhaps that *we* are the enemy. She is rude and truculent, but I think she doesn't really want to be that way. This is her lifeline, her way of reaching out. If we ignore it or don't handle it properly, then she will retreat further into herself.'

'You've thought about this a lot,' Lord Westcroft said. Selina wasn't sure if there was admiration or disbelief in his voice.

'*This* is my job,' Selina said with more passion than she had planned. 'And those girls need someone to care about them.'

A stony silence fell between them as the implication of her words registered.

'What do you propose, Miss Salinger?' Lord Westcroft asked coldly.

'I think we should take them out to visit their mother's grave. Acknowledge their pain, but do something practical about it.'

'We?'

'Yes, we,' she ground out.

Lord Westcroft leaned back in his chair. Eventually he spoke. 'I can spare two hours tomorrow morning. We will take the carriage.'

'Thank you,' Selina said, rising to her feet. She'd got what she wanted, although she wished for a little more emotion from Lord Westcroft.

Slowly, slowly, she told herself. They just needed to spend more time together and tomorrow would be a start.

Chapter Five

'Lady Theodosia,' Lord Westcroft said, taking his younger niece's hand and helping her up into the carriage. 'Lady Priscilla.' Selina stepped behind them and was surprised when he held out his hand for her. She slipped her hand into his, feeling the warmth and the slight calluses on his fingers. They were hands that had worked before, even if he held a title now.

'Miss Salinger.' He looked her in the eye as he said her name and Selina felt her breath catch in her throat. Then she was up in the carriage and the moment was gone.

She stepped up, thinking she would sit next to one of the girls, but they had huddled together and the carriage seats were only small, leaving no room for her next to them. She sat down, pushing her body into the corner as Lord Westcroft settled himself next to her.

After a moment the carriage lurched forward and Selina almost flew from her seat, only the restraining arm Lord Westcroft put out stopped her.

'Thank you,' she said.

'Where are we going? Is it to town, to buy new dresses? Or to the seaside? Oh, I do want to go to the seaside.' Theodosia was bouncing up and down on her seat, unable to sit still for even a moment.

Selina sat back, giving Lord Westcroft a meaningful look. He sighed and she thought he had been about to roll his eyes at her, but something held him back.

'Miss Salinger showed me your writing, Priscilla,' he said gently. He held up a hand to halt the tirade that looked about to explode from his niece's mouth. 'I would understand if you were angry, but it was the right thing for Miss Salinger to do.'

'Where are we going?' Priscilla asked, her voice filled with barely restrained anger. Selina wondered at the maturity of this young girl. Most would shout and scream, but once again Priscilla was able to hold it all inside.

'To visit your mother's grave.'

Selina was surprised at the tenderness in Lord Westcroft's voice. All she'd seen of him so far had been distant and formal. This was a different version of the man.

'Her grave?'

Lord Westcroft nodded. 'It is hard losing a parent, much harder losing two. Especially at such a young age...' He paused and Selina saw raw emotion in his eyes. 'I don't know if your father told you about your grandmother, my mother?'

The girls both shook their heads.

'She was kind and gentle and loving. I remember that about her, although sometimes I'm not sure I can remember her face. She died when I was eight.' He smiled gently. 'I used to go and sit by her grave, tell her all the things that had happened, all the things I was proud of, all my grievances. It made me feel closer to her.'

Selina could see by the sincerity in his eyes that he was telling the truth. Lord Westcroft projected himself as a cold, hard businessman so it was easy to believe the deception and forget that underneath was a living, breathing, *feeling* person, someone who had mourned the death of his mother and someone who was making the effort to comfort his nieces despite his initial reluctance.

'It's not the same,' Priscilla said, a brittle edge to her voice. 'Your mother would have been buried in the churchyard, given a proper place. *Our* mother is buried on a rough bit of land outside the church.'

Lord Westcroft nodded. 'You're right, it's not the same. I had somewhere to go and sit, to feel closer to my mother. That is why we're going to visit today. It might not be in the churchyard, but that doesn't mean you can't find some peace there.'

'I wish we had some flowers,' Theodosia said quietly. 'Mama loved flowers.'

'I cut a few stems from the garden before we left,' Lord Westcroft said, surprising them all. Selina felt her eyebrows raise. It was a thoughtful gesture, one she wouldn't have thought he would even have considered.

She was surprised to find the carriage pulling to a halt after they had only been travelling for ten minutes. She hadn't realised the village was so close. In better weather, when the wind wasn't gusting across the moors, it would probably make a pleasant walk.

Lord Westcroft stepped down from the carriage and helped each of the children and then Selina in turn. He reached up and took two small bouquets of flowers from the coachman, handing one to each of the girls.

'Go on,' Selina, urged them gently and after a moment's hesitation the two little girls linked arms and walked across the grass around the side of the church. Selina made to follow, but Lord Westcroft placed a hand on her arm to hold her back.

'They won't want us there,' he said.

'They might…'

'They won't,' he said firmly. 'Walk with me, we will go and check on them in a few minutes.'

'I'm sorry about your mother,' she said.

He shrugged. 'Everyone loses their parents at some point. I was just unfortunate to lose the kind, caring one first.'

'Your father wasn't caring?' It was too intimate a question, but Selina felt it slipping out anyway. She needed to remember they weren't friends, just an employer and his employee.

'No.'

'Sorry, I shouldn't have pried.'

'Are your parents alive?'

Selina shook her head, feeling the tears welling up in her eyes. If only they were, if only her father was still around to explain why he had pretended to care for her so deeply, but had ultimately decided she was not worth providing for.

'I lost my father eighteen months ago and my mother a few years before that.'

'Eighteen months,' he mused. 'That was when you became a governess?'

'Yes.' She smiled brightly, hoping the pain wouldn't show through. Before then she hadn't had a reason to work for her living. She'd been the treasured daughter of a very wealthy man. She'd spent her days reading and socialising with other young ladies in Cambridge and her nights attending balls and music recitals and dinner parties. It was quite different from her life now.

'You didn't have any other relatives to take you in?'

'No,' she said abruptly, pushing the image of her half-brother from her mind. He'd made it perfectly clear that he never wanted to set eyes on her again, even providing his carriage to whisk her away from the city she knew and deposit her far away in London.

'Pity,' he said, 'although not for me.' He paused, turning slightly to her. 'You have a way with the girls. I can see them doing very well with you.'

'Thank you. They are lovely children under all the layers of grief.'

'I am pleased they have you.'

Selina felt her body stiffen—he was going to try to distance himself from his nieces again.

'They have you, too.'

'Yes. Although I will return to India once everything here is settled.'

'India?'

'Yes, that is where my business is based.'

'That's a long way away.'

'I shall wait until the children are settled into a routine with you and you are familiar with the house.'

'Lord Westcroft...' Selina said, hesitating, but deciding to press on. No one else was going to tell him how much his nieces needed him and it didn't seem as though he would realise it himself. 'Priscilla and Theodosia have lost their parents at a very young age. They will be looking for someone to step up and fill that void.'

He looked straight ahead, over the moor beyond the village, and for a moment Selina thought he might ignore her comment entirely.

'They have each other.'

'That's not enough.'

'It will have to be.'

'You could—'

'Miss Salinger,' he said sharply, 'you are employed to

teach the children and attend to their welfare. Anything else is none of your concern. Is that understood?'

Selina stepped back as if she had been slapped.

'Entirely,' she said. 'Please accept my apology. Clearly I have overstepped.'

Without looking back she walked away, moving towards the grave where the two little girls were crouched. She hesitated a moment before approaching, taking a minute to blink away the tears that were forming in her eyes. She knew all about being alone in the world, but at least she hadn't found out how cruel those who were meant to love them could be until she was an adult.

Matthew perched on the low stone wall that surrounded the churchyard and closed his eyes. Somewhere to his left his nieces and Miss Salinger were tidying the grave, pulling up the weeds and laying down the flowers he'd brought. He knew he should be over there with them, he wouldn't have to do anything, his presence would be enough.

'Coward,' he muttered to himself. He had never meant to speak to Miss Salinger in such a fashion, but as she'd confronted him again on his relationship with his nieces he'd felt overcome with dread. He'd needed to say anything to push her away, to stop her from seeing the fear that lay beneath his refusal to get close to the girls.

The look of surprise on her face had seared itself into his mind, as had the expression of disgust that had followed. Of course she was disgusted. He might have only been acquainted with the governess for a few days, but that was long enough to know she was generous and caring. The idea that he wouldn't want to ease the suffering of his nieces would be difficult for her to comprehend.

He shook his head. He had to stay strong. He'd learnt

a long time ago that caring wasn't always the best option. Trying to conform to everyone's wishes, trying to *do the right thing* could end up in disaster. No, he knew his strengths and caring for two young girls was not one of them. The last time he'd been asked to care for someone vulnerable it had not been a success. He was smart enough not to make the same mistake twice.

He felt his resolve strengthen. This wasn't his life, it wasn't the life he had ever asked for or expected. His brother had been raised to be the Earl, his lesser importance had been made clear from a very young age by his father. He'd built a life for himself, been successful in the navy and then his shipping business, without any help from his family. *That* was his life and there was no room for two little girls in it. There was no point in them becoming attached to him or him developing an affection for them. In a few weeks, maybe months, he would be going back to India and it would be easier for everyone if they barely noticed him gone.

Still, he needed to apologise to Miss Salinger. There was never an excuse for rudeness, especially not to someone whose only motivation was trying to protect a child.

Rising, he walked over, crouching down as he reached the grave.

'There,' Miss Salinger said, pulling at the last of the weeds. 'That looks better.'

Priscilla was quiet, her serious little face white and unreadable, but she gripped Theodosia's hand tightly.

'Goodbye, Mama,' Theodosia said as they stood up.

Priscilla turned to Miss Salinger, fixing her with her wide eyes. 'Thank you,' she said, so quietly it could hardly be heard above the wind.

'You're welcome, Priscilla.'

'Can we come back?'

'Of course. Perhaps every couple of weeks we could bring fresh flowers and tidy things up. If Lord Westcroft would be kind enough to allow us the carriage.'

He nodded, not trusting himself to speak.

Priscilla acknowledged him with the briefest look, then edged a little closer to Miss Salinger, allowing the governess to take her hand to steady her over the rough ground. It was a breakthrough, one that was well deserved on the part of Miss Salinger.

'Shall we walk into the village before returning home?' Matthew suggested. 'It's pleasant to be out.'

Miss Salinger eyed the dark clouds and trees blowing in the wind, gathering her shawl closer around her shoulders.

'We should show Miss Salinger the local area, it is to be her home after all.'

As they emerged on to the road he informed the coachman that they would be a few minutes longer and then walked briskly to catch up.

'Lead the way, girls,' he instructed. Theodosia skipped on ahead, seemingly undisturbed by their trip to the grave. Priscilla lingered for a moment, but soon hurried to join her sister.

Matthew offered Miss Salinger his arm. It would have been impolite for her to refuse, but he could see her contemplating doing just that. Eventually she relented, slipping her hand into the crook of his elbow.

'I wanted to apologise,' he said quietly. 'I was rude.'

Miss Salinger looked at him expectantly.

'Go on,' she said.

'Go on?'

'You said you want to apologise.'

He paused, wondering if any other woman of lower rank would challenge him like this. He stopped walking, waiting for her to turn towards him and lift her chin so she was looking him in the eye.

'I'm sorry,' he said. 'I spoke harshly.'

She studied his face and then nodded.

'Would you allow me to explain?'

'There is no need, Lord Westcroft. I understand my place.'

'No,' he said with feeling. 'I *want* to explain.' He realised it was the truth. It wasn't just about keeping Miss Salinger here in Yorkshire, although that was one of his main concerns. He realised he didn't want her to think too poorly of him.

That thought made him pause. For the past ten years he'd perfected *not* caring about what anyone else thought of him. He'd ignored the disappointment from first his father and then his brother when he had broken away from the family to make his own path in life and ever since he'd learned to not worry about other people's opinions of him. But now here was this governess, a woman he'd only known for a few days, and he didn't want her to think too badly of him.

'I wasn't born to be an earl. It wasn't the future I was prepared for. I've built my life, a life I enjoy, in India. I *will* be going back there in a few months, I have to.' As he spoke Miss Salinger gave him her full attention, her head tilted a little to one side as if weighing his words. 'I love my nieces and I want to provide well for their future. Manresa House will always be their home more than mine and I hope with you they will be happy there.'

'But you won't be there,' Miss Salinger said quietly.

'No. I won't. I don't want Priscilla and Theodosia to form too much of an attachment to me, not if I will be gone out of their lives in a few months.'

'You could stay.'

'No. It isn't an option.' It was an option, just not one he would consider. Nor would he tell Miss Salinger the true reason for keeping his nieces at a distance. No one ever needed to know his shame, his inability to protect someone as vulnerable as Elizabeth had been.

Miss Salinger searched his face, her eyes flitting over him, assessing.

'I understand,' she said eventually, 'but you're wrong.'

'Wrong?'

'To keep the girls at a distance. You might be leaving soon, but right now they need you. They've lost both their parents…their whole world has changed. You're not protecting them by pushing them away, you're hurting them. They crave your attention, your love.'

'I don't think…' He trailed off. He felt a panic rising inside him.

'It doesn't have to be much,' she said softly. 'An outing every so often, perhaps a few impromptu visits to the schoolroom. Dinner together once a week.'

'You are a very persuasive woman, Miss Salinger,' Matthew said quietly. He watched as she blushed at the compliment and not for the first time he had the urge to reach out and trail his fingers over her cheek, to tuck the stray strands of dark hair behind her ear and let his hand linger for a moment.

'Does that mean you'll do it?'

'One outing. No more.'

Chapter Six

Swallowing hard, Selina put on her sunniest smile and ushered the two girls into the study, knocking briefly as they piled through the door.

'Good afternoon, Lord Westcroft,' she said, bobbing into the shallowest curtsy she could get away with. 'We're ready for a walk on the moors.'

Lord Westcroft looked at her from behind the huge desk, a frown forming on his face. She watched as his eyes narrowed. He was quick and clever, a hard man to outwit, and she could see he already knew what she was trying to do.

'You enjoy that,' he said evenly.

'It's going to be so much fun,' Theodosia said, skipping over to his side, peering unabashedly at the documents spread over his desk. 'I shall walk with you if you like.'

Selina saw him consider. She had gambled on Lord Westcroft's softer side, hoped that he would not refuse a direct request from his nieces to spend time with them, even if she had shamelessly engineered the situation.

'Go find your coats, girls,' he said, his voice restrained. He stood, waiting until they were out of the study before crossing to the door and closing it behind them. Selina tried to keep her breathing level, but as he turned around he was standing close, his broad shoulders brushing against hers.

Nervously she licked her lips. For a long few seconds he didn't move, standing just out of her line of vision, and she wondered if he was about to send her to pack her bags.

'I could have just refused Theodosia there and then,' he said, his voice barely more than a whisper, but still managing to be forceful.

'Yes.'

'It would have upset her.'

'Yes.'

'But that is none of my concern. It would not have been my fault.'

He stepped closer and Selina caught a hint of his scent, a mixture of soap and something more exotic, something she couldn't identify. She looked up, having to tilt her chin to meet his eye, and felt her heart begin to hammer in her chest. He was an attractive man, powerfully built with thick dark hair and a strong jaw. The sort of man her friends in Cambridge would have whispered about, hoping he would notice them.

She swallowed, feeling her mouth turn dry.

'Why didn't you?' she asked quietly.

He took another step closer. Their bodies were almost touching now and Selina had the irrational urge to reach out and place a hand on his chest, to trail her fingers over the soft material of his waistcoat and feel the muscles underneath.

'Why didn't I?' he repeated, as if he couldn't believe she had the audacity to ask the question.

Every inch of her skin felt hot, unbearably so, and she

couldn't tear her eyes away from his. It was as though she were being hypnotised, her body coming under the spell of a man she would normally keep her distance from.

'You could have said no.'

'Perhaps I will.'

She shook her head, holding his gaze. Reminding herself she was doing this for the children, she dropped her shoulders and tilted her chin another notch. Now was not the time to be overcome with such irrational thoughts of desire.

'No,' she said quietly but firmly. 'You won't. No matter what you say you don't want to hurt those girls.'

He looked at her silently for well over a minute, time in which Selina had to battle with herself to stay focused. Never would it be appropriate to let her body sway towards his, but she felt the pull, the primal urge to move closer to him.

'This time I will overlook your behaviour,' he said eventually. 'But understand this, Miss Salinger, I will not be manipulated.'

'Understood.'

He stepped away and Selina let out the breath she had been holding. Her body felt as though it was on fire, every sense was heightened and as Lord Westcroft moved back towards his desk she had to pinch the skin of her hand to bring herself back to reality.

'Five minutes,' he said abruptly. 'I shall meet you in the hall.'

Selina stepped out of the study, knowing once again she'd been lucky to stay on the fine line between looking out for her charges and insubordination. As she walked through the dingy entrance hall she couldn't help but let a smile creep on to her face. Lord Westcroft might protest his very hardest that he didn't care, that he was capable of turning his back on his nieces and returning to India, but when faced with disappointing them he just wouldn't do it, would he?

'It's only a little wind,' Selina said in her most persuasive voice. Three pairs of eyes looked back at her dubiously.

'There is no such thing as *a little wind* up here on the moors, Miss Salinger,' Lord Westcroft said sternly. 'The weather is a dangerous foe and none more so than the blowing winds from the east.'

'It'll be bracing, bring some colour to our cheeks.'

'It'll be cold,' Priscilla countered.

'And the exercise will be good for us.'

'Unless we fall down a hole or get blown off a cliff.'

Selina wagged a finger admonishingly. 'I might not know the area well, but I am well aware that we are at least five miles from the sea. There are no cliffs to fall off on the estate.' She looked at all three in turn, trying out her most winning smile. 'It is either this or two hours of Aristotle in the schoolroom.'

'A threat indeed,' Lord Westcroft murmured.

Silently Priscilla and Theodosia filed out, fastening their coats as they did so. Selina followed, feeling the presence of Lord Westcroft right behind her. Despite the biting wind she felt a warm glow deep inside. *This* was what the girls needed, time and attention from their guardian.

'We'll head out through the formal gardens and east over the parkland,' he instructed the girls, watching as they linked arms and bent their heads to the wind.

Selina shivered. It was colder than she had first thought.

'Regretting your suggestion?'

'A little wind never hurt anyone.'

'Apart from the thousands of sailors lost at sea each year in storms.'

'Well, yes. Apart from them,' she conceded. 'It's not good for the girls to be cooped up inside all day long.'

In truth, she had been the one becoming restless. She'd never been very good at staying inside for a whole day. In her old life in Cambridge she had often ventured out into the slippery cobbled streets even in the pouring rain to avoid a whole day spent inside.

'Perhaps you are right,' he conceded, 'but personally I prefer a little warmth when I venture outside.' He looked off into the distance, his eyes glazing over ever so slightly.

'You're imagining you're back in India?' she asked, watching as he turned his face up to the pale sun behind a fast-moving cloud.

'Always. The heat is wonderful there and when the wind blows it's a welcome reprieve from the humidity, not an icy blast that cuts right through you.' His tone had softened a little as he spoke about the country he clearly considered to be his home.

'Don't you miss anything from England when you are away?'

Selina knew it was intrusive of her to ask such a personal question, but she was intrigued. Lord Westcroft was shrouded in mystery. She hardly knew anything about her employer apart from his eagerness to leave England at the earliest opportunity. The servants at Manresa House were a sullen group who seemed to disappear whenever she entered a room as if they didn't want to engage with her and as such she hadn't even heard any of the usual gossip servants were sometimes happy to share.

That in itself wasn't altogether unusual. Selina had

learned over the past year governesses occupied a strange position in the household. Not quite a servant, but still far removed from the family—it was a lonely position to be in.

'No,' he said quietly. 'What is there to miss?'

'I think I'd miss plenty. The way the earth smells after long-awaited rain. How the sun reflects off the stone of the colleges in Cambridge. The rivers and lakes and hills and farmland.'

'You sound as though you love your home.'

Selina felt the hot sting of tears in her eyes as she always did when thinking of her father's house, nestled in the very heart of Cambridge. She missed the cosy rooms and the ornate fireplaces and the pretty little garden where she had sat reading in the summer. Most of all she missed her father. The long talks, the feeling of being safe and loved. The security. Even when they had travelled the few miles to their country estate she had missed the cosy house in Cambridge where they'd spent most of their time.

'I did.'

'Did?'

'When my father died eighteen months ago the house…' She trailed off, blinking back the tears.

'It went to someone else?'

She nodded. Even after all this time she couldn't voice her half-brother's name and the cruel glint in his eye as he'd demanded she leave.

'My brother,' she said eventually.

'Your brother? But surely he should provide for you?'

Selina laughed, hearing the note of bitterness and stopping abruptly. She'd always promised herself she wouldn't let her brother's final act taint all her memories of home, all her memories of her parents.

'No.'

She was saved from further questioning by the return of Priscilla and Theodosia, who had run ahead and were now returning, battling against the wind that whipped at their skirts.

'I want to show you the folly, Miss Salinger,' Theodosia said, taking her hand. Selina was glad of the distraction, aware of Lord Westcroft's curious eyes probing hers. She'd never told anyone of her disgrace, of the circumstances surrounding her banishment from the family home, and she wasn't going to start now, no matter how much she wished to scream and curse her brother.

'You can climb to the top if you're very, very careful,' Theodosia said as she pulled Selina along by the hand. 'And then you can see all the way to the sea.'

'Apparently,' Priscilla added quietly. '*We've* never been able to see that far.'

'Father did,' Theodosia insisted.

'So he said.'

'He wouldn't lie.'

'I used to come up here when I was a boy,' Lord Westcroft said, interrupting the quiet squabbling. 'And on a very clear day you can see the cliffs and the sea beyond.'

In front of them, at the top of a small hill, rose a tower that looked like something out of a fairy tale. It was made of grey stone with windows dotted at intervals up the walls. A wooden door stood closed at the bottom and at the very top there were crenulations surrounding what she assumed must be a small viewing platform.

'It is out of character with the rest of the house,' she observed.

Manresa House was imposing and severe whereas the folly was whimsical.

'Courtesy of my great-grandfather,' Lord Westcroft

said quietly. 'I understand he was quite mad. His father built Manresa House.'

At the front of their little group Priscilla pushed open the door to the folly, revealing a spiral set of stairs winding up. Before Selina was inside Priscilla and Theodosia had started clattering up the wooden stairs, their blonde hair trailing out behind then as they ran.

'After you,' Lord Westcroft murmured, allowing Selina to ascend first. It was surprisingly tall, with the spiral staircase winding round and round again and again before opening out on to a platform at the top of the folly. With the girls already up there it was a tight squeeze for Selina and then Lord Westcroft to step up on to the wooden flooring.

'Steady,' Lord Westcroft said as she stepped back almost on to his foot. Selina glanced around, aware of his proximity, knowing she should press herself against the wall to make room.

'No chance of seeing the sea today,' Priscilla said, throwing a challenging look at Selina.

'The conditions aren't the clearest,' Selina admitted. 'But it is still pleasant to be out exploring the countryside.'

Theodosia was standing on her tiptoes, squinting out into the distance and trying her very hardest to see the cliffs and the sea beyond. It was cloudy, the visibility poor beyond the immediate area, but Selina's heart squeezed for the little girl as she looked, scrunching her nose with concentration.

'This way,' Lord Westcroft said quietly, directing his niece's gaze. 'If you look hard enough, you might see the white crest of a wave.'

Priscilla rolled her eyes, slouching against the stonework.

Stepping back to give Lord Westcroft the opportunity

to move closer to his nieces, Selina stumbled, correcting herself quickly. Even before she had reached out a hand to grasp the parapet she felt Lord Westcroft's hands on her waist.

'Careful,' he said quietly, his words tickling her ear. 'It's a long way down.'

He held her for a moment longer, his hands seeming to burn through the fabric of her dress. Selina swallowed as his body brushed against hers momentarily before he released her and stepped to one side.

As he leaned his forearms on the stone wall that ran round the edge of the tower Selina risked a glance sideways at him. Her heart was still pounding in her chest and she wasn't entirely convinced it was because of her little stumble. No, her body was reacting to what had come after, that feather-light touch from a man she wasn't even sure she liked.

Lord Westcroft was attractive, there was no denying it. As well as his looks he exuded a self-confidence and sense of authority that were powerful.

Selina looked away, gripping on to the parapet herself to give her a distraction. Thoughts of attraction were inappropriate and unhelpful. He was her employer, but more than that he was a man of the aristocracy. A man not to be trusted.

'Shall we continue?' Lord Westcroft motioned to the stairs.

Obediently the girls clattered down, Selina following. She had to squeeze past Lord Westcroft to duck her head back through the low doorway and as she did so she felt a steadying hand on her arm.

'Watch your footing,' he said quietly, his eyes meeting hers.

They descended the tower in silence, emerging once

again into the ferocious wind at the bottom, the girls flattening themselves against the stonework to shelter from the gusts.

'I think you are going to have to admit defeat,' Lord Westcroft called above the wind.

Selina chewed on her lip. She wanted longer, wanted to stride across the moors, to allow the girls to burn off some of the restless energy that had been building for the past few days. Even more than that she wanted a little longer with Lord Westcroft. For the children, of course, but if she was being completely honest with herself, for her, too. It was lonely here, with only the children for company during the day and servants who barely acknowledged her.

'Theodosia will blow away if we venture any further,' Lord Westcroft said, a fleeting smile passing over his lips. Selina was pleased he was no longer angry with her—fresh air did wonders for everyone. 'Come, girls,' he said, holding out his arms to usher his nieces back towards the house. 'We can continue our exploration of the estate another day. A day when the weather is a little kinder.'

Selina studied the faces of her two charges, saw the hint of disappointment there despite both girls having protested initially to the excursion. She suspected it was disappointment that their time with their uncle was going to be cut short.

'Instead I propose hot chocolate and biscuits in front of the fire in the library,' Lord Westcroft said. Theodosia and Priscilla both smiled, linked hands and began to hurry back towards the house.

'Thank you,' she said quietly.

'What for?'

'You saw their disappointment and you didn't ignore it.'

'I was worried if I did you might march us all the way to the sea.'

'You can joke all you want, Lord Westcroft, but what you did there was kind.'

'I'm not a complete monster then,' he murmured quietly.

'No, not completely.'

With a smile he offered Selina his arm and she felt a thrill of anticipation as she took it. It was reckless speaking to her employer like this, but it was very hard for her to act meek and submissive. Her upbringing hadn't trained her for a position in service and, despite all her practice, Selina still often thought of herself as the respectable daughter of a wealthy man.

Chapter Seven

'You enjoyed yourself today,' Miss Salinger murmured as they watched the girls slumped on the sofa. It was warm in the library with the roaring fire and the sofa had proved too inviting and comfortable for the young girls. Theodosia had nodded off soon after she'd finished her steaming cup of hot chocolate and the little girl had biscuit crumbs all over her lap. Priscilla had managed to hold out for longer, talking to the adults in her solemn, grown-up way as the light faded outside the window and the evening drew in.

'Anyone who says they don't enjoy chocolate and biscuits is a liar,' he said.

'You know I didn't mean that.'

'Have you ever been told you're exceedingly persistent, Miss Salinger?'

The governess grimaced and nodded. 'My father's favourite adjective for me was tenacious.'

'Your father was right.'

'In many things,' she said and he thought he heard a hint of sadness in her voice.

Matthew shifted. They were sitting on armchairs positioned half-facing one another and over the course of the afternoon Miss Salinger had lost some of her upright bearing and now looked comfortable propped up by cushions. To anyone looking in it would appear to be a happily domestic scene, with the two little girls asleep on the sofa and he and a pretty young woman relaxing in front of the fire.

It was a disturbing thought and quickly Matthew stood, poking at the fire to cover his sudden restlessness.

Part of him wanted to flee, to make his excuses and stride back to his study. It would be perfectly acceptable for him to do so. He'd spent more time than he'd planned with Miss Salinger and his nieces already, but something made him sit back down.

'Tell me about your family,' he said, watching as the governess's eyes widened just a little at his request. Whenever she mentioned her father there was something in her manner that made him want to find out more.

'I come from Cambridge,' she said slowly. 'My father met my mother later in life, after his first wife died in childbirth. I have an older half-brother, much older, who I barely know. My mother passed away four years ago, my father a couple of years later.' Her words were measured and careful and not for the first time Matthew wondered what secrets she was hiding. 'I had a very happy life in Cambridge when my father was alive. He was kind, doting…' she paused, smiling to herself as if remembering '…indulgent, perhaps.'

'He clearly placed a great importance on your education,' Matthew prompted.

'Yes. I had a governess when I was young, but he enjoyed sharing his knowledge, too.'

Matthew frowned, his eyes narrowing. Only the wealthiest families could afford to educate their children in their own homes with tutors and governesses. Those even of the gentry class would often send their children to school, but would never be able to employ a governess.

'A governess?'

Miss Salinger's eyes widened as she realised what she had let slip. Slowly she nodded. 'My father was quite wealthy,' she said quietly.

It wasn't unheard of for the daughter of a wealthy man to need to seek employment. Fortunes were built and lost every week, families were divided, wealth was locked in entailed property.

'How did you end up here, Miss Salinger?' he asked bluntly. He wanted to ask her who her family was, who her father had been. Although he'd been out of the country for many years he'd grown up in the world of the rich and powerful. He knew most of the wealthy families, but he didn't recall any Salingers among them.

She swallowed, staring into the fire for a moment and he knew she was considering whether to lie to him.

'First let me get you a drink, then you can tell me.' He stood, crossing to the side of the room and opening a small cupboard hidden in the panelling of the wood to reveal a decanter of brandy and a couple of glasses. He poured two generous measures and passed one to Miss Salinger. She took a sip, grimaced, but soon followed it up with another.

'My father and my half-brother were estranged,' Miss Salinger said as she took another mouthful of the brandy. 'I've only met William half a dozen times over the course of my life. He objected to my mother, to my father marrying beneath him. So he objected to me.'

Matthew knew only too well the rifts that could arise in a family and tear them apart.

'When he was alive my father always told me I was

well provided for, that I would never have to worry about my future.'

She paused and Matthew saw the tears brimming in her eyes. Although he had split away from the rest of his family many years ago he'd done so on his own terms. He couldn't imagine being forced out.

'That wasn't the case?'

She shook her head, causing a tear to spill on to her cheek. He had the urge to reach across and wipe it away with his thumb, but thankfully she quickly raised a delicate hand and stopped him from doing something foolish.

'Everything went to my brother,' she said quietly.

'Everything?'

'Yes. And *he* was never going to provide for me.' There was an edge to her voice that told Matthew there was more to this story.

'You saw your father's will?'

Miss Salinger shook her head, biting her lip. 'But the solicitors confirmed everything.'

'Your brother put you out on the street?'

'He paid my coach fare to London and escorted me to the stop himself.'

'He gave you no money? Nothing?'

'Nothing. I had a little saved, enough for a few weeks' food and rent in London before I found a position as a governess.' She said the words nonchalantly, but Matthew could see there was a world of pain in her eyes. He doubted things had been that straightforward, that her path from her father's home to her new situation as a governess had been that smooth. 'I suppose I should be grateful, I had my education, enough to get me a job. Many don't have even that.'

'While your brother sits in your house and spends your father's money.'

'His money now.'

Matthew felt the first stirrings of anger. There was much injustice in the world, but for a man to turn away his own sister, to put her on the street, was disgusting. Miss Salinger had been lucky, finding a position. If she hadn't, her money would have soon run out and who knew where she would have ended up then.

'Your brother's behaviour was unacceptable.'

Miss Salinger nodded, turning her face away. He could see further tears spilling on to her cheeks. Without thinking through the consequences he moved from his chair, kneeling down in front of her, and took her hand.

'Your position here is secure,' he said softly, 'You don't need to worry about being turned out again. I know it's not the same as having your own home, but you will have a place here for as long as you desire.'

'Thank you.'

He saw something soften in her eyes, saw her cheeks flush, felt the minuscule movements of the muscles as she squeezed his hand. They stayed locked in that position for another second, their eyes searching the other's.

Slowly he backed away. Thinking of anything but Miss Salinger's safety was inappropriate right now. He should ignore the hint of desire in her eyes, the way her lips had parted ever so slightly. He should ignore the voice in his head that was urging him to reach out and kiss her.

'I should take the girls up to bed,' he said.

'Yes. That would be kind.' She stood, wiping the last traces of tears from her cheeks, and busied herself gently pulling the blankets from Priscilla and Theodosia.

He carried Priscilla up first to the nursery, lingering as she burrowed her head into his shoulder, murmuring in her sleep. Theodosia stirred as he lifted her from the sofa, but when he placed her in her bed upstairs she was back asleep. He sat on the edge of the bed for a moment, smoothing down the young girl's hair, thinking of how different his life had become in just a few weeks.

Steady, he told himself. One afternoon of happy domesticity and he was forgetting his life, the life he'd worked so hard to build. And forgetting the reasons he'd turned his back on a conventional life a decade ago. He wouldn't be pushed into anything for the sake of family ever again. The girls would be perfectly content with Miss Salinger—him staying would just add a layer of complication. A layer no one needed.

He resisted a look back over his shoulder as he turned the light out in the girls' bedroom. It would just make it harder to step away.

Matthew turned, barrelling in to Miss Salinger. She bounced off him and quickly he reached out to steady her before she could stumble.

'I'm sorry,' she said quickly. 'I just came to check the girls were settled.'

'Both asleep.'

'Good. They were tired. It was a lovely afternoon for them.'

He still had hold of her upper arms even though she was now in no danger of stumbling. Something was stopping him from letting go, an invisible pull that he couldn't quite explain.

'And for you, Miss Salinger?' he asked, his voice low.

'For me?'

'Are you settling in? Do you like it here at Manresa House?'

He watched her lips as they parted, seeing the words form even before he heard them. She had beautiful lips, lips that begged to be kissed.

Quickly he drew back. Kissing the governess was the

quickest way to send her running, even if he did detect a spark of something that looked like desire in her eyes when she glanced at him. By her account Miss Salinger had been raised to follow the rules of society and those rules were very clear about not succumbing to the attentions of your employer in a dark corridor.

'Yes, Lord Westcroft, I enjoy my work very much.' It was a measured answer, crafted not to give too much away.

'You can see yourself staying here?'

'I can.'

'Good.'

Silence fell between them. Matthew knew he should excuse himself, return to his neglected accounts and maps, but he wanted to stretch this moment just a little longer.

'Join me for a drink,' he said, midway between a request and an order.

'I'm not sure...'

'One drink, Miss Salinger. What could be the harm in that?'

She swallowed, her eyes darting up to meet his, and he knew in that moment she could read his darkest thoughts. Slowly she nodded and Matthew knew if he was a gentleman he would withdraw the offer, make it easier for them both to walk away.

Instead he offered her his arm, waiting as she hesitated for only a second before slipping her hand into the crook of his elbow and moving to his side.

Foolish, foolish, foolish! the little voice in her head was screaming. There had been so many opportunities for Selina to take her leave, to make her excuses and escape, but each and every one she'd allowed to pass her by and now she was sitting in the library with her knees almost touching Lord Westcroft's and a heavy glass of brandy in her hand.

'Would you tell me about your life in India?' She was hoping to steer the conversation on to a safe topic.

'What would you like to know?'

'Anything. Everything. It is a life so far removed from what I have experienced, I can't even begin to imagine it.'

For a moment Lord Westcroft was silent, looking into the distance, his eyes clouded. Then he smiled, a devastating smile that made her heart pound in her chest and her whole body scream to inch a little closer.

'To be able to imagine India it is first important to picture the voyage that takes you there,' he said. 'Close your eyes.'

'I don't think…' Selina started to protest.

'Close your eyes.' The command was gentle but firm and she found herself sitting up straighter in the chair, clutching the arms and closing her eyes.

'Imagine the soft sway of the ship beneath your feet, the warm salty air on your lips, the rustle of the wind in the sails. You've been sailing for months, through stormy seas, rough passages, past pirate-laden coasts. Now things are calmer, warmer, the air is tropical, your movements are slower, your energy sapped quicker, your skin always damp. Even the slightest breeze is a welcome relief.'

Selina felt her breathing deepen and her neck arch back ever so slightly as she imagined all he was describing. His voice was low and melodic and with her eyes closed it felt exquisitely intimate.

'Land when it is sighted is a mass of greenery, with golden sand beaches. Tight mangrove forests line the waterways, but the country within is worth the battle to get to.'

She could hear him shifting in his seat and had to resist the urge to open her eyes. As he spoke her skin was prickling with anticipation and her blood pounding around her body. Never had someone's words managed to conjure such a visceral response and part of her wanted him to continue while the rest of her wanted to run away while she still had a modicum of control over herself.

'The land is beautiful, rolling hills with the sparkling sea in the background, and though the villages are mostly primitive the people are in many ways much more able than those in England. They have an affinity with their land, with the weather and the seasons and the crops, and a sense of fairness and equality that means no man in a village will let another go hungry.'

'It sounds like paradise,' Selina murmured.

'All places have their flaws. The cities are crowded and dirty, the people there often hungry and living in poor conditions. There is exploitation, as there is any-where in the world.' He paused and Selina could sense he was smiling again. 'But it is the most beautiful coun-try. The air is fresh and the land is lush.'

She heard him shift and stand and just as her eyes were about to flicker open she thought she felt the faint-est touch on the back of her neck. Selina stiffened, not knowing whether she wanted to flee or to beg for more.

'I think you would like it there, Miss Salinger,' Lord Westcroft said from somewhere across the room.

Selina's eyes shot open. She must have imagined the touch, conjuring up what she wished to happen. She was in dangerous waters, sitting here alone in Lord West-croft's study, and not because of how the man in front of her was acting. He hadn't made a single inappropriate move, but here she was wishing for things that could never be. Things that she knew were both impossible and unwise.

'Please excuse me, Lord Westcroft,' she said, standing quickly. She needed to get out of this room, to get away from the man who had awakened something inside her she'd never felt before.

Before he could answer Selina had hurried from the room, aware her behaviour would seem odd, even perhaps a little rude.

'Rude you can apologise for,' she muttered to herself. 'Wantonness you cannot.'

Quickly she walked through the dark hall and up the stairs, stopping only when she'd closed the door to her bedroom firmly behind her. She paused for a moment, resting her forehead on the thick wood, and made an effort to calm her pounding heart.

Perhaps it was inevitable, this attraction she felt for her employer. He was an attractive man and he could be charming when he wanted to be. She just needed to remind herself how dangerous men of his class could be. How they could promise a woman the world, but didn't always carry through on that promise, especially to someone of a lower social standing.

She'd seen the way he'd looked at her, seen the flashes of desire in his eyes, hastily hidden, but there all the same. But he wasn't looking at her as an equal, as a woman he might take as a wife. If anything were ever to happen between them, it would not lead to marriage, Selina was sure of that. She was a governess, inferior in society's eyes, and she'd seen first hand how men of Lord Westcroft's class wheedled out of any commitments to a woman who wasn't socially their equal.

Selina thought of her mother, beautiful and young. Her

father had been besotted, he'd always said he was completely in love with his second wife, and had mourned her fiercely when she'd died.

'Not enough to marry her,' Selina said to herself. Despite living her whole life thinking her parents had married, that they had defied convention, that love had overcome the differences in social status, her half-brother had taken great pleasure in telling her that wasn't actually true. Instead their father had taken the housekeeper's daughter as a mistress, moved to Cambridge to shield the family from the worst of the gossip and fathered Selina, a daughter he doted on, but had never deigned to tell she was actually illegitimate.

That was why she would never trust a gentleman. It was a cautionary tale, one that had already cost Selina everything she had once known, and she wasn't about to make the same mistakes as her mother. There would be no more fantasising about Lord Westcroft, not even when he was at his most charming.

Chapter Eight

'She must be pretty,' Richard Rowlands said as he squinted out over the rolling fields.

'Mmm…' Matthew said non-committally. He'd known Rowlands his whole life and the man had a knack of getting straight to the heart of a problem.

'Something more than just a pretty face, though,' the other man mused. 'You must have come across a lot of attractive women in the course of your travels…'

'Shall we ride the boundary?' Matthew suggested, hoping to change the subject.

'Wouldn't be the end of the world…'

'Riding the boundary?'

'Falling for someone. You deserve a bit of happiness. It's high time you stopped punishing yourself for what happened with Elizabeth.'

Elizabeth. As always when he heard that name his throat tightened and a great pressure began to build behind his eyes.

'I'm not falling for her,' he said curtly. 'I merely mentioned I don't detest having a bit of company at Manresa House. It's a dreary pile of bricks.'

'Whatever you say, my lord.'

'Cheeky sod.'

'I can doff my cap if you prefer?'

'That'd be a fine sight.'

Rowlands grinned. There had always been a friendly camaraderie between the two men, despite Rowlands having worked for the Hampton family since he was a lad. He had risen to the position of land steward when Matthew's brother was in charge of the estate and now Matthew was determined to do whatever it took to keep the steward managing the farmland and tenants and grounds of Manresa House. He would be invaluable when the time came for Matthew to return to India.

'Perhaps I might come and introduce myself to this governess of yours if you have no interest in her,' Rowlands said, grinning as Matthew rolled his eyes at him.

'Did I mention she's invaluable? I don't want you scaring her away.'

'I've been declared the most charming man in north Yorkshire three years running.'

'*That* I struggle to believe.'

Rowlands stroked his thick moustache and beard. 'What can I say, the ladies love a man with a silver tongue and a full beard.'

'You haven't thought about marrying again?' Matthew asked quietly. His friend had been widowed young, left with a son who must be approaching adulthood now.

'Mary was the only one for me,' Rowlands said softly, his voice full of sincerity.

For a moment Matthew envied the steward's relationship, short lived though it had been. He had never known love, had never experienced feeling as though you couldn't survive without the other person. And he wouldn't, not now. After Elizabeth, after those disastrous few months as a married man, he had made himself a promise that he would never be pushed into something he knew was wrong again. More than that, though, he had decided he wouldn't entangle anyone else in his life. He'd been entrusted with a wife once and it had been an unmitigated disaster. Never again would he put himself or anyone else through that.

'Come on,' the steward said, urging his horse forward. 'We have a lot of boundary to check before nightfall.'

Matthew followed the other man's lead, feeling the whip of the wind on his face and the chill that was slowly penetrating his thick coat. Yorkshire was the only place he'd ever known such a wind, blowing with an icy ferocity that could cut right through you. Just like the sight of the wild heather and the sound of the red grouse's call, it was one of the things that he would always think of when he remembered his childhood home.

They rode towards the house, planning on cutting past the formal gardens and out to the west of the estate where manicured lawns gave way to the wilder countryside and where in the distance the white forms of the sheep could be seen dotted over the fields. As they approached the gardens Matthew heard a shriek of laughter and instinctively flinched. Miss Salinger and the girls might be handling the bow and arrows again.

He wriggled his toes, remembering the sharp pain as the arrow had penetrated his boot and embedded itself in his skin. Luckily the wound had been shallow and hadn't plagued him for more than a day.

Sharply he pulled on the reins as Theodosia shot out in front of them. She was giggling, her hair flying behind her as she ran, and Matthew thought back to his childhood. After his mother's death there had been no more merriment at Manresa House. His father had expected him and his brother to grow up, to act like men despite only being eight and ten. Games and laughter had been heavily frowned upon. And his tutors had been much less rebellious than Miss Salinger.

Theodosia put her finger to her lips, grinned, then shot off again, hiding herself behind a plinth with a granite urn on top of it.

'Ready or not, here I come.' Miss Salinger's voice was carried on the wind from the other side of the formal gardens.

Matthew watched as she began striding in their direction, stopping to check every possible hiding place on the way. She looked graceful as well as purposeful and he found his eyes tracking her every movement.

This was why he'd been avoiding her for the past week. Ever since that evening in the library, the evening where he'd come so close to kissing her despite knowing it was highly inadvisable, he'd found excuse after excuse to keep his distance. First he'd needed to travel to Whitby, then he'd decided it was time he reacquainted himself with the furthest corners of his estate. He'd hoped that during the days he'd spent away from Miss Salinger he would have refound his sense, but the stirring inside him as he watched the slender form of the governess battle against the wind disabused him of that idea.

'Good morning,' he greeted her as she came to the path they were on.

'Good morning, Lord Westcroft.' Up close he could see the flush of her cheeks where the wind had suffused them with colour.

'May I introduce Mr Rowlands? He is steward of the estate.'

'It is a pleasure to meet you, Mr Rowlands.'

'And you, Miss Salinger. I hope you're settling in well here.'

'I am, thank you,' she said giving him a warm smile.

'Theodosia seemed in high spirits,' Matthew said, watching as his words made Miss Salinger stiffen. They hadn't been meant as a rebuke, but he knew his tone was gruff and disapproving.

'We shall return to our lessons imminently,' she said, meeting his eyes with a look of defiance. 'Arithmetic, one of your approved subjects.'

'Good.'

'The girls concentrate better if they have breaks from the schoolroom, breaks to run around and play, just like the children they are.'

He inclined his head. He hadn't meant for this to develop into an argument.

'Perhaps one day you might grace the nursery with your presence and you would see for yourself.' With a formal little curtsy and a nod to Mr Rowlands Miss Salinger left them, striding off to where Theodosia was crouching and making the young girl giggle as she was found.

'I think I rather like Miss Salinger,' Rowlands said after a minute, still watching where the governess and young girl were walking hand in hand, searching for Priscilla.

'Hmm.'

'She certainly doesn't seem to believe servants should be meek and submissive.'

'Heaven forbid I be blessed with someone easy to deal with.'

Rowlands shot him a knowing look. 'I don't think you'd replace Miss Salinger with an obedient young governess without a backbone...' He paused. 'I don't think you'd replace her with anyone.'

'Remind me again why I allow you such liberties.'

'Who was it who rescued you from the roof of the barn

in the summer of ninety-five? And who fished you out of the lake when you made a wager with your brother you could swim its length in the middle of December? And who…?'

Matthew held up a hand, unable to stop himself from smiling. Memories from his childhood were not often pleasant, but he *had* enjoyed the competitiveness with his brother, when Henry had been just his brother, not being groomed all the time as the *heir to the title*. Until he was eight and Henry ten they'd played together, fought one another, learned together, and Matthew had loved his older brother with a fierce devotion. It had only been later, when their mother was dead and Henry had been subjected to years of their father's indoctrination that the boys had drifted apart. The final act that had severed their relationship permanently was Henry's support of their father on the Elizabeth issue. It had been one betrayal too many and once Matthew had made his escape from the oppressive family home he had cut ties with his brother as well as his father.

Elizabeth, the woman he'd been persuaded into marrying. She had been the daughter of Lord Mewbry, a viscount from the next county over. Lord Mewbry was a wealthy man, a man in possession of a daughter with a huge dowry. A dowry his father had been coveting for years. At the age of eighteen he'd been informed he was betrothed to Elizabeth, instructed that they would marry a few months later. As usual he'd been given no say in the matter, just a firm instruction of how his life would turn out.

For a few weeks he'd convinced himself it was his duty, his contribution to the family. Then he had begun making subtle enquiries about his betrothed. What he found out had horrified him. Elizabeth was ten years his senior, never married and by all accounts had the mind of a child. He'd returned straight to his father and refused the match.

Three weeks later they were wed. His father had threatened to cut him off entirely and at eighteen that had been a terrifying prospect. His brother had told him he must step up and do his duty, provide for the family. And Elizabeth's father had come to visit, telling him that a marriage between them was the only way to protect Elizabeth. He was determined to see her married and the only other option was for Elizabeth to marry Matthew's father. Of course it had all been manipulation, he could see that now.

It had been the biggest mistake of his life. The marriage had been in name only, he'd refused to consummate their union, and for the six months of their marriage he had tried to do penance for his weakness of being unable to stand up to his father by giving Elizabeth a comfortable life. He'd employed a companion, a kind and patient woman from the village, and had ensured she wanted for nothing, but still she had been unhappy, nervous in her new surroundings. Six months after they had married Elizabeth had suddenly dropped down dead while walking out in the garden. No one could explain why.

The relief that came after, the feeling of freedom, was another thing to feel guilty for and that had been when Matthew had decided to step away from the family. He'd been bullied and controlled for the last time and was determined to make his own way in the world.

Even over a decade later he still felt guilty when he thought of Elizabeth. He should have been stronger, should have refused the union. Never again would he be pushed into something he knew wasn't right and never again would he make the mistake of thinking he was fit to care for someone.

In the distance he heard the happy chatter of his nieces, their voices pulling him back to the present, and felt a sudden pang of sadness. They were alone in the world…they'd lost the people who should be ensuring their happiness. He knew how that felt.

'Rowlands, would you excuse me?' he said, slipping from the back of his horse. 'I've remembered something important.'

'Not a problem, my lord. I'll take your horse back to the stable. We can ride the perimeter another day.'

Matthew nodded his thanks, already halfway down the path. He was almost running by the time he reached Miss Salinger and his nieces and had to stop abruptly so as not to barrel into them.

'Is anything amiss, my lord?' Miss Salinger had a note of real concern in her voice.

'Yes, I mean, no.'

'Lord Westcroft?'

'It's all right,' Theodosia said, reaching up and taking his hand. 'We haven't finished playing yet. There's still time for you to join us.'

'I'm not sure…' Miss Salinger said.

He turned his sunniest smile on the governess and saw with satisfaction how she took a deep breath as she looked at him. Crouching down, he took Theodosia by the hand.

'You're right, I was worried I had missed out on all the fun,' he said, giving her a conspiratorial wink.

'Missed out?' Miss Salinger echoed.

'Hide and seek, wasn't it?'

'You want to play?'

'Of course he does, Miss Salinger,' Theodosia said

slowly as if talking to someone who had lost their wits. 'Who *wouldn't* want to play hide and seek?'

'People with no legs, people with no eyes. *Grumpy* people…' Priscilla said to list under her breath.

'I want to play,' Matthew said and with that admission he felt the weight of responsibility lift from his shoulders briefly.

'Priscilla and I will count, you both hide,' Theodosia instructed.

'Separately,' Miss Salinger confirmed.

Theodosia shrugged as if she didn't much care, promptly covered her eyes and started counting.

Matthew looked around. He wasn't sure how long he had, but the garden provided a wealth of hiding places. A youth spent trying to avoid his father meant he had expert knowledge of hidden places all round Manresa House.

With a quick glance over his shoulder just in time to see Miss Salinger slipping behind the curve of the steps that linked the terrace with the formal gardens, he crouched down behind the wild tangle of the rose bed.

A minute passed and then another.

'Found you,' Theodosia shouted, tugging him by the arm. 'That really was much too easy. Miss Salinger is always easy to find as well.'

'I was going easy on you,' Matthew said, allowing himself to be pulled back to the bottom of the steps by his younger niece.

'We've been running round these gardens our whole lives,' Theodosia said. 'We could find you in less than five minutes no matter where you hid.'

'Lord Westcroft grew up here, too,' Miss Salinger, who had also been discovered, reminded the young girl gently.

'But he's old. And he hasn't lived here for a very long time.' She considered for a moment. 'And he's old.'

'So old you had to mention it twice,' Matthew murmured.

He caught Miss Salinger repressing a smile and felt wonderfully carefree. For this moment at least he was determined to forget his responsibilities, his expectations of himself. It had been an impulse that had driven him to slip off his horse and come and join his nieces, the desire to forget his maudlin thoughts about Elizabeth, but one he wasn't regretting. There had been a moment of clarity, a moment of realisation, that he had suffered a lonely childhood after his mother had died and he was reproducing exactly the same environment for his nieces. It wasn't what he wanted for the two little girls in his care.

'Let's make a wager,' Priscilla said and Matthew turned to her in surprise. The elder of his two nieces was so often quiet it sometimes meant he forgot she was there. Especially when faced with the boisterousness of her little sister.

'A wager?'

'Yes, Father used to make them all the time,' Priscilla said. The memory hit Matthew in the chest, almost making him stagger backwards. Henry grinning while wagering he could beat Matthew at some dangerous feat. 'You take Miss Salinger to hide somewhere in the garden, somewhere you don't think we can find you. We shall count to one hundred. You can then time five minutes on that little pocket watch you have in your jacket. If we find you before the time is up, then we win. If we don't, then you win.'

'And the stakes?'

'A horse. No, a new dress. No...' Theodosia started to gush.

Priscilla interrupted her sister, 'A trip to the seaside. A whole day.'

'And if we win?'

Priscilla considered, tilting her head to one side in a gesture that reminded him of his brother. 'I will agree to the dancing lessons Miss Salinger keeps mentioning.'

'Dancing lessons?'

'You said you wanted them to be proper young ladies,' she murmured.

'I thought you were too preoccupied with teaching them to rebel. Shoot their guardian with a bow and arrow and the like.'

She looked at him, her expression haughty, 'We can do both.' Inclining her head towards Priscilla, she dropped her voice a little. 'Priscilla has been resisting the idea of learning to dance.'

'I have no intention of marrying. Ever. So I have no need to learn to dance.'

'But dancing is about so much more than courtship,' Miss Salinger said. Matthew noticed the dreamy quality to her words, the faraway look in her eyes. He could imagine her in the local assembly hall, dancing and laughing and without a care in the world, not knowing her whole life was about to change.

'Why don't you ever want to marry?' Matthew turned to his niece as he spoke. She had a strong character, strong views, that much he'd learned since returning to Manresa House a few months ago, but declaring at the age of nine she was never going to marry was quite a statement to make.

'That doesn't matter,' Priscilla said firmly. 'Are we going to play or not?' She held out her hand and Matthew didn't hesitate to take it, shaking it firmly. In ten weeks Priscilla had only said a very few words to him directly—he wasn't about to break this fragile moment of communication.

'Go,' Theodosia said, pushing him and Miss Salinger gently but insistently. They watched as the girls turned around and faced the house, then began to count to one hundred.

Matthew caught Miss Salinger's eye, pleased to see she was thrown by this turn of events. He knew she saw him as stuffy, especially when it came to the girls, and he was glad to defy her expectations of him. Silently he put a finger to his lips, reached out and took her hand and pulled her along beside him.

He would enjoy this moment of being carefree.

'This way,' he said quietly when they were out of ear-shot.

They skirted around the formal flowerbeds, past the statues and urns and took a sharp left turn just before the walled garden. He led her round the perimeter wall to one corner where the stones jutted out further in one direction, to give a space to store equipment without it being seen when taking a stroll around the grounds. There they ducked behind the wall, completely hidden from the path in both directions. He took out his pocket watch, noting the time.

Matthew peered out, checking the girls hadn't been following, before turning back to Miss Salinger. He swallowed, blinking hard. She looked beautiful standing in front of him with rosy cheeks and her hair falling loose from its fastenings, whipped by the wind. She was wearing her thick, dark cloak, fastened at the neck, but even the tiny triangle of skin that poked out underneath it seemed to tease and taunt him.

Control, he told himself silently. For years he'd prided himself on being a master of self-control. After the Elizabeth fiasco he had vowed he would never dance to another man's tune again. He would stand up for what he knew was right, but more than that he would examine his own motives for doing things carefully before agreeing to anything.

Right now all that resolve seemed to have deserted him. He knew a dalliance with Miss Salinger would be disastrous. He *needed* her, needed her to look after the children, and any intimacy between them could only jeopardise that much more important relationship.

He knew all that, but still he couldn't stop imagining the way she would taste if he kissed her, the softness of her skin under his fingertips, how she would arch her neck and moan as he ran his lips over her body.

'Lord Westcroft,' Miss Salinger whispered. 'Are you unwell?'

He shook himself, regaining control. 'Quite well, Miss Salinger.'

Looking down, he realised he was still holding her hand, the soft skin warm against his despite the cool temperature and ever-present wind. He should let go, release her, allow her to step away, but he held on for a moment longer, gently pulling her towards him.

'Step in closer,' he murmured, 'so you're properly hidden from the path.'

After a moment's hesitation Miss Salinger did, moving closer until their bodies were almost touching, the gap between them tantalising and teasing.

As she moved closer he caught a hint of her scent, a mix of lavender and honey, and he had a wonderfully vivid image of Miss Salinger in the bath smoothing honey into her skin.

Matthew was aware of every inch of her, aware of how her breathing had become more rapid, aware of the minuscule movement of her lips as she caught them between her teeth. He wanted to catch hold of her, to tilt her chin to meet his, to kiss her until they both forgot all the reasons it would be a bad idea.

'The Yorkshire air suits you, Miss Salinger,' he murmured quietly.

She looked at him with a puzzled expression.

'The colour in your cheeks, the wind in your hair. It suits you.' He reached out, managing to stop his hand before his fingers touched her cheek, but he knew she had seen the gesture. He expected her to pull away, to step back and put some distance between them, but she didn't. Instead her lips parted almost imperceptibly and her eyes flicked up to meet his.

Unable to stop himself, he completed the movement, trailing his fingertips from her temple down to the contour of her jaw.

'You plague me, Miss Salinger,' he murmured. 'You occupy my every thought, distract my every action.'

'I don't believe you.'

'You don't believe I think about your smile when I wake up in the morning, or imagine your—'

'Stop,' she whispered, interrupting him, her voice ragged. 'We both know this is unwise.'

'Ten years. Ten years I've done what is right and good and wise. Perhaps for once I want to do something reckless.' He felt all the pent-up emotion about to burst from him. He wanted her, wanted to kiss her, to bury himself inside her, not coming up for air until they were both gasping.

'Something reckless,' she murmured and he could tell she was considering it.

He looped an arm gently around her waist, nudging her towards him. It was a suggestion more than a pull, giving her ample opportunity to move away. He might want her fiercely, but he'd never taken advantage of a woman. No, he wanted her to come to him willingly.

'Lord Westcroft,' she said, her eyes meeting his. It was neither statement nor question, pitched somewhere in between.

Gently he placed a finger under her chin and tilted it up. Her lips were full and inviting, and he knew with a burning certainty that he was going to kiss her and it would be sublime.

'Found you,' Theodosia's voice called triumphantly.

Miss Salinger took a hurried step back, her foot catching in her skirt in her haste. She began to topple, her arms shooting out from her sides to try to regain her balance. Matthew leapt forward, sweeping her into his arms, her body fitting perfectly against his chest.

'Well done, girls,' Matthew said smoothly, setting Miss Salinger on her feet and striding out from behind the wall as if he didn't have a care in the world.

Chapter Nine

Selina tucked her feet underneath her and looked out of the window. It was her favourite spot in the nursery, the generous window seat having a view over the formal gardens and to the farmland beyond. Today the view was not great. Thick clouds hung low and heavy in the sky and a thin sheen of drizzle covered everything. Hardly the best day to go to the seaside. Perhaps Lord Westcroft would postpone, perhaps he would tell the girls they would wait for a sunnier day, or at least a day that was dry.

'Are you ready?' Lord Westcroft called as he stepped into the nursery. Priscilla and Theodosia were playing quietly in the corner with a large doll's house, but as their uncle came in Theodosia jumped up in excitement.

'Have you seen the weather, Lord Westcroft?'

'A beautiful Yorkshire day.'

'It's raining.'

'I've definitely heard you say before a little rain never hurt anyone.'

It was one of her favourite phrases. She cursed his good memory. Today she would have taken any excuse not to spend a whole day with this unpredictable man in front of her.

'A little rain never did hurt anyone,' she conceded. 'But it makes for a miserable trip to the seaside.'

'You can't cancel, you just can't,' Theodosia said with vehemence.

'They won't cancel, Thea,' Priscilla said quietly. 'They promised.'

'We did promise,' Lord Westcroft said quietly, leaning in just a little too close.

Selina hesitated, then forced a smile. They had promised. And the girls had been looking forward to the outing all week. It shouldn't matter that the last time she'd spent any time in close proximity to her employer she'd begged him to kiss her with her body language. In the intervening week she had reminded herself why it would be inadvisable to have anything but a respectable relationship with Lord Westcroft. She was strong. She was determined. Two hours in a carriage would not change that.

'We shall need your thickest coats,' she said, standing up and starting to bustle about. 'When do you wish to leave, Lord Westcroft?'

'As soon as possible.'

'I'm going to paddle in the sea and eat ices and let my hair fly loose in the wind,' Theodosia started to chatter excitedly away to her sister.

Twenty minutes later they were standing outside the front of the house as the carriage pulled around. Lord Westcroft helped the girls up first, then offered his hand to Selina. She took it, avoiding eye contact, stepping up into the comfortable carriage and taking her seat opposite the girls.

Feeling every touch, every accidental contact between their bodies far too much, Selina decided she would use the journey productively. She would start negotiating for the things she thought the girls would benefit from.

'Lord Westcroft,' she said.

'Miss Salinger…' he turned to her with a smile '…may I say you're looking very well. Isn't she, girls?'

Priscilla and Theodosia looked her over dubiously. Selina knew she looked as she always did outside in Yorkshire, windswept and a little dishevelled.

'Lord Westcroft,' she said again. 'I wanted to discuss the girls' lessons. They are doing very well in mathematics, music and history, the subjects you are keen on.'

'Important subjects.'

'Indeed. And we have dabbled in a little literature and art. Priscilla is very talented with her watercolours.'

Priscilla flashed her a rebellious look. Selina had endured a long tirade from the girl as to why painting was a waste of time and how if she had been born a boy she wouldn't be limited to such useless pursuits.

'I wonder, though, if we should be thinking about the girls' futures and expanding their education a little.'

'Expanding?'

Priscilla shook her head quietly and Selina caught her eye. It was heartbreaking, the worldliness of this young girl. She trusted so little at the tender age of nine.

'Young ladies should know how to ride,' Selina said, holding up a finger as if ticking that item off. 'They should know how to dance. They should perhaps speak a little French. They should be aware of how a household is run.'

Lord Westcroft sat back in his seat and regarded her thoughtfully.

'Tell me, Miss Salinger, what lessons did you have when you were a child?'

'I hardly think…'

'You were well educated. I merely wish to know what your father deemed suitable.'

'I had lessons in mathematics, history, French, literature and geography. My father was interested in classics so he taught me much of what he knew. He also taught me to read in Latin and Greek. I had a dance teacher when I was a little older to teach me to dance and an art teacher to instruct me on how to draw and paint. I learned to play the piano and sing and when I was a little older than Priscilla I had a dedicated music teacher who taught me how to play the harp.'

'The harp,' Lord Westcroft murmured.

'I was also instructed in sword fighting and archery, and my mother did her very best to teach me how to cook, but I'm afraid it isn't a strength of mine.'

She looked around the carriage at the three amazed faces.

'Sword fighting?' Theodosia asked, her eyes lighting up.

'Who are you, Miss Salinger?' Priscilla shook her head in disbelief as she spoke.

'Yes, who *are* you?' Lord Westcroft murmured.

'I had a very full education and parents who wanted me to be as well educated as any man, for my sex not to hold me back.'

'We've had four governesses before you,' Priscilla said slowly. 'And they all just went to school until they were of an age to leave and become governesses.'

'Who was your father, Miss Salinger?'

'It doesn't matter.'

'It does. A man who can afford to give his daughter that thorough an education must be wealthy, if not titled.'

'Salinger is my mother's name,' Selina said quietly.

'Who was your father?'

'I hardly think it…'

'Who was your father, Miss Salinger?' Lord Westcroft asked softly. He'd been wanting to ask her since she had first let slip her family were wealthy.

'Viscount Northrop.'

Three stunned faces looked back at her.

'Why are you a governess if your father was a viscount?' Priscilla said, frowning slightly.

Selina swallowed—voicing the words was still too painful.

'Fortunes change,' Lord Westcroft said gently. 'I think that is one of the reasons Miss Salinger wants you to have such a rounded education, so you are equipped for anything that might befall you.'

Considering her next words carefully, Selina spoke, 'Women have none of the power in this world. We are told what to do by our fathers, our husbands, our guardians, our brothers. They can give us everything and they can take it away. All you can be left with are the skills and knowledge you have amassed.'

'Were you wealthy once, Miss Salinger?' Theodosia sat looking at Selina, her eyes wide.

Selina thought of the dozens of fine silk dresses she had owned, the pearls and her treasured set of diamonds, all claimed by her half-brother after her father's death.

'I was.' She smiled brightly, trying to push the maudlin thoughts of the past away, 'But wealth does not give you happiness. You have to find that elsewhere.'

'Do you *actually* believe that?' Priscilla asked.

Selina looked at the young girl. 'Yes. I do. Poverty can make you unhappy, but wealth alone is not the only ingredient in the recipe for happiness.'

'Well said,' Lord Westcroft murmured.

'Why are you a governess when your father was a viscount?' Priscilla asked again.

'My father died. Everything was left to my half-brother. He'd never liked me so he told me to leave.'

'He sounds horrible,' Theodosia said with a scowl. 'If I ever meet him, I'll kick him in the shins for you.'

'Proper young ladies don't kick people in the shins,' Lord Westcroft said.

Theodosia leaned across the space in the carriage, whispering, 'I'll do it anyway, for you, Miss Salinger.'

'Thank you, Thea.'

Selina sat back in her chair, feeling warmed by the fierce emotion stirred in the little girl by her predicament. Next to her she could feel Lord Westcroft's eyes on her, but she refused to look up. She knew she risked losing all ability to think if she looked into his eyes, but even without a single glance in his direction she could feel the heat rising inside her.

'Whitby,' Matthew announced as he helped his nieces down from the carriage. It had taken just over an hour to reach the seaside, an hour of listening to the friendly squabbling between Priscilla and Theodosia and sitting comfortably with Miss Salinger by his side. She had spent most of the journey resolutely trying not to look at him, which had been curious. Just to be perverse he had spent most of the journey trying to make her look at him. He'd always enjoyed a challenge. She'd given in about twenty minutes from Whitby when he'd made a series of ludicrous comments and she'd been unable to stop herself from turning to him to look at him with raised eyebrows. He'd given her his most winning smile and been pleased to see the flush of her cheeks and the shudder of her breath as it caught in her throat.

He'd spent much of the rest of the journey trying to recall what he could about Miss Salinger's father. The name Viscount Northrop was vaguely familiar, tainted with a hint of notoriety. He couldn't remember all the details, but there had been something about an unsuitable marriage and subsequent shun from society. At some point he would get the whole truth from Miss Salinger and perhaps it would explain why she looked so sad when she spoke of her father.

Miss Salinger looked around her appraisingly. Matthew did the same. Ever since he was a child he'd been visiting Whitby. It was a bustling town, with busy shipyards and sailors aplenty. Despite this it still had a genteel air and two beautiful sandy beaches on either side of the river. The fish sold in the markets was as fresh as it got and when his parents had entertained they'd always sent to Whitby for the seafood.

Today it looked a little dull, with the grey sky threatening yet more rain blending in with the dark and moody sea on the horizon. Paint was peeling off the little fishing boats that bobbed nearby and everyone was going about their business hurriedly with their heads bent against the wind.

'It's charming,' Miss Salinger said and Matthew could tell she really thought so. 'I knew it had a booming boat-building industry, but I wasn't aware there would be quite so many little boats. It looks quaint.' She grimaced as a gust of wind whipped at her skirt and cloak and made Theodosia stumble a couple of steps away. 'Although perhaps better enjoyed on a nice summer's day.'

'Let's get ices first,' Theodosia said, skipping with excitement. 'There's a shop by the harbour that Mama took us to.'

Miss Salinger shivered. 'Are you sure you want ices on a day as cold as today?'

She was met by two perplexed stares.

'Of course,' Theodosia said, speaking slowly as if Miss Salinger had just recovered from a knock on the head.

'Come. I think I know the place you mean.' Matthew leaned in to Miss Salinger. 'Never fear, they do hot coffee as well.'

He felt unexpectedly jolly. The weather might be less than perfect for a day at the seaside, but the girls were in fine spirits and he got to spend the day with Miss Salinger. Glancing across at her as he offered the governess his arm, he felt a tingle of anticipation. He remembered the last time they'd been together, that almost kiss, the thrum of desire that had passed between them, drawing them together. It might be entirely inadvisable to try to replicate that feeling, but Matthew knew on his part at least it was inevitable.

The girls skipped on ahead, darting backwards and forward along the esplanade as they giggled at the antics of a squabbling group of seagulls.

'The trip is already a success with the children,' Miss Salinger said, her eyes fixed on the girls in front of them.

'Good. It may not be a sunny day, or warm, but I don't think children notice these things as much as we do.'

Miss Salinger nodded. She was biting her lip and he could tell she had something she wanted to say to him.

'Why the change of heart?' she demanded after a minute.

'The change of heart?'

'For nearly three months you have refused to get close to the girls, refused to get to know them. Then suddenly you're playing hide and seek and taking them on trips to the seaside. It doesn't make any sense. It's confusing and, where children are concerned, you can't keep changing the rules, especially the rules of affection.'

'I wasn't aware there were any rules of affection,' Matthew said, his tone light.

'You don't dally with a child's hopes. You can't build a relationship one week and then completely ignore them again the next.'

'For a governess you have a lot of opinions on what her master can and can't do,' he said quietly. It was a sentence meant to provoke, to raise the fire inside Miss Salinger. He loved her passion, her dedication to the happiness of two little girls she'd only known a few weeks.

'*Someone* has to be their advocate.'

Matthew held up free hand. 'I don't wish to argue about this again.'

'I'm sorry,' she said after a pause. 'It should be enough that we are here today.'

'It should be,' he teased. He reached across and squeezed the hand that was tucked into the crook of his arm with his free hand. 'I realised I was forcing Priscilla and Theodosia into precisely the same childhood I had despised. One full of rules and a man at the head of the family who was more monster than father or guardian.'

'You're not a monster.'

'No,' he agreed readily, 'but I have absolutely no idea how to raise two little girls.'

For a man used to excelling at whatever he did it was quite the admission. These past few years he'd been extraordinarily successful, first in the navy and then building his own business. He'd excelled and enjoyed for the first time in his life not having that constant criticism that had followed him through childhood.

'Most people don't when they become parents for the

first time. And you didn't get the gradual introduction, the luxury of getting to know them little by little as they grew from baby to child. You were presented with two little girls already formed, with opinions and personalities all of their own.'

'Mmm,' he said thoughtfully.

'Was your childhood truly that awful?' Miss Salinger spoke quietly, the question surprising him.

Normally he would laugh such an enquiry off. Over the years he'd learned to keep his past close to his chest. No one needed to hear about the bitterness he still held inside over the time his father had pitted him and his brother against each other in a sword fight, under the guise of teaching them swordplay. His brother had won and Matthew's punishment, alongside the deep gash on his arm that still burned white when he tanned, was to be locked in the attic for three days. He'd been seven. Or the time his father had caught him by his mother's grave, talking to her, and the old Earl had thrashed him for being weak.

'It was,' he said quietly. 'My father was a cold man, he should never have had children, he didn't know how to care, how to love. Henry he tolerated because he was the heir. I was inconsequential, not worth the effort.' He paused, remembering the loneliness and solitude after his mother had died. 'When my mother was alive she protected me to some extent, at least most of the time he wasn't overtly cruel. When she died...' He trailed off and shrugged.

They continued on silently for another few steps. To their right the sea lapped against the harbour wall and little boats bobbed up and down. Every so often a stronger gust of wind would howl through the town and made the wood of the fishing boats creak and snap.

'My father was a cruel and distant man, and I hated every moment I was under his control.' He glanced sideways at Miss Salinger. She was looking at him, her face a mixture of sympathy and anger. 'But he's long dead and I cannot carry round the grudges from childhood my entire life.'

'Many people do,' Miss Salinger said softly.

'I saw myself the other day, when you were playing hide and seek with the girls, as the distant, cold figure sitting up on the horse. It looked far too much like my father.'

'You could never be like that.'

'You hardly know me, Miss Salinger.'

'I think you can know someone's character within a very short time of meeting them. You're not cruel.'

'Those girls have lost their mother and father. I cannot replace them, I cannot be what you wish me to be to them, but I can give them a safe environment to grow up in, I can provide a little merriment and adventure.'

'You say you don't know how to raise children, but I think you do. That is all they need—everything else is nice but unnecessary.'

'Perhaps.'

They looked ahead to where Theodosia was swinging off the metal railing that separated the esplanade from the water in the harbour, her feet dangling precariously over the water every time she swung backwards and forward. As if one, they broke out into a run, Matthew outpacing the governess, but only a little. He pulled to a stop and looped an arm around the little girl just as the strength in her little muscles gave out and she collapsed laughing into him.

'*That* was dangerous, little imp,' he scolded her gently.

'It was fun, though.'

'Don't think I'd go diving into the murky waters of Whitby harbour to save you if you fell in.'

Theodosia turned her serious face to him, for once devoid of a smile. 'Mother was teaching us how to swim, before she died. I can do a little.'

'Where was she teaching you?'

'The lake.'

Matthew shivered. It was beautiful in summer, but damp and dreary this time of year.

'Perhaps…' He trailed off. He'd been about to offer to teach the girls to swim in the summer. He couldn't make promises like that. In a few months he would be headed back to India and who knew when he would return to England again. The girls would be at least a few years older, maybe even young ladies thinking about their debuts. 'Perhaps in the summer we could find someone to give you lessons.'

He glanced at Miss Salinger and immediately imagined her lithe naked body submerged in the blue waters of the lake. Quickly he looked away, but he knew that image would stay with him for a long time.

'Will you do it, Miss Salinger?' Theodosia asked.

'I can't swim,' the governess admitted. 'Cambridge is landlocked and there never seemed to be any need for me to learn.'

'You can't swim?' he echoed, surprised that the young woman who could seemingly master any skill hadn't ever learned to swim.

'I fell in the River Cam once, splashed around for a few seconds in panic and a passing student had to dive in and save me.'

'Lucky man,' Matthew murmured. He was besieged by a thousand images of Miss Salinger emerging dripping from the river. He *knew* she would have been fully clothed, but in his imagination she was clad in the white cotton nightgown he'd seen her in on her first night at Manresa House. And it was wet. And it was clinging to all the curves he knew hid under the thick wool of her clothes.

'Excuse me?'

'Lucky man,' he repeated a little louder. 'Every gentleman wishes for a chance to prove himself gallant.'

Miss Salinger gave him a sharp look, but he just smiled serenely.

'We've arrived,' he said, motioning to the shop front across the street. Miss Salinger took the girls by their hands, leaving him to watch as she glided away from him, his mind still caught on the image of her emerging naked from the river.

Chapter Ten

'I'm very sorry, sir, we do not make ice cream out of season,' the waiter said, bowing low with his apology. 'I can offer you hot drinks and a selection of cakes.'

Theodosia frowned as if she didn't comprehend.

'October is a little late in the year to be wanting ice cream,' Priscilla said to her sister.

'But I've only ever had it once before and it was delicious. I thought they always had it at the seaside.'

'How about warm milk, girls? Or hot chocolate?'

They nodded, but there was visible disappointment on the girls' faces.

'Wait here,' Lord Westcroft said, jumping up from his seat and disappearing behind the counter. Selina marvelled at his self-assurance—only a titled man or a very wealthy one would have the audacity to walk around a serving counter in that way.

'What is he doing?' Priscilla was peering in curiosity.

'I've no idea.'

A minute later he re-emerged, brandishing a piece of paper.

'What is that?' Theodosia asked.

'The recipe for ice cream.'

Selina frowned, wondering if he meant for the dour cook at Manresa House to try out the recipe one evening.

'We have an ice house on the estate, we can get all the ingredients. The method doesn't look too taxing.'

Three pairs of eyes stared at him in confusion.

'You mean for Cook to make it?' Priscilla was as sceptical as Selina. 'If you knew Cook, you'd know she's old, mean and resistant to change.' It was a harsh summary of the servant's character, but Selina couldn't deny it was accurate. 'I don't think even you could get her to make ice cream for dessert.'

'Then we shall make it,' he said, his tone implying it was completely normal for an earl to take over the kitchen to make ice cream.

'Us?' Priscilla asked.

'Why not?'

'Have you ever made ice cream before, Lord Westcroft?' Selina couldn't help but smile at the image.

'No, but you forget I have the recipe.'

She hadn't forgotten, but for a delicacy such as ice cream she suspected there was a little more to it than measuring the right quantities of ingredients into a bowl.

'You really mean it?' Theodosia was inching to the edge of her chair, her eyes wide.

'Of course. You asked for ice cream and ice cream is what you shall get.'

'Can we do it tomorrow? And can we make lots of different flavours?'

'Tomorrow I go away on business, but we can make it as soon as I return.'

Selina watched as Theodosia threw herself at her uncle, settling on his lap and burying her head in the front of his jacket. It seemed he meant to continue involving himself in his nieces' lives, at least where it didn't interfere with his business.

Unfair, she chided herself. Lord Westcroft was really making an effort and Priscilla and Theodosia were blooming under his attention. She had to remind herself that most parents and guardians were not as involved as her own father had been and many did go away for extended periods of time. It would be unfair to expect anything else from Lord Westcroft.

Still, she knew the girls would feel the upheaval deeply when it was time for their guardian to leave for India.

'Don't be so foolish,' she muttered to herself, earning her a curious look from Lord Westcroft. She felt foolish, she had told him time and time again that his involvement in the girls' lives was the most important thing. He'd warned her he would eventually have to leave, used it as a reason for not becoming too close to them. Now he was doing what she wished and she was worrying about how him becoming closer to Priscilla and Theodosia might affect them when it was time for him to leave.

The cups of hot chocolate arrived, steaming and sweet, and Priscilla and Theodosia took theirs to the window, watching the activity on the boats as they sipped the sweet liquid.

'You're hiding something from me,' Lord Westcroft said as Selina glanced at him over the rim of her cup.

'What makes you say that?'

'Something about your background.'

Selina shook her head. He already knew far more than she'd ever told anyone before. Her previous employers had assumed she was the poor but well-educated daughter of some minor gentry family, exactly what Selina had wanted them to think. Only Lord Westcroft had probed further, only he had seen through the thin veil of deception.

'You know who my father was, how my brother turned me out. You know everything.' It wasn't quite the truth, but no one needed to share in her complete humiliation. He bowed his head and Selina saw his fingers twitch as if he were about to reach out across the table towards her. Silently she shook her head—of course he wasn't. He was an earl, sympathetic to her background, but not about to take her hand in public to comfort her. Her thoughts were running away from her.

'And your friends? They didn't step in?'

Selina swallowed.

'I thought not,' he murmured. 'They didn't know, did they?'

'Why do you want to know so much?'

Tilting his head to one side slightly, he regarded her for a minute before speaking. 'Do you know, I'm not sure. You intrigue me, Miss Salinger, and I want to know why.'

Selina looked into his eyes. They were dark, the deep brown of his irises almost merging with the black of his pupils, and the intensity of his gaze made her cheeks burn under the scrutiny.

'You won't give up, will you?'

'No.'

Selina toyed with the handle of the empty cup in front of her, trying to decide whether to make something up, to see if he would believe a half-truth, but even as she considered she knew he would see through any lie.

'Before I was born my father was married to Lady Portia Wesendale. She gave birth to my brother a few years into the marriage, but they struggled to have any more children. By all accounts it was not the happiest of unions, but they managed to get through the animosity between them by simply not seeing each other very much at all. Lady Portia became pregnant when my brother was fifteen. She died in childbirth and the baby only survived four days.'

Selina glanced over at the girls. Although she didn't mind them knowing portions of her family history, she would rather they were not privy to her deepest secrets.

'Pregnant even though they did not see each other much?' Lord Westcroft asked.

'Apparently so...' Selina shrugged. 'My mother was the daughter of my father's housekeeper. She was thirty years younger than him, stunningly beautiful, and they fell in love.' Selina blinked back the tears. She missed both her parents terribly, wished that they could have been here to guide her through the past few years of hardship. 'The difference in their social status meant they would not be accepted by society, so Father abandoned London for good and they lived a happy life in Cambridge. A year later I was born.'

She was assailed by all the memories of her childhood. Her father lifting her up on his shoulders to explore the cloisters of the Cambridge colleges. Her mother strolling along the banks of the Cam, parasol protecting her porcelain-white skin. The whole family gathered in their cosy library, listening to her father read one of the classics.

'I had a wonderful childhood. Without the pressures of his duties in London my father had a lot of time to give to me and he had a love of learning that meant he saw me well educated.'

'And where was your half-brother in this new happy family?'

'On the periphery,' Selina said sadly. 'My mother would never have excluded him, but he *hated* her with a passion. He hated that she'd replaced his mother in becoming the lady of the house, he hated that my father cared for her in the way he never had for William's mother and he hated me. When he came home from university he would only spend a few days in Cambridge with us, then he would leave for Northrop Hall where my father had appointed a distant cousin to look after the estate. After university he stopped visiting at all. I barely knew him.'

'I can understand a child carrying that much hatred,' Matthew said, spinning his cup on the table, 'but there was no reason to take it out on you.'

'When my father died I knew my brother would inherit the title and the estate, but my father had always told me I would be well provided for.' She blinked back the tears. 'I believed him.'

'What happened?'

'William came with three solicitors and told me they had possession of Father's will. As his heir he inherited everything. I was left with nothing.'

'But you didn't see it.'

She shook her head. At first she'd thought it was a deception, but William's next revelation had pushed that suspicion away.

'There's more,' she said, lifting her eyes to meet his. She'd never told anyone this next part, never spoken the words out loud.

'William told me that my father and mother had never been married, that their union had been one of sin...' she paused, taking a deep breath '...that I was illegitimate.'

Lord Westcroft frowned, 'How do you know he wasn't lying?'

'My mother would always point out the church where she'd said they'd got married, a pretty little church in the village of Trumpington. I called my brother a liar and he escorted me to that church. He told me to question the vicar, who denied all knowledge of a marriage between my parents and placed the parish records in front of me to check for myself. There was no record of marriage between Viscount Northrop and Amelia Salinger.'

The cup clattered across the table as she let go of the handle, looking up to see Lord Westcroft's reaction.

'And that is why your father didn't leave you anything?'

Selina shrugged. 'He was a liar. He told my mother he loved her every day, but what sort of man puts a woman in that position? Makes her live as his mistress when all the world thinks they're married? It wouldn't have cost him anything to actually marry her, nothing but his pride.'

'From how you describe him it sounds out of character.'

Selina bit her lip, 'Perhaps I never really knew him. I *thought* he loved me, that he loved us, but that clearly wasn't true. And I thought he was a good man, but he was just like every other *gentleman*—more worried about his title and family name than the people who loved him, whom he professed to love.'

She sniffed, determined not to cry again over her father. For two weeks after William had thrown her out of the house she'd been overcome with tears again and again, but now she'd moved on. Built a life for herself. It was a very different life from the one she'd planned, but it was a life all the same.

'Do you see now why I had to change my life completely? I couldn't rely on friends to take me in. They all thought I was the legitimate daughter of a viscount and I couldn't bear to sully their reputation alongside my own.'

This time Lord Westcroft did reach out a hand, laying it on the table so his fingertips just touched hers. She looked up, saw the sympathy in his eyes and wished she could throw herself on to his chest and sob until all the pain had subsided.

She thought of the suitors, the young gentlemen in Cambridge, the men she knew would have faded away as soon as they knew she was not born in wedlock. They were all the same, *gentlemen*, all wanting connections and power and not caring who they hurt to get it.

Quickly she slid her hand away. That was why she needed to be careful. Lord Westcroft was attractive and charming when he wanted to be. Kind, too, and she knew the sympathy in his eyes was genuine, but he was still a gentleman like all the rest. Her body might thrum when he walked into the room, her lips yearn to be kissed by him, but her head needed to remember that nothing good could come out of it. He would never consider an illegitimate governess as a woman to be taken seriously and Selina refused to ever be a man's mistress, no matter how attractive she found him.

'Come, girls,' she said, her voice shaking. 'Let us go down to the beach.'

Without looking back, she ushered the children out of the door and started to march them briskly down the street. As they crossed the road she felt Lord Westcroft's presence behind her and it took all of her self-control not to turn to him, not to take his arm and welcome him in.

Chapter Eleven

Matthew stood, watching Miss Salinger crouching down at the seashore. She had carefully picked a place just out of reach of the crashing waves, but every so often would look up and check she wasn't about to be swept out to sea.

The sky above them was filled with heavy dark clouds which looked about to burst and the relentless Yorkshire wind was whipping up sand all around them. All in all it wasn't really the perfect day to spend on the beach, but Priscilla and Theodosia didn't seem to notice.

Miss Salinger and Priscilla were intently searching the shore for seashells, collecting them up for some project back home, and Theodosia was running up and down the beach, each time getting a little closer to the waves, waiting for them to crash and break near her boots before dashing away shrieking with excitement.

'Can I show you a game?' Matthew strode over to Theodosia. She looked up at him with her eyes shining. 'It's a game I used to play with your father when we were boys.'

'How do you play?'

'It is a game of nerve. You both stand on the shoreline and wait for the next big wave. The winner is the person who holds their nerve longest before jumping out of the way, still without getting wet, of course. Shall we try it?'

Theodosia nodded, hitching up her skirt and holding it round her knees. With her free hand she reached out for his and Matthew felt a pocket of warmth as he took her fingers in his own.

'Look, there's a big one,' Theodosia said excitedly as she looked over her shoulder. The wave came crashing closer and his little niece jumped forward, squealing with exhilaration. 'You win that one,' she said, jigging up and down on the spot. 'Let's play again.'

'I warn you I'm very good at this game.'

'Did you always used to beat Papa?'

'Always.' He felt a spark of happiness as he remembered the days spent on the beach at Whitby, the carefree hours running in the wet sand and splashing in the shallows.

They stood with their backs to the sea again, looking over their shoulders at the waves coming in, waiting for the next big one.

'Look. There.' Theodosia pointed at a wave bigger than the rest as she hopped up and down.

They both watched it approach, Matthew able to feel the little girl's excited energy through the way her fingers wriggled in his own. At the very last moment he jumped forward, pulling Theodosia with him to stop her getting soaked.

'You win,' he said grinning at her. 'I lost my nerve.'

'Again. Again.'

'Theodosia Hampton,' Miss Salinger called, walking closer, 'I hope you're not going to get too wet, otherwise we'll have to go straight home.'

'I'm jumping out of the way of the waves,' Theodosia said. 'Don't worry, miss, I'm too quick to get wet.'

As Miss Salinger turned her attention to him Matthew felt the air being sucked out of his lungs. She looked beautiful with her hair whipped by the wind, her cheeks rosy from the fresh air and her eyes shining.

Steady, he told himself. She'd revealed a lot of herself when they'd been talking over their steaming cups of coffee, but one thing had been very clear—her reluctance to trust anyone again and certainly not someone of his social rank.

She shouldn't trust him, sensible woman. All his thoughts of her were decidedly ungentlemanly. Even now as she crossed the sand with a frown on her face he couldn't stop himself from imagining tangling his fingers in her hair and pulling her into the surf with him.

'I don't want Theodosia to catch a cold,' she said, a note of accusation to her voice.

'You play instead, then,' he offered, holding out his free hand to her.

'Yes, yes, yes,' Theodosia said, clapping her hands. 'And I shall be the judge.'

'I'm not going to play,' Miss Salinger said firmly.

'Are you afraid of a little water?'

'I'm loath to be wet and uncomfortable all afternoon.'

'Then all you have to do is beat me. Unless you don't think you're capable.'

'I'm not falling for that,' she said, standing in her governess stance, feet planted slightly apart, hands on her hips.

'If you won't play, then I will,' Theodosia said, grinning up at her governess. 'And then I might fall in the sea and catch a chill and it would be all your fault.'

'You will not,' Miss Salinger said, taking a step towards them. 'Come away from the sea right this instant or we will go straight home.'

Theodosia pouted, but it was a credit to the governess's discipline that the young girl slipped her hand out of his and dragged her feet a little further from the shoreline.

'I think we should make it into a wager,' Matthew said, his eyes locking on to Miss Salinger's.

'There is no point in proposing a wager because I'm not going to do it.'

'If I win, you let me seek out your brother and satisfy myself this whole business with your father's will was above board.'

'No,' she said, shaking her head. 'No. Most definitely not.'

'Let me put it another way, then,' he said, holding out his hand to her. 'If you win, then I forget all about it. If I win, or if you refuse to play, then I ride straight down south, find your brother and question him.'

'Why do you even care?'

'I don't like injustice. Or the strong taking advantage of the weak.'

'I'm not weak.'

He looked her up and down. 'No, you're not. But when faced with a viscount and his solicitors you don't stand much chance alone.'

'I knew I should never have told you the truth.'

Matthew wriggled his fingers, gesturing for her to step forward. With a sigh she complied, placing her hand in his.

'*When* I win, you promise to forget all about it?' she said, the frown back on her face.

'On my oath.' As he spoke he crossed his fingers behind his back as he had done as a child whenever promising something his father had asked of him.

'Tell me the rules.'

'We stand hand in hand,' he said, giving her hand a

squeeze just to remind her they were already entwined. 'Then we wait for one of the big waves. Whoever moves first is the loser, whoever stays for longer is the winner, unless they get wet.'

'I have to warn you I like to win,' Miss Salinger said.

'So do I.' He leaned in closer, 'You may want to hold your skirts up a fraction, just so they don't get wet.'

'I couldn't.'

'There's no one else here.'

'You're here.'

'I promise not to look.'

'I don't believe you.'

'Sensible woman. All the same, the sea is a little cold at this time of year.'

She looked him in the eye as she gathered a handful of her skirt in her free hand, inching it up from the ground to reveal her boots underneath. Matthew swallowed, knowing she was testing him, but unable to resist the urge to look down.

'Nice boots,' he murmured.

'You promised not to look.'

'We all knew that wasn't a promise I was going to keep.' He straightened up, gripped her hand a little tighter, and began to walk backwards towards the shoreline. 'Are you ready, judge?' He looked at Theodosia, waiting for her response.

'Ready.'

'Best of three?'

Miss Salinger nodded, her eyes fixed intently on the approaching waves.

They waited, watching as the smaller waves broke until a little way out a large wave began to build.

'Feel free to jump now,' he murmured.

'I'm fine here. But you jump if you want to.'

The wave crashed, the water sped towards them and at the very last moment they both jumped forward.

'You jumped first, Miss Salinger,' Theodosia called. 'My uncle wins the first game.'

He smiled at her, laughing as her frown deepened.

'Shall we go again?' she asked, pulling him back towards the waves.

Again they waited, watching the smaller waves lap the shore a foot away, waiting for something bigger.

'Don't get those pretty boots wet,' he murmured into her ear as a larger wave began to build out at sea.

She didn't reply, her focus completely on the water rushing towards them. He rose on to his toes, ready to spring, waiting until the very last moment before jumping forward. Even before he landed he knew Miss Salinger had won that round.

'Miss Salinger won,' Theodosia declared. 'Whoever wins the next one is the overall winner.'

She slipped her hand into his again, pulling him back to the shoreline, and he felt a momentary warmth flow through him. It had been a very long time since anyone had held his hand. Of course there had been women, in India and before that during his time in the navy. Beautiful women, the bored wives of indifferent officers, even once a cool and haughty Indian princess, all of them passionate encounters, filled with heady desire, but not once in all his adult years had he been close enough to anyone to hold their hand.

Beside him Miss Salinger leaped forward. Matthew reacted too late, too lost in the sadness of the realisation that his closest contact these past few years was a governess who had made it perfectly clear what she thought of men of his social class. The water sloshed over his boots, darkening the leather, but thankfully not seeping inside.

'Miss Salinger is the winner,' Theodosia called, running to the governess and throwing her arms around her.

'I told you I like to win,' she murmured as Theodosia danced off to join her sister.

'You did. I congratulate you on your victory.'

'You remember your promise.'

'I remember. I won't go seeking out your brother. At least not until I have your permission to do so.'

She sucked in a breath, her chin dipping down a fraction.

'That wasn't what we agreed.'

He took her hand in his own again, knowing it was a bold act to do so outside the constraints of the game, that anyone could walk past and see them, draw the wrong conclusions. Matthew didn't care. There was something so *right* about holding her hand in his own.

'I will not go and confront your brother,' he said as he looked her in the eye, 'but we will talk further on the matter.'

'You have no right—' Miss Salinger said.

'I know,' he interrupted her. 'I just can't seem to help myself.'

With a glance to check the girls were occupied he leaned forward, running his fingers of his free hand down the length of her cheek. The skin was cool and soft and he wondered how the rest of her would feel under his fingertips. Before he could think through all the reasons this was a terrible idea, he kissed her, tasting the sweetness under the tang of the salt from the sea. Her lips were soft and warm and inviting and after a moment he felt her pulling towards him, drawing him in. He wanted to gather her to him, to pull her body tight against his, but he knew this kiss could only be fleeting. Still, his body reacted with the full force of desire surging through him and the primal part of him wanted to lay her down on the sand and explore every inch of her.

Instead he pulled away, his eyes lingering on her for a moment before he turned to check the girls hadn't seen anything.

'Why did you do that?' Her voice was strong despite the slight tremble he detected and he cursed himself for poor timing. Now he couldn't think of anything else but kissing her again and it was impossible, here in the open where even once had been too much of a risk.

'I wanted to, I've wanted to for a long time.'

'And you just do what you want.' It was said as a statement, her voice flat, and Matthew realised the error in his words.

'No,' he said, catching her hand as she turned away. 'Don't pretend you didn't want it, too.'

'I wanted it,' she said, her eyes burning with suppressed fury, 'but us mere mortals don't get to act on our wants and desires above all else. We have to think of consequences.'

'It was just a kiss,' he said, trying to stop himself from leaning forward and tucking a stray strand of hair behind her ear.

'Would you have kissed me if you hadn't known about my background?' she asked quietly. 'Would you have kissed me if you didn't know I was illegitimate?'

'What has that got to do with anything?'

'Everything. I tell you that story, that horrible little dirty secret, and suddenly you think I'm the sort of woman who will allow herself to be seduced by a gentleman. I will never be any man's mistress.'

'It was just a kiss,' he said, although his body screamed it was so much more.

'I will not be your mistress.'

He looked at her, the fear mixed with sadness in her eyes, and felt a surge of anger. Not at her, never at her, but at the men who had made her so suspicious. The men who had taken her innocence and stamped on it, her father and brother for not protecting her as they should have.

Carefully he stepped towards her, placing a hand on each of her arms, making sure the touch was firm but gentle.

'I'm sorry,' he said. 'I never meant for it to be anything more than a kiss.' He smiled. 'You're an attractive woman, Miss Salinger, a woman I can't seem to stop thinking about. You invade my thoughts, my dreams, and I could see on some level you desired me, too.'

She didn't protest, although he saw the faint blush as the blood rushed to her cheeks.

'I didn't think of your birth or your position. I didn't think of anything except my overwhelming desire to kiss you.'

Tears began to form in her eyes, but Matthew forced his hands back to his side instead of raising them to brush the moisture away.

'That's the whole point, isn't it?' she said softly. 'You didn't think. You didn't have to. If someone sees you kissing your governess on the beach, they'd probably give you a slap on the back and a knowing wink. There are no consequences for you.'

'There are for you?'

'If I became your mistress one day, you would get bored of me.' She held up her hand stopping him from interrupting. 'Or you would return to India, the girls would grow up and I would need to move on.' There was no arguing with that. 'But I would have a reputation as a governess who overstepped her place, who abandoned her morals. Either I wouldn't get another position, or I would and my next employer would think I was the kind of woman they could take advantage of.' She shook her head. 'I have no protection, no family to take me in. My reputation is everything.'

The tears were flowing down her cheeks now and Matthew saw the loneliness in her eyes. She'd been ripped from her world of privilege and abandoned by everyone who should care, forced into a new life she knew hardly anything about.

'I'm sorry,' he said again. 'I didn't think, you're right, I don't have to.' He offered her his arm, 'Walk with me, I promise I will behave like the perfect gentleman.'

'There is no such thing.'

'Then I promise I will behave impeccably.'

Chapter Twelve

Selina turned her face up to the sky and felt the first fat raindrop fall on to her cheek. The clouds were dark and heavy and she knew that now the rain had started soon a deluge would follow.

'We need to shelter,' she called, gripping hold of Theodosia's hand a little tighter.

Another drop hit her in the face, then another and another. She pulled the hood of her cloak further up over her hair, looking around in desperation for somewhere to get out of the rain.

'This way,' Lord Westcroft shouted above the howl of the wind, gripping hold of Priscilla's arm and guiding her over the slippery grass.

After the girls had exhausted themselves on the beach Lord Westcroft had suggested they head home, but Priscilla had asked in that quiet, unassuming way of hers if they could go and visit the ruined abbey up on the cliff. Despite the impending storm neither Selina nor Lord Westcroft had been able to deny a request from the girl who never asked for anything, so they'd started the climb.

'There's no roof,' Selina said as they reached the shell of a building. Once it would have been magnificent, the large smooth stones placed so carefully on top of each other in a feat of engineering so advanced for its time. It towered high above their heads, the stonework around the windows intricately carved even though they had long since lost their glass.

'It looks sad,' Theodosia said, looking up at the ruined building.

'Quick, in here,' Lord Westcroft said, pulling them through a stone archway and into the empty heart of the building. Here there was still no roof, but the walls were so thick the archways provided some shelter. They dashed through, stopping under one by the far wall, the angle of the outer wall protecting them from the worst of the rain.

It was pouring now, heavy drops that hit the floor with such force they bounced and splattered. At least in the ruins of the abbey they were sheltered from the relentless wind, although Selina felt the chill of the air settle deep inside her and knew it would take a long time to warm up even in front of a roaring fire.

'We may be trapped here for a while,' Lord Westcroft said, peering out from the archway at the clouds above.

'I'm sorry,' Priscilla murmured quietly, her voice barely audible.

'There is nothing to be sorry for. We all wanted to see the abbey,' Selina said, pulling her cloak tighter about her to try to ward off the chill that was already seeping into her bones.

'Come, girls, stand in closer to the wall, you'll keep drier here.' It was touching to see his concern for his nieces, the two girls he'd been determined not to form a connection with. Selina could see the affection in his eyes when he looked at them.

Without thinking she brought her fingers to her lips.

Still she could feel the fizz and burn from his kiss—the memory would be seared into her for all eternity.

Your first kiss, she mocked herself. It was true. While her friends had been busy scurrying into dark corners with their admirers, allowing a kiss, a touch, a squeeze, Selina hadn't ever been tempted. Not until Lord Westcroft.

Despite her angry outburst after the kiss she couldn't deny she'd wanted it, desire had burned through her, consuming her, until she had thought of nothing else every time he was close. When he'd gathered her in his arms and brought his lips down on hers she'd felt her whole body fizz. It had been sublime, wonderful, until he'd pulled away. Then Selina had been reminded of all the reasons she should never desire a man like Lord Westcroft.

Quickly she glanced at him. He was doing his utmost to pretend to be looking out at the rain, but she knew the very edge of his gaze was on her. There was still that thrum of desire present, that unspoken pull between them. Never before had Selina felt anything like it. It was disconcerting, but not totally unwelcomed. For so long she'd felt numbed by everything that had happened to her, but *this* she was truly feeling.

'The clouds are moving quickly,' Lord Westcroft said, poking his head out of the archway. Flecks of water were splattered on his dark hair and coat, but he didn't seem to notice. She wondered if the rainstorms in India compared to this.

'Perhaps we should run down the hill when it gets a little lighter,' Selina said. 'If we stay here, we'll all catch a chill.'

'We will wait another five minutes.'

They waited, all tucked together in the confined space

under the archway. Selina was acutely aware of Lord Westcroft's every movement: the brush of his hand as he flicked water from his shoulders, the swish of his coat against hers as he shifted from foot to foot. She thought of his hand encircling hers, his arms pulling her close, his lips descending on to hers...

'We need to go,' she declared, stepping out of the archway into the rain.

A hand shot out, gripping her arm, and Selina had to take a deep breath to steady herself before she turned to face him.

'The ground will be treacherous,' Lord Westcroft said.

'Take care of the girls. I do not need any assistance.' As soon as the words were out of her mouth her foot slipped an inch, sliding over a muddy patch. Immediately Lord Westcroft's hand was on hers, but Selina shrugged it off. The last thing she needed was any further distraction. From now on she would do her utmost to keep her distance from her employer.

'Walk quickly, but keep your eyes on the ground in front of you,' Lord Westcroft instructed his nieces. 'We don't want anyone breaking a leg.'

They hurried out of the shelter of the abbey, crossing the grass as the rain pelted them from above. Selina could feel her cloak grow heavy with the weight of the water soaking in and she gripped a handful of her skirt to keep the hem dragging in the worst of the mud. She would be filthy no matter what, but there was no need for her to bring home half of Whitby's soil with her.

Retracing their steps, they began the descent down the hill. Twice Theodosia slipped, her feet sliding almost out from under her, but Lord Westcroft gripped her firmly, each time grasping hold of her and pausing a moment while she regained her balance before he urged them forward again.

'Nearly there,' Selina called over her shoulder. They were almost back down at sea level, the wind a little less ferocious with the shelter of the hill behind them. Selina could see the carriage waiting for them where Lord Westcroft had instructed and she held on to the thought that in two more minutes they would be snug inside the wooden structure.

As she turned back to check once again on the girls Selina felt one of her feet begin to slip out from under her. If she'd been facing forward, she probably would have been able to save herself, but as it was the twisting movement sent her off balance. She fell, her cloak billowing out and exposing the material of her dress, and as she hit the ground she felt her body jar and tense. For a moment she couldn't move, despite the dampness seeping in through her skirts, and she half-sat, half-knelt, until Priscilla came hurrying over, touching her lightly on the arm.

'Are you hurt, Miss Salinger?' he asked, her voice filled with concern.

Selina shook her head. She wasn't, not really. Her body had been jolted by the fall, but she didn't have any sharp pains that indicated a sprain or strain.

'No, just wet and cold,' she said with a smile. She might be cold and wet and muddy, much like the first time she'd knocked on the door at Manresa House, but she was warmed by the concern in Priscilla's eyes. Despite her best efforts Priscilla had still remained aloof and cool towards her this past week. She was no longer confrontational or defiant, but she had not interacted much either.

Selina felt Lord Westcroft's hand under her arm and before she could protest to the touch he was hauling her up to her feet. He didn't let go immediately, even though the girls were standing right there next to them and it seemed as though a thousand unspoken words flew between them.

'Go,' he commanded, ushering all of them towards the carriage. Selina happily obliged, she was beginning to shiver and she knew the girls would be feeling the cold. It would not be warm inside the carriage, but at least they would be sheltered from the elements.

Quickly they crossed to the carriage, Selina feeling the mud dragging on her skirt and didn't dare look too closely at the state of her clothes. She must look completely bedraggled. Glancing back at Lord Westcroft, she grimaced. He, of course, looked none the worse for his dash through the pounding rain and howling wind.

They settled into the carriage and Lord Westcroft thumped on the roof to let the coachman know they were ready to depart. It would feel like a long hour's journey back home and all Selina could think of was sinking into a hot bath and washing the grime from her body.

She exhaled slowly, trying not to notice the way her wet clothes clung to her body or the way, even after everything they'd just endured, she could sense every movement of the man sitting next to her.

'We will be home soon,' she said, trying to reassure the girls.

'I don't think we'll forget this trip to the seaside for a while,' Lord Westcroft said.

The carriage had only travelled a few hundred yards when there was an almighty jolt, throwing Selina out of her seat and into the space between everyone's legs. The girls were hurled backwards into their seats and Lord Westcroft almost ended up on the floor with her. The carriage lurched again, this time tilting to one side, and Selina tumbled into Lord Westcroft's lap. She felt his arms encircle her to stop her from falling any further, but before she could think about where she was she was hit squarely in the chest by Priscilla as she came flying from her seat.

Underneath them the wood creaked and groaned and Selina braced herself for another shift in position, tensing as they lurched a few inches in each direction before it seemed to settle. Theodosia was still sitting on the seat opposite, clinging on to the plush material underneath her so hard her knuckles were turning white. Priscilla, thin and waif-like though she was, was pressed against Selina's chest in a way that was making it hard for Selina to take a breath. She was all too aware of how her bottom was resting squarely in Lord Westcroft's lap, his arms around her waist in the most intimate of embraces, had they not just been thrown around the carriage like fish struggling in a fisherman's net.

'Is anyone hurt?' Lord Westcroft recovered his voice first.

'No,' Selina said. She would have a couple more bruises to add to the ones she'd sustained tumbling on the hillside, but she wasn't seriously hurt. Opposite her Theodosia shook her head.

'Priscilla?'

'No.'

'Good.'

'What happened?' Theodosia's voice was shaky, her hands still gripping the seat even though the carriage had seemingly settled.

'I think we've lost a wheel,' Lord Westcroft said, peering out of the window.

Before anyone in the carriage could move the door was flung open. It was the left side of the carriage, the side that was now angled higher in the air than the right, and the coachman's worried face appeared in the gap.

'Is anyone hurt?' he asked, raising his voice over the hammering rain.

'No. What happened?' Lord Westcroft shifted slightly as he spoke to the man, gripping on to the edge of the carriage a little tighter.

'We hit a rut in the road, the wheel has come off.'

'Can it be fixed?'

'Not tonight,' the coachman said grimly.

Lord Westcroft looked at Selina and the girls. 'We'll have to find somewhere to stay tonight and make the journey home in the morning.'

'There's an inn just back the way we came, The Red Lion. A respectable establishment, my lord.'

'Very well. We shall enquire about rooms there to-night. Hold the horses while I get Miss Salinger and my nieces down. The last thing we want is for them to get frightened and bolt.'

'Yes, sir.'

'When we get to the inn I'll ask then to send a couple of men to help you unharness the horses and secure the carriage.'

The coachman's head disappeared from view and momentarily Selina felt Lord Westcroft's hands tighten around her waist. Carefully he lifted her from him, placing her and Priscilla in the seat next to him. Moving slowly so as not to unbalance the precarious angle of the carriage, he pulled himself up to the door and swung himself out. Selina had to admire the ease of the movement. He looked as though he was familiar with this sort of acrobatics and she wondered if it was his time in the navy that had taught him to be so agile.

'It's a little drop to the ground,' he said as his face

reappeared. 'Miss Salinger, could you help the girls out one at a time?'

'Priscilla, can you go first?' Selina asked. Slowly the hammering in her chest was beginning to subside and the fear she'd felt coursing through her body as the coach lurched was ebbing away. Selina supported the little girl as she swung her leg out through the door and watched as her uncle deftly caught her and lifted her to the ground.

'I'm scared,' Theodosia said, shaking her head as Selina held out her hand.

'Your uncle is right outside the door. He *will* catch you.'

'I don't want to fall.'

'You won't fall. I promise.'

Theodosia looked into her eyes, the little girl's face more solemn that Selina had ever seen it before and after a long pause she nodded once.

'Come, take my hand. I'll help you climb over the edge and then your uncle will catch you.'

She supported Theodosia as she swung her legs over, smiling to cover a grimace as the little girl gripped her hand so tightly Selina felt as though her fingers might snap. Outside she could hear Lord Westcroft murmuring reassuringly to Theodosia and as she watched he took his niece into his arms, hugging her tight to his chest before he set her down on the ground.

'Your turn, Miss Salinger,' he called up, his face appearing through the door again. 'I will be here to catch you.'

Selina felt her body tense at the idea of falling, quite literally, into his arms. Right now she was cold and scared and tired and she wanted nothing more than for him to embrace her, to hold her to his chest and make everything right. It was a dangerous urge to have, the sort of urge that could land a respectable young woman in a scandalous situation.

'I will be able to climb down myself.'

'Don't be so stubborn,' Lord Westcroft said abruptly.

Selina frowned at him, hitching up her skirt to allow herself to throw one leg up and out through the door, taking a moment to find her balance before doing the same with the second. Carefully she eased herself out, feeling the patter of the rain on her skirt as she emerged into the downpour. She glanced down—it really wasn't all that far to the ground—and began to lower herself.

As she moved she felt the carriage judder slightly underneath her and immediately she stiffened, clinging on tighter to the edge of the doorway.

'Just drop down, I'll catch you,' Lord Westcroft said, a note of urgency in his voice.

Selina felt the carriage shift again and before she could talk herself out of it she pushed back, dropping into Lord Westcroft's arms.

She knew she wasn't a petite, dainty young woman. She'd stood half a foot taller than many of the debutantes during her first Season, but the *oof* that slipped from Lord Westcroft's mouth seemed a little unnecessary. He didn't drop her, though, his strong arms encircled her waist and he lowered her gently to the ground. For a moment they just stood there, Selina cradled against his chest, the soothing beat of his heart calming her own. Then with a creak the carriage toppled further on to its side and Selina felt herself being pulled backwards out of the way of the splintered wood.

'What a disaster,' Lord Westcroft said, standing and looking at the wrecked carriage. 'And all from a rut in the road.' He gathered the girls to him, sheltering them as much as he could, seemingly unable to tear his eyes away from the carriage.

'We need to get inside,' Selina said. She could feel the rainwater soaking through every layer of her clothing and knew the girls would be equally soaked to the skin.

'Can you hold the horses?' Lord Westcroft shouted to the coachman.

'Yes, sir. They're calm enough, considering.'

'As I said, I'll send a few men to help you as soon as we get to the inn.'

They dashed off down the street, aware of the slippery conditions underfoot. As the coachman had promised The Red Lion was only a few hundred feet away, the freshly painted sign swinging in the wind, giving them something to aim for.

Selina felt winded as they staggered in through the door, glad of the arm Lord Westcroft offered. They had entered the main bar area, populated with a few hardy locals who all turned to look at the bedraggled newcomers as they let the wind and rain in.

'Has something happened, sir?' A middle-aged woman appeared from behind the bar, bustling forward at the sight of Priscilla and Theodosia's pale faces.

'Our carriage has overturned just a little further along the road. Have you any men who could hold the horses while they are unharnessed?'

'Of course, come in, warm yourselves by the fire.' She turned and disappeared for a moment and Selina could hear her calling to someone. A moment later a portly man appeared, concern etched on his face.

'My wife says there's been an accident, is anyone harmed?'

'No, thankfully. We were travelling home and the carriage struck a rut in the road. The wheel has come off and the carriage overturned.'

Three strong young men hurried past and out into the dusk, all pulling on coats. Even from the briefest glimpse Selina could tell they were the sons of the landlord—all had the same stocky build and fair hair.

'My boys will help your man see to the horses. Will you be wanting rooms for the night?'

'Yes, please.'

The landlord eyed Selina and the girls.

'I've got a fine double room for you and your wife, and a comfortable room next door for the children.'

At that Theodosia laughed, the first sound she'd made since slipping out of the carriage.

'Miss Salinger isn't my uncle's wife,' she said. 'She's our governess.'

'My apologies, sir. Perhaps I should show you the rooms available and you can choose the best for your needs.'

'Wonderful.'

'Would you like to come through to the private parlour?' the landlord's wife asked, bustling over. 'I've got a lovely fire roaring in there and we can see about some dry clothes.'

'Thank you,' Selina said, allowing herself to be ushered through, away from the curious gazes of the Whitby men.

Once in the parlour Selina wished for nothing more than to sink into the comfortable rocking chair positioned directly in front of the fire, but she knew it would be a long time until she would be able to relax. First she would need to see to getting the children dry and warm and then think about their accommodation for the night.

'Take off your coats, girls,' she said, fiddling with

the fastenings on Theodosia's coat, her fingers numb and fumbling.

'You're soaked to the skin,' the landlord's wife said, shaking her head. 'I can lend you some clothes, but they might swamp you a little. And for the little darlings it will have to be clothes from my boys. We've only had sons, no daughters.'

'Anything would be greatly appreciated,' Lord Westcroft said. 'Dry and not quite the right fit is better than wet and cold.'

'I'll bring them to you directly, sir. My name is Mrs Ruthers, anything you need you just ask.'

'Thank you. I am Matthew Hampton, Lord Westcroft, this is Miss Salinger and these are my nieces, Lady Priscilla and Lady Theodosia. We are very grateful for your hospitality.'

Selina saw the woman's eyes widen as she realised the status of her guest. North Yorkshire was not an area Selina knew well, but by the size of the estate and the grandeur of Manresa House she knew Lord Westcroft must be one of the wealthiest landowners in the area. And he was an earl. It would be quite intimidating for Mrs Ruthers to be hosting such a man.

She bustled out and Selina glanced at her employer. He was drenched like the rest of them, but otherwise looked unruffled at the events of the evening. She supposed his time in the navy and sailing backwards and forward to India had prepared him for any situation.

He knelt down next to her, gently helping Priscilla out of her coat, smiling reassuringly at his two nieces. Selina felt some of the tension she'd been carrying seep from her. They were safe and soon would be warm and dry. Given the circumstances there wasn't much more she could ask for.

Chapter Thirteen

Matthew pulled the shirt over his head, twisting his shoulders from one side to the other to try to relieve the tension that had gathered there. It had been an odd day, the trip to the seaside more enjoyable than he'd expected and then the disaster of the carriage accident.

And the kiss. Even now, even after everything that had happened since, he couldn't stop thinking about the way Miss Salinger had folded into his arms, the sweetness of her lips under the salty tang of the sea spray and the reaction of his body as they'd come together. He knew it had been ill-advised, a kiss that could only complicate and jeopardise the delicate relationship between him and Miss Salinger, but he hadn't been able to resist. She'd looked so perfect standing there with the wind whipping at her clothes and her dress, her expression defiant and her eyes always searching, always finding his.

'You're a fool,' he muttered to himself. Only a fool would kiss a woman he needed quite so much. Without Miss Salinger he would have no one to look after the girls, no one to teach them, no one to be their constant, their advocate when he returned to India. He *knew* all of this, but still he hadn't been able put sense before desire.

He began to unfasten his trousers, imagining her in the room next door lifting off the oversized dress Mrs Ruthers had provided her with for dinner. He imagined her slipping between the sheets, completely naked, her body brushing tantalisingly against the cotton as she turned.

For a long moment he savoured the image, knowing it could never be more than a fantasy. He'd had a wife once. He wasn't going to make that mistake again. He never wanted to have someone relying on him so completely— his history had shown he could not always be trusted to make the right decisions.

Not a wife... Matthew laughed, knowing the reaction he would elicit from Miss Salinger if he even hinted they should become lovers. It wasn't the lack of desire, he could see she was attracted to him with every look, every action, but she would never act on it. He thought of the story she had told, her history, her mother's history. She would never allow herself to be treated as her mother had been—a mistress with an illegitimate child.

Still, a man could dream. Vivid, sensual dreams of the woman just on the other side of the wall.

Just as he stepped out of his trousers there was a faint knock on the door. Matthew frowned. It was late, after eleven, and the inn had fallen quiet a little while ago with most of the patrons returning home during a let up in the rain.

After a few seconds there was another knock, slightly louder. Quickly he pulled the trousers back on and moved to the door, opening it to reveal the dark corridor beyond.

Miss Salinger stood outside, a huge white nightgown dwarfing her slender frame, looking like a spirit summoned from a dream. Her feet were bare and as she moved he caught a glimpse of slim ankles and calves underneath the billowing cotton.

'Is anything amiss?' He could see the concerned expression on her face, the lines of worry where she had been frowning.

Her eyes darted over him, lingering for a moment on his bare chest before she raked them back up to meet his gaze.

'Priscilla,' she said, her voice no more than a whisper. 'She's restless, mumbling in her sleep. I'm worried she may have a fever.'

'I'll come,' he said, grabbing the shirt he had discarded over the chairback and pulling it on over his head.

She led the way, bypassing the first door which was her small single room and slipping inside the comfortable bedroom the landlord had suggested for the girls. They lay together in a high double bed, the sheets pulled up to their chins. Miss Salinger had opened the curtains allowing some faint light to filter in, but the sky was still cloudy and there was little moonlight to see by.

As they entered the room Priscilla shifted in the bed, rolling around. She began mumbling incomprehensible words, then as suddenly as she had started she fell quiet.

'I always check on the girls at night,' Miss Salinger said, her voice laced with concern. 'Priscilla normally sleeps soundly.'

He crossed to the bed, taking in the silent, still form of Theodosia on one side and Priscilla with her hair tangled behind her on the pillow. Carefully he placed a hand on her forehead, holding it there for a minute before stepping away.

'She does not feel overly hot,' he said quietly, 'And it would be very quick for a fever to take hold after getting a chill only earlier today.'

'Mama,' the little girl called out, her eyes still closed, but an expression of fear on her face. 'Mama, no.'

'Hush.' Miss Salinger instinctively went to Priscilla's side, wrapping her arms around the thin body and beginning to stroke her hair.

'She's dreaming of her mother.'

'Please, Mama, come back.'

It was heartbreaking to hear the words tumble from her lips, to see the fear and desperation in her voice.

'You're safe, Priscilla. There's nothing to worry about,' Miss Salinger murmured reassuringly. Matthew watched as she perched on the bed beside her young charge and began rocking her gently. 'Should we wake her?' she asked.

'No. If it is just a bad dream, it'll come to an end soon enough. If we wake her, she'll be terrified, unsure of where she is and what is happening.'

The governess gave him a piercing look. 'You've had nightmares?'

Matthew shook his head. 'Henry did, my brother. After our mother died he suffered terribly from nightmares. We shared a room when we were young. I woke him a few times, but it was never a success. It was better to just let him settle naturally.' He remembered his brother's troubled tossing and turning, the older boy reduced to shivering in his sleep from fear, and felt a pang of regret. He missed his brother, not so much the man who had sided with their father at the pivotal moment of Matthew's life, but the boy he'd once been, the companion Matthew had done everything with.

'Mama, Mama, Mama,' Priscilla muttered again, her words becoming more slurred as her breathing deepened a little.

'Hush. I've got you. You're safe. You're loved.'

Feeling surplus to requirements, he stepped to the other side of the bed and checked on Theodosia. She was sleeping peacefully, undisturbed by her sister's tossing and turning.

'I think she's settling,' Miss Salinger said, easing herself off the bed, moving slowly so as not to disturb either of the girls. They stood watching them for another few minutes, only moving once they were both satisfied Priscilla was no longer dreaming. Quietly they crept out of the room.

'I'm sorry for disturbing you,' Miss Salinger said, shifting quickly from foot to foot. She was barefoot, the cold floor turning her toes to ice.

'Hopefully it was just a nightmare,' he said as their eyes locked. Fever and congestion on the chest could be deadly and could strike down even the healthiest of children.

'Hopefully.'

She hesitated and then turned to return to her room. Without thinking, Matthew reached out and gripped her hand.

'Come have a drink with me,' he said, not knowing himself why he was making the suggestion. He prided himself on his sensibility and a sensible man would be putting a solid wooden door and a lock between himself and temptation.

'I think the landlord has gone to bed...' It wasn't a *no* and Matthew felt something leap and flare inside of him.

'I'm sure they won't protest if we help ourselves to one drink.'

'They might think we're thieves or vagabonds, broken in and drinking away their livelihood.'

'What if I promise to pay them handsomely—three times what the alcohol is worth?'

She hesitated and Matthew could see the internal struggle waging inside her. She *wanted* to come and sit with him, to laugh and talk and banish some of the thoughts of the day, but he could see she didn't quite trust herself.

'And I promise to be on my best behaviour,' he said, not able to resist giving her his most charming smile. 'And if I'm not, I hear you have the most wonderful imagination for punishments—Priscilla tells me you favour a heavy Latin translation for when they've disobeyed.'

'It seems to focus them,' Miss Salinger said with a smile.

She *wanted* to go downstairs, to let go of her caution for a little while. Perhaps it was the shock of the accident, or perhaps it was an inevitable realisation that, no matter how hard she protested to Lord Westcroft, she enjoyed his company more than she dared admit. His company and his kisses.

Downstairs he pulled out a stool at the bar, watching as the governess elegantly climbed up and perched on the edge. He should have guessed about her upbringing earlier—there was a grace to Miss Salinger that seemed to be bred into ladies of a certain social class. She glided rather than walked, stood completely still without even the slightest hint of a fidget when the occasion arose and had perfect posture.

'What can I get you, my lady?' He gestured to the array of spirits behind the bar.

'Brandy,' she said decisively.

'A woman after my own heart,' he murmured.

He chose the good stuff, a deep rich colour, strong and fragrant, and poured two generous measures out into the glasses. Placing the bottle down on the counter, he came and joined her on the other side, pulling up a stool so his legs were almost touching hers.

Miss Salinger sighed as she took a sip of the brandy, closing her eyes for a moment and allowing her head to loll back, revealing the length of her delicate neck peeping out from the much-too-large nightgown.

'It has been quite a day,' he agreed. 'Not what I envisaged when I agreed to this trip to the seaside.'

'Until the very end I think it was a success,' Miss Salinger said slowly. He saw the exact moment she remembered their kiss as she recalled the events of the day, saw her cheeks pinken in that delightful way he was becoming so accustomed to.

'A success,' he agreed, raising his glass in toast to her.

She bit her lip, worrying it for a few seconds before raising her eyes to meet his.

'It is certainly a day I won't ever forget,' he said.

'This…what happened today must be nothing compared with your adventures in India.'

'There have been one or two little scrapes. A walk through the jungle being stalked by a man-eating tiger, being chased from a village after being accused of doing magic and a rather hairy encounter with a great king cobra with a body as wide as a tree trunk.'

'A little downpour and a minor carriage accident must seem dull in comparison.'

He looked at her, tilting his head to one side. He *had* enjoyed the day, disasters and all. When he had agreed to take his nieces to the seaside it had felt like an obligation. Although he was determined they wouldn't grow up in the same stifled, unhappy environment he had, he still wasn't sure how much to leave to Miss Salinger. His goal was to be fun, to be present, but not to be an essential feature in his nieces' lives. All too soon he would have to leave, but in the meantime he was struggling to know how involved to be.

'Not dull,' he said, his eyes skimming over her. 'Never dull.'

Matthew felt a bubble of desire starting somewhere deep inside of him and working its way past his common sense to the surface. He wanted to reach across and unlace the oversized nightgown, to push it from her creamy shoulders and reveal the body underneath. With a hand on the rough wooden counter to steady himself he felt his body shift imperceptibly closer.

'I'm sure this is a little different from the life you were leading a few years ago, too,' he said.

She smiled. 'Just a little. Sometimes, looking back, I can't believe I'm the same person.'

'I know exactly what you mean.'

Miss Salinger gave him a questioning look, tilting her head to one side as if to encourage him to go on.

'I was a very different man the last time I was in residence at Manresa House. It feels like a lifetime has passed between then and now.'

'Surely just the same man, with a different perspective on life?'

'I hope not,' he murmured. He paused, knowing he should say no more. Miss Salinger didn't need to know about his marriage and she certainly didn't need to know about the weakness of his character that had allowed the marriage to go ahead when he knew it was wrong. There was something calm about her that urged him to spill his secrets and he found himself leaning in a little more as if about to take her into his confidence. 'When I was a young man my father and brother wanted me to do something I knew was wrong,' he said slowly, thinking back to the day his father had declared he would be wed within the month.

Miss Salinger leaned forward, too, her fingers nearly touching his on the scarred wood of the bar.

'They told me it was for the good of the family and I let them convince me.' He shook his head. He'd been so desperate for their approval he had lost sight of his moral compass. 'Because of my actions someone was unhappy. I'd known it might be the case, but I allowed it to happen anyway.'

'It can be hard to stand up to family when you're young and unsure of yourself,' Miss Salinger said, her eyes glinting in the darkness.

'I didn't like the man I was, how easily I'd been convinced to do something I'd known was wrong. That was when I decided to make my own way in life, to make my own decisions, to be responsible for them.' He'd left Manresa House and hadn't returned for over a decade. 'I think I *did* become a different man in the years I was away.'

'Away from the influences of your father and brother?'

'Precisely.'

'And who are you now, Lord Westcroft?' Miss Salinger asked quietly. It was a loaded question, filled with curiosity and a hint of desire.

'Who do you think I am?'

She regarded him. 'I think like everyone you have two sides. There's your public face, the successful businessman who likes order and discipline. Then there's your private face, the one that allows himself to jump from the waves on the beach and play hide and seek with his nieces. The man the world sees is a mixture of the two.'

'Which do you prefer, Miss Salinger?'

'Even I know, inexperienced as I am, not to answer that question from my employer.'

He smiled, wondering not for the first time why she had agreed to come and have a drink with him. The right thing to do, the *safe* thing, would have been to politely decline when he invited her downstairs. Instead she'd allowed herself to be persuaded. And now here she was, looking at him with a mix of apprehension and anticipation, as if half-hoping he would take her in his arms.

Selina felt her head spinning. She knew she was playing a dangerous game, but she couldn't seem to help herself. Carefully she swirled the remnants of her brandy around in the glass, trying to distract herself from Lord Westcroft's dark eyes that she knew were just waiting for her to look up.

'What is your name, Miss Salinger?' He spoke suddenly, his voice low but his tone insistent.

'My name?'

'I'd like to know.'

She imagined her name slipping from his lips and felt a shiver run through her body.

'Selina.'

'Selina,' he murmured. 'It suits you.'

She'd always thought it was a little too exotic for her.

'It's unusual, exotic,' he said.

'I always worried people expected more from someone with a name like that. More than plain little me.'

'Plain?' he asked, incredulous.

'I'm not angling for a compliment,' she said hurriedly.

'You are many things, Selina, but you're not plain.'

Self-consciously she brushed her dark hair back from her face. As the daughter of a viscount she'd always been told she was beautiful, elegant, desirable. It was easy to be all those things when you had a maid dedicated to styling your hair and an unlimited budget for buying beautiful gowns. She'd bathed every couple of days, rubbed her hair with the finest soaps, applied creams to her skin each night before bed.

Since her dramatic change in circumstances her hair had lost some of its shine, her skin some of its healthy glow. Her clothes were plain and functional, her hair swept back into a simple bun most of the time. When she looked in the mirror she saw herself as she truly was, without all the trappings of wealth and privilege, and it was decidedly unsettling.

'I don't necessarily mind being plain.' It had its advantages. She hadn't found it hard to blend in which had been important in her new life.

'You're not plain.'

'It really—'

'You're not plain,' he said forcefully.

Selina looked up, her eyes meeting his.

'I have sailed around half the world, mixed with women from almost every continent. I know what plain looks like, Selina, and it does not look like you.'

'I think...'

He leaned forward, shaking his head, a rueful smile on his face. 'Trust me, Selina, I can't stop thinking about you. You are not plain.' His voice was low and dangerous and his eyes fixed on hers.

Selina felt her heart begin to hammer in her chest and the warm flush as the blood raced to her skin.

'That would be questioning my judgement. And I can assure you over the last few years I've honed my judgement to perfection.'

This was the point where she should walk away, where she should slip from the stool and run as fast as she could. Staying would be dangerous. Staying meant acknowledging she wanted him to kiss her again, that she wanted

him to trail those fingers of his across her skin as he ex-
plored every inch of her body.

'You're deciding whether to leave?' he asked, his voice
soft, a smile playing on his lips.

'It would be the sensible thing to do.'

'Do you know what I think, Selina?' He waited until
she shook her head to continue. 'I think you've had far
too long where you've had to be sensible. I think you
want to be a little reckless.'

'Would it be reckless?' she asked. Every part of her
skin felt as though it were on fire and he hadn't even
touched her yet.

'It already is. Alone, in a dark room, drinking with a
man who finds you exquisitely attractive.'

Selina swallowed. This was a new experience for her.
Never had she wanted to be kissed before Lord Westcroft,
never had she wanted to throw caution to the wind and
find out how it would feel to have a man take her in his
arms and explore the places only she had ever touched.

'Decision time,' he murmured. 'Will you stay or will
you go?'

Despite the circumstances, despite being alone in the
dark with a man who was physically much stronger than
her Selina knew she didn't have to worry about her safety.
If she walked away, he wouldn't chase after her.

'I'm quite comfortable here, thank you very much,' she
said, trying to inject a lightness to her voice, but hearing
the words rasp out, betraying the dryness of her mouth
and the roil of apprehension inside her.

He smiled and she half-expected him to reach out
for her there and then, but he didn't move more than his
fingers, brushing his fingertips against hers as they lay
on the counter. It was enough to send little jolts through

her body, to make her arch her back ever so slightly as if anticipating what was to come.

'You never asked my name,' he said.

'I know your name. Lord Westcroft.'

'That's my title. Not my name.'

'You want me to know your name?' She felt her head begin to spin. She'd heard him say his full name earlier on, when they had first come into the inn, but she wasn't about to break the moment by reminding him of that now.

He leaned in, his lips almost brushing her ear. 'I want you to moan my name when you can't think of anything else but my lips on your skin. I want you to say Matthew, not Lord Westcroft.'

Slowly she moved her head around, letting out an involuntary little sigh as he laced a hand through her loose hair and kissed her. They came together hard, body against body, lips against lips, and he kissed her as though they were both drowning. Selina could think of nothing else but the pleasure that raced through her body, the pucker of her skin as he brushed against her, the deep yearning for more even as he pressed her tighter to him.

'Selina,' he whispered into the skin of her neck as he broke away to pepper kisses down the velvety skin to her collarbone. It felt wonderful to have someone say her name again, to hear it come from this man's lips and, as he came back to kiss her again, she felt more whole than she had in a long time.

As they kissed again Selina realised she wanted more. She wanted everything. Her common sense would stop her from that, but she wanted just a tiny bit longer to be caught up in the moment. Tentatively she dipped her hands under the hem of Matthew's shirt, trailing her fingers up his back and feeling him react, pulling her ever closer. Their bodies were entwined now and Selina had a hard time working out where she ended and he began.

Matthew pulled away slightly, toying with the edge of her oversized nightdress, looking her in the eye as he tugged at the neckline, pulling it down over her shoulders. Once it had slipped from her shoulders, due to its size, there was nothing to hold it up before her waist and the thin cotton pooled on her hips. Selina looked down, watched as Matthew trailed his fingers over her chest, grazing over the soft skin of her breasts. She felt her back arch, begging for more, subconsciously asking for his hands to move lower.

'And you think you're plain,' he murmured as he smiled at her, then dipped his head to catch one of her nipples in his mouth. She cried out, clutching his head, letting her neck arch and her head fall back. For a moment she felt as though she were taken out of her body, then as his teeth grazed her she came crashing back, a jolt of pleasure shooting through her.

Selina lost all concept of time as he nipped and kissed her, aware of nothing but his lips on her skin, his body pressed to hers. Only when he straightened and kissed her did she remember who and where she was. And even that wasn't enough for her to push him away. How could anything that felt this good, this right, be wrong?

Matthew's hands were trailing lower, down over her waist and hips, and Selina knew very soon she would have to make a decision as to how far she could allow this to go. Her body screamed at her to let it continue, to take every moment of pleasure. The more sensible voice in her head seemed to be being drowned out, suppressed by the part that was enjoying this so much.

The decision was taken out of her hands when they both stiffened, hearing the creak of the floorboards on the landing above followed by footsteps on the stairs. With her heart pounding Selina hurriedly pulled at her nightgown, slipping her arms back into the sleeves and adjusting the front before perching back on the stool at the bar. She glanced across at Matthew, noted his tousled hair, but nothing else was out of place. He looked calm and serene, not as if he'd just been ravishing his wards' governess in the public rooms of a tavern.

'Oh, it's you,' Mr Ruthers, the landlord, said, letting the long wooden stick he was carrying fall to his side. 'I heard noises and thought someone had broken in.'

'I'm sorry we disturbed you,' Lord Westcroft said. 'After the ordeal of the accident neither Miss Salinger nor I could sleep. We helped ourselves to some brandy, I hope you don't mind. Add the bottle to my bill.'

'Of course, my lord. I'll be going back to bed then.' Mr Ruthers turned and swiftly retreated up the stairs.

'Where were we?' Lord Westcroft murmured as they heard the landlord's bedroom door close somewhere above them.

'I was just about to go to bed myself,' Selina said, slipping from her stool.

He inclined his head, not pressing the matter. Selina wondered if this was a regular occurrence for him, seducing women who should really know better.

Before she could change her mind she hurried to the stairs and climbed back to the first floor, only stopping once she'd closed her bedroom door behind her. Silently she slipped between the sheets and closed her eyes, knowing sleep would not come. There were far too many warring thoughts circling in her head and far too many wonderful echoes of the pleasure she'd felt only a few minutes before.

Chapter Fourteen

At dawn Selina gave up trying to sleep and rose, crossing to the curtains and pulling them open to let the soft light of the morning in through the window. The tavern was stirring, with footsteps padding backwards and forward along the corridor and the quiet clatter of pots below. She fingered her dress that Mrs Ruthers had hung by the fire in the kitchen the night before after washing off the worst of the mud. The hem was still a little damp, but the rest was dry and overall it was presentable, if not completely clean.

Slowly she slipped the cotton nightgown from her shoulders, assailed with the memory of Lord Westcroft's hands doing the same thing last night. She felt the heat rise up inside her as she remembered how his fingers had danced across her skin, how his lips had nipped and teased until she felt as though her whole world was spinning.

'Enough,' she said, pushing the nightgown down over her hips and stepping out of it, hastily beginning to pull on her functional woollen dress to combat the early morning chill in the air.

Last night had been madness. Perhaps she could blame it on hysteria, a delayed reaction to the carriage accident.

It hadn't felt mad, though. It had felt right. Even though every lesson in how a young lady should conduct herself, in morality, told her it was wrong. If the landlord hadn't interrupted them when he did, who knew how far things would have gone.

'That would have been a bad idea,' Selina told herself sternly, unable to ignore completely the residue of desire burning deep inside her. It would have been a bad idea. She knew how men of Lord Westcroft's class treated women who were their social inferiors. It wasn't that she thought Lord Westcroft a bad man, far from it, but he had been brought up to believe women of inferior social status were not worth the same considerations he would show his social equal.

He's not your father, she told herself. Even eighteen months on Selina still couldn't quite believe the man who had doted on her had been capable of treating her mother so poorly, of treating his only daughter so poorly. Plus his total inconsideration of what life would be like for her when she had to hear she was illegitimate from her half-brother who had taken great pleasure in turning her from her home.

Quickly she suppressed all thoughts of her father. Now her problem was Lord Westcroft, or more precisely her reaction to him. She couldn't pretend she was the innocent party in a seduction. Lord Westcroft might be vastly more experienced than she, but she had been a willing participant each and every step of the way. She'd known what was going to happen the moment she had agreed to go downstairs with him for a drink in the deserted tavern.

'Everyone is allowed to make one little mistake,' she told herself as she looked critically into the small mirror set on the dressing table. Her face was pale, her hair lacklustre, her eyes flat and tired and without any sparkle.

One mistake. Perhaps two if you counted the kiss on the beach, but certainly no more. Lord Westcroft might make her body burn with desire, but no man was worth abandoning her principles for, not when those principles were solely there to protect her.

'Head high, back straight, shoulders down,' she instructed herself, looking into the mirror to check she looked suitably determined.

Selina opened the door and stepped into the corridor, meaning to go and check on the girls. One step out of the door and she came crashing into Lord Westcroft, who was striding down the corridor, a frown on his face.

They both stiffened, then took a couple of steps back. Selina had the ridiculous urge to curtsy, but instead looked resolutely at the worn wooden floorboards.

'Good morning, Miss Salinger,' Lord Westcroft said, his voice holding none of the tenderness of the night before. And gone was the intimate use of her first name.

'I trust you slept well, Lord Westcroft,' she forced herself to say.

'No.'

She looked up at his abrupt answer and saw the frown on his face deepen.

'I did not.'

Selina got the feeling he blamed her for his lack of sleep.

'I was just about to check on Priscilla and Theodosia.'

'I shall accompany you.'

He motioned for her to go first, walking a pace behind her with his hands held straight down by his sides as if making sure no part of him inadvertently brushed against her.

Selina risked a glance back at his face and felt all the muscles in her body tensing in response. It was an abrupt change—only a few hours ago he was kissing her as though they were the most intimate of lovers and now he could barely stand to be within a few feet of her.

This was why it was a terrible idea to be seduced by your employer.

Quietly Selina opened the door to the girls' room, seeing the two forms still lying peacefully in the bed. She crept over to satisfy herself neither was burning up with fever and then hastily retreated before she could disturb them.

'Let them sleep,' Lord Westcroft commanded. 'It was a tiring day.'

'I will check on them again soon,' Selina said, hoping her reassurance would prompt him to return to his own room. Either that or investigate the enticing smells wafting up the stairs.

Lord Westcroft hesitated, then something in him seemed to soften and he motioned for Selina to follow him.

'Accompany me to breakfast,' he said, walking off down the corridor before she had a chance to answer.

She contemplated returning to her room instead, but knew she would have to properly face Lord Westcroft some time. Better to do it now when there was no one else around to witness the awkwardness.

Matthew stomped down the stairs, not bothering to turn and check to see if Selina was following him. He was in a foul mood. All night he'd been tormented by vivid images of Selina. Selina dropping her head back as he pushed her nightgown from her shoulders, Selina arching against him as he kissed her breasts, Selina underneath him as their bodies came together again and again. The last one was, of course, pure imagination, but Matthew had always been blessed with a vivid imagination and last night it had spun image after image until he was tense and frustrated.

The lack of sleep wasn't the main reason for his foul mood. As he'd lain awake, trying his hardest to occupy his mind with anything but Selina's naked body writhing underneath him, he'd had plenty of time to think. Plenty of time to remind himself why even a flirtation with his nieces' governess was a bad idea.

He couldn't deny it was a bad idea. Of all the women in England she should be the last he was imagining taking to his bed. He *needed* her, for the future of his nieces, but also for his future. Selina's presence in his life meant he would one day soon be able to return to India and take up his old life again. That was what he wanted.

He stomped a little harder on the stairs to quiet the voice that asked him if that was really what he wanted. In India he was a success. A self-made success. Here in England he was constantly reminded of an unhappier time and of the foolish young man he'd once been. In India he could forget his shame, forget his weakness in not standing up to his father and brother. Here there were reminders around every corner.

Good manners prevented him from slouching in a chair as soon as he reached the private parlour downstairs. Instead he held out the chair for Selina, felt a rush of guilt for the rude way he was treating her and noticed his resolve already beginning to crumble.

'Please accept my apology,' he said as he sat down.

Selina was prevented from saying anything by the bustling into the room of Mrs Ruthers.

'Good morning. It's lovely to see you up so bright

and early. I trust you slept well. Have you seen the sunshine? I think finally our luck with the weather may
have changed.' She spoke as she moved around the room,
drawing the curtains and setting down a pot of tea on the
table between them.

'What are you apologising for?' Selina waited until
they were alone again to speak.

Not last night. Never last night. He knew he *should*
regret it, but he couldn't. Last night when he'd been kissing Selina he had felt a thrill like he'd never experienced
before. He couldn't bring himself to regret that.

'This morning. I was rude. I apologise.'

She blinked a few times as if trying to get his words
straight in her head, then dipped her head in acceptance.

'I didn't sleep very well,' he said in explanation.

'Nor I,' Selina said, her eyes not able to meet his.

'Perhaps we should discuss what happened.'

Quickly she shook her head, busying herself with preparing two cups of tea. 'There is no need. It was a moment of foolishness on both our parts. We were overcome
by the events of the day and allowed ourselves to forget
our relationship to one another.'

'A mistake, then?' he asked mildly.

Emphatically Selina nodded. 'A mistake,' she agreed.

'Even though we both wanted it.'

As her eyes met his he saw a moment of panic in them
and realised that however difficult this was for him it was
ten times that for Selina. She had her position to consider,
her livelihood. And her home.

'Yes,' she said curtly.

'And what if we both happen to want it again?'

'That will not happen.'

He felt a sinking inside him, a disappointment that
he barely dared to acknowledge. He might know noth-

ing good could come from a dalliance between him and Selina, but that didn't stop him from wanting it anyway.

'Who knows what may happen in the future?' he mused quietly, jumping a little as Selina crashed her tea-cup back down on the table.

'I know,' she said firmly. 'I know that the next man I kiss, the only man I kiss, will be my husband. I will not be anyone's mistress or lover. And if I never marry then so be it.'

'So be it?'

'I will live a life without any passion.'

'Then our kiss will have been your only one? The one to remember—' He broke off with a frown. 'You haven't ever kissed anyone before?' The idea of an over-eager suitor pressing her into a dark corner occupied his mind and he found himself jealous at the thought.

'I do not think that is any of your concern,' she said primly.

'No,' he mused, 'I don't think you have.'

'Can we talk of something else?'

'Certainly. What do you wish to converse about? The weather? The children?'

'The children,' she declared, standing up with purpose, even if that purpose was to flee. 'I should check on the girls.'

Matthew didn't stop her. It would have been cruel when she was so flustered. As he took a sip of the perfectly made tea he asked himself what he wanted from Selina. What he *truly* wanted.

His first priority had to be securing her services as governess to Priscilla and Theodosia, that was what he needed most. In a world of his design he would also have Selina in his bed, his lover for the few short months he had remaining in England. That was what he wanted—

her to look after his nieces during the day and slip between the sheets with him at night.

Matthew grimaced. He'd heard her protestations, her reasons why she didn't want to become his mistress. He felt a slither of guilt at thinking about trying to persuade her when her reasons made so much sense, but he couldn't give up on the idea of the pleasure and passion they could share. And if he was cautious they could have the pleasure without any of the scandal Selina was so afraid of.

Carefully he replaced the teacup in its saucer and drummed his fingers on the table. Now he knew what he wanted it was just a matter of making it a reality.

Chapter Fifteen

Matthew urged his horse forward, leaning low across his neck and revelling in the whip of the wind against his face. He rode at full gallop for another twenty seconds and then allowed Autumn to slow. The chestnut-coloured horse snorted, stamping its hooves in appreciation of the gallop and tossing his head once and then again.

'Calm, Autumn,' Matthew instructed, laying a reassuring hand on the horse's neck.

'He's a spirited beast,' Richard Rowlands said as he arrived at a more sedate pace on the back of his own horse.

'He is.' Like everything else on the estate Matthew had inherited a whole stable of horses from his brother. It still felt strange to think they were his now, that everything here was his. He felt like an impostor much of the time, as if his father or brother would suddenly pop up and demand to know what he was doing on their land. It was one of the reasons he wished he was back in India. There he was master of his own business, not just a successful man but a man who had been responsible for his own success. Here he felt as though he didn't belong.

'I heard about your trip to Whitby,' Rowlands said.

An image of Selina with her nightgown slipped from

her shoulders popped into his mind and he had trouble refocusing on what Rowlands was saying.

'It was a pleasant day out until the accident.'

'No one was hurt?'

'No. At least not then. Priscilla is in bed with a chill from being out in the abysmal weather.'

'I wish her a speedy recovery,' Rowlands said, his expression serious. A chill could turn to something much more deadly in no time at all.

'The rest of the trip was delightful,' Matthew said.

'Whitby in winter?'

It wasn't the typical time to visit the seaside, but Matthew knew he would never forget the day. It had been eventful in more ways than one.

'Must have been the company,' Rowlands said quietly.

'Indeed.' Matthew smiled, unable to stop himself. He seemed to be smiling a lot recently.

'Did the delightful Miss Salinger enjoy herself?'

'Very much so.'

The land steward gave him a sidelong look. 'I'm glad you're doing something to make you happy. You deserve it.'

Matthew grimaced as he slid down from Autumn's back. For the last decade, ever since Elizabeth had passed away and he'd regained his freedom, he had felt as though he needed to do penance. It wasn't that he denied himself pleasure, but everything he had done had been tinged with the need to prove to himself that he wasn't a completely lost cause. He'd worked hard, built a life he could be proud of, and that had often meant sacrifice. While other men of his class were gallivanting around London he had been serving in the navy, duty had superseded fun. And even when he had moved on, starting the shipping business, there had rarely been any time to devote to leisure.

Carefully he crouched, inspecting the old stone wall that ran around this part of the perimeter. It was waist high, built of cracked and worn stones, falling down in places. The wall was the only thing separating his estate from the moorland beyond.

'We need to rebuild here,' he said, testing out the adjacent portions to the crumbling part. For a structure with nothing to stick the stones together it was surprisingly sturdy.

'I'll get a couple of the labourers to bring their tools up tomorrow,' Rowlands said.

Matthew paused for a moment, looking out to the moor beyond the wall. It was beautiful even at this time of year with the trees half-bare and the plants died back. It was his home, more so than anywhere else, but still even after a few months back here it didn't feel like it. He yearned for the turquoise of the ocean off the very tip of India, the scorching sun, the rolling hills.

For an instant he pictured taking Selina back there with him, swimming with her in the warm waters and taking her to see the majestic elephants and deadly tigers. He could imagine sharing his world with her, imagine her expressions as she came across something completely new, imagine her in his arms as they built a life together away from the social confines of England.

Matthew physically shook himself. It was a ridiculous thing to imagine. He'd kissed her twice, no more, and she'd made it perfectly clear there would be nothing further between them.

'You're thinking about her,' Rowlands said as Matthew remounted. There was no need to ask who Rowlands meant, the man was as sharp as a carefully honed sword-point and had spotted the desire coursing backwards and forward between Matthew and Selina even after seeing them together for a mere few seconds.

'She does seem to occupy my thoughts much of the time.'

'You're smitten.'

'Perhaps I am. She is an attractive woman.' Selina was attractive, but there was so much more to her than just her appearance.

'A governess isn't that far beneath you on the social ladder,' Rowlands said quietly. 'Especially if you don't care too much what the rest of your equals think of you. She could make a fine wife.'

Matthew gently urged Autumn forward, trying to hide his surprise at the direction of Rowland's mind.

'Wife?' he managed to ask eventually.

'Miss Salinger didn't strike me as the kind of woman who would be happy being a man's mistress.'

'No...' Although that was what he was contemplating trying to persuade her to be. She was a sensual woman, three nights ago in the tavern in Whitby had shown that, a woman who could be ruled by her passion. She would get as much pleasure out of an affair as he, if only she could be persuaded.

'And if she won't be your mistress...'

Anything else was out of the question. He would never marry again, not after the first disastrous union. It was a secret liaison or nothing, no matter how much he wanted her.

'I'll not marry again,' Matthew said, pushing on ahead to close the subject. Rowlands urged his horse on to keep pace, his face set as if he had more to say.

'Never?'

'Never.'

'One bad experience when you were eighteen shouldn't put you off for the rest of your life.'

'I'm better off single,' he said, trying to inject a note of finality into his voice.

'Nonsense. No one is better off alone. We are made to be mating pairs, just like in nature.'

'Not everyone is.'

Rowlands considered this for a long moment, looking out thoughtfully over the moors as they rode along the perimeter boundary.

'Think about it: a loving wife at home, looking after your estate and your nieces, a good woman to slip into bed beside every night. Tell me that isn't a tempting proposal.'

Matthew couldn't deny it. What man wouldn't want a woman looking after his interests, looking after him *and* warming his bed? Especially a woman like Selina. But he couldn't, no matter how much he wanted her in his life. Even having her as his mistress would be a little too close, but the benefits would overshadow the feeling that he was risking too much.

'I'll never marry,' he repeated quietly. Rowlands must have seen something in his expression because the older man fell quiet, a sadness permeating his features.

The schoolroom felt empty without Priscilla sitting scowling in her usual seat. Selina had spent her morning dashing backwards and forward between Priscilla's bedroom and the little room off the nursery she used for the children's lessons. Theodosia had been unusually subdued, worried about her older sister and unable to concentrate on anything for more than a few minutes at a time. Whenever Selina went out to see if Priscilla needed anything she returned to find Theodosia staring out the window with a vacant expression on her face. In the end they had given up on trying to learn anything useful and Selina had placed a piece of paper and some paints in front of the little girl and told her to make her sister a painting to wish her a quick recovery.

Theodosia was now painting with more concentration that she had ever shown a single of her lessons, her little pink tongue sticking out the corner of her mouth. Selina suspected Theodosia thought the quality of her artwork would impact how quickly her sister recovered.

Fifteen minutes ago when Selina had gone to check on Priscilla the little girl was tucked up under her sheets sleeping peacefully with her hair spread out on her pillow. She was healthy but small and Selina had a fear of winter chills—they could all too easily turn into a congestion on the chest which was often deadly.

With Theodosia occupied Selina took out a sheet of paper of her own and began to write. She hadn't written a letter for eighteen months, not a personal one at least. She had felt so adrift in the world she hadn't wanted to drag anyone into her misery.

Something Lord Westcroft had said a few days ago had been circling in her mind. He'd asked if none of her friends would have helped her. Many of her acquaintances would have shied away from scandal such as the one Selina had been caught up in, but not Violet or Felicity. They were kind, generous, and Selina knew if she had turned to them they would have defied the gossips and the snobs and given her refuge.

Selina wasn't entirely sure why she hadn't asked for their help. It hadn't just been pride, more a mix of grief and shock over what had happened, the feeling of needing time to understand everything that had befallen her before she shared it with anyone else.

Now she was ready. Not to reach out for help—in a strange way she felt secure here despite only having been in her position a matter of weeks—but to let her friends know why she had vanished, to reassure them she was well.

Carefully she began the first letter, the familiar scratching of the pen across the paper taking her back to her little desk in the corner of her father's library where she used to spend an hour a day writing correspondence in her old life.

Dear Violet,
I apologise for not writing sooner. My life has changed so much this past year and a half I felt the need to be at least a little settled before I could put pen to paper and explain what has taken me from Cambridge.
I am living in north Yorkshire, as far north from Cambridge as you could get without crossing the border, and a stark contrast to the flat meadows of our city. After a series of less-than-ideal positions I have taken a job as a governess to two lovely young girls in the household of Lord Westcroft. They are his nieces. He was appointed guardian when both their parents died.

Selina paused, wondering what to say about Lord Westcroft. She desperately wanted to confide in some-one, to tell them exactly what she thought of the man who should be nothing more than her employer. She wanted to tell them how her body felt as though it were on fire whenever he walked into a room, how every moment of every day he occupied a small corner of her mind. She wanted to tell them about the dreams that plagued her sleep, making her wake pent up with desire and longing.

Selina felt the heat rise in her cheeks. She could never tell anyone about those dreams. Her upbringing hadn't been the strictest, but a woman of her birth wasn't meant to succumb to the pleasures of life. Always there had been this message that she should remain in control of her baser instincts, project a façade of cool uninterest.

Letting a little laugh escape her lips, Selina looked up to check Theodosia hadn't noticed. Cool uninterest wasn't likely to happen when Lord Westcroft was nearby.

Tapping her pen on the table, she thought for a moment before continuing her letter. She would not tell of her illegitimacy—even now that revelation still had a sting to it she could not bear to put to paper.

As you will know my father passed away eighteen months ago. After his death my half-brother, the new Viscount Northrop, was not keen on my remaining at home. I ventured out into the world and found a position as a governess in London. That lasted for a few months before the little boy I was teaching went to school, then I was employed to teach two young siblings in Surrey.

This latest position is suiting me well. I enjoy my work and Theodosia and Priscilla are sweet children, if a little sensitive due to the early death of their parents. I feel that here I can make a difference.

Lord Westcroft is hoping to return to India soon and, if he does, I will stay on and look after the children in his absence.

I miss Cambridge. I miss you and Felicity. I miss our walks to Grantchester and our picnics in the meadows. My life is very different now from how I had thought it would be, but I think I am beginning to feel happy again. For a long time after my father died I felt nothing but sadness and loneliness, but here I feel as though I am part of something again.

Please write and tell me your news. Did you accept the proposal from Mr Huntsworth? How have you fared these past eighteen months?
I long to hear from you.
With love and affection,
Selina

She sat back and read through the letter. It contained barely any of the turmoil she was feeling, the rush of emotions. If Violet had been sitting here across from her, then Selina would not have been able to hide the truth of her feelings, but in a letter it was so easy to put down only what you wished to tell.

She would give almost anything to have one of her friends here, someone friendly to discuss every aspect of life with, to plan and worry about what she should do for the best. At Manresa House there wasn't anyone Selina could get close to. The servants were quiet and scurried about their work without stopping to talk and Mrs Fellows, the housekeeper, was sour and disliked idle conversation. Here she was alone.

Not quite, the little voice in her head told her. Lord Westcroft didn't count, not really. Not when her feelings for him were what she wished to talk about.

It wasn't as though she could go and talk to him and expect an impartial opinion when she told him she was falling for him, that she was developing feelings for him a governess shouldn't have for her employer. He likely wouldn't even answer her—just run for the door and find the fastest ship back to India.

Selina just wanted one of her friends to hold her hand and tell her that desire and love were two very different things and, as she was very inexperienced in both, she was merely getting them mixed up. Desire was acceptable, as long as she was strong enough not to act on it again, but these last few days Selina had begun to wonder if the feelings she was having ran deeper than desire. If they did, it would be a disaster. Love meant heartbreak, at least when the man you thought you loved was set on sailing off to the other side of the world in a few weeks, and Selina wasn't sure her heart could withstand any more blows.

'Miss Salinger?' Theodosia's voice broke through her thoughts.

'Yes, Thea?'

'Do you think Priscilla will like my painting?'

Selina took the proffered artwork and inspected it carefully. Normally a little careless in her work, Theodosia had taken a lot of time and care over making the offering for her sister. She had painted a beautiful, brightly coloured flower on the front, complete with green stem and leaves. On the back she had carefully written a get well message and signed her name.

'I think she will like it very much, it's beautiful.'

Theodosia nodded seriously.

'Will she…?' The little girl faltered and Selina held out her hand, letting Theodosia clamber on to her lap before urging her to continue. 'Will she get better?'

Selina squeezed her eyes tight shut to stop the tears from falling on to her cheeks. Someone so young shouldn't have to worry about life and death like this. After losing both her parents in a relatively short space of time it was no wonder Theodosia was petrified she might lose her beloved sister as well.

'Your sister is a fighter. She's strong and stubborn and she wouldn't let something as insignificant as a little chill get the better of her,' Selina said, trying to inject a note of levity into her voice. In truth, she didn't know if Priscilla would recover. The fever did not seem to be too bad at the moment, but illnesses and fevers could be unpredictable, worsening in a matter of hours and killing indiscriminately.

'I don't want her to die,' Theodosia said in a small voice.

'We will look after her and I'm sure she will be back on her feet in a couple of days.'

'My papa never got better.'

Selina swallowed. She had never asked Lord Westcroft how his brother had died. He couldn't have been very old, Lord Westcroft had talked of their time together as children and from his stories it sounded as though they were only a few years apart in age. She found it difficult to judge people's ages, but Lord Westcroft must be in his early thirties, so his brother couldn't have been more than thirty-five. A man in his prime, too young to die, although it wasn't unheard of. She wondered if it had been a fever or an accident or something else entirely.

'What happened with your father?' She spoke gently, not wanting to upset the little girl.

'He was very sad after Mama died,' Theodosia said, snuggling into Selina's arms and half-burying her face in Selina's chest. 'He used to go away for weeks at a time. Weeks and weeks and we wouldn't see him. Then one day when he came home he was ill. He went straight to bed and never got up again.'

Selina stroked Theodosia's smooth blonde hair. No

wonder she was worried about her sister. The last member of her family who had been ill in bed had died and now Priscilla was in bed and Theodosia was imagining history repeating itself.

'Do you miss him very much?'

Theodosia shrugged, her little shoulders moving against Selina's arms.

'I miss Mama every single day. She used to sing to me and tuck me into bed and kiss me better when I hurt myself. At least she did when she had her happy days.'

Selina's heart almost broke. At seven the little girl in her arms shouldn't have to know about sadness and suicide. Or be worrying that the last member of her immediate family was going to slip away from a fever.

'Did she have many sad days?'

Theodosia nodded, 'Sometimes for months at a time. Papa would have to force her to eat and she wouldn't come out of her room for days on end. And she cried at night. I used to creep down the stairs and listen.'

It was an upsetting image, little Theodosia creeping downstairs to hear if her mother was crying.

'I missed her very much when she was gone.'

Gently Selina kissed the top of her head, holding her a little tighter. Her own mother had died when Selina was seventeen, her father when she was twenty. It had been hard enough losing the two people she had loved most in the world as an adult, she couldn't begin to imagine what it would be like for a child.

'Would you like to visit her grave again when Priscilla is a little better? We could take some fresh flowers. You can tell her everything you've been doing.'

Theodosia nodded. 'Do you think she can hear us when we talk to her?'

'Without a doubt. Your mama will be up in heaven

watching over you, so proud of the brave and courageous girls you and Priscilla have become.'

'Sam Taylor from the village said she wouldn't go to heaven because of how she died.'

'Nonsense,' Selina said in her firmest voice. 'Your mother was a kind woman, a good woman, that is all that matters.'

Theodosia fingered the painting she was holding and Selina sat up slightly, knowing they needed to move on. Theodosia needed to talk about her mother and her father, but at the tender age of seven it would have to be done very delicately, very gradually. For now they'd made a good start, but it wouldn't do to dwell on the sadness of the past for too long, not when she was scared about her sister's condition.

'Shall we go and visit Priscilla? You can give her the painting.'

Slipping down from her lap, Theodosia gave Selina her hand and side by side they made their way out of the schoolroom and into the bedroom.

As they walked into the darkened room Selina almost shouted out in surprise when a figure rose from a seat beside the bed. Lord Westcroft stepped forward, crouching down to speak to Theodosia.

'Priscilla just woke up, she was asking for you, but she's fallen back to sleep now.'

'I painted her a flower,' Theodosia said, brandishing the painting.

'I'm sure she'll love it. Shall we put it by her bedside so she will see it as soon as she wakes up?'

Theodosia hopped into the chair by her sister's bed and started chattering away, telling her all that she'd been doing in Priscilla's absence. The worried look was still on her face, but she talked and talked none the less.

Lord Westcroft touched Selina gently on the elbow, guiding her to the door.

'I've sent Jim for the doctor again, he should be here in the next few hours.'

'Do you think she's improving?'

'It's difficult to say. She was lucid when she woke up this time, which has to be a good sign, but more than that I really don't know.'

He looked tired and drawn and Selina wondered if he had ever felt this sort of worry before, the kind of worry you only experienced when an innocent child was very unwell.

Impulsively Selina reached out to him, laying her hand on the sleeve of his jacket.

'Priscilla is a strong girl,' she said, repeating the words she'd said earlier to Theodosia. 'She will fight this.'

'I hope so. I couldn't...' He trailed off, his eyes seeking out Selina's.

'We don't have to worry about that,' she said firmly. 'She will get better. Soon.'

He nodded, not looking entirely convinced, then walked out of the room. Selina had to fight the urge to run after him, to wrap him in her arms and provide the comfort he sorely needed.

Chapter Sixteen

Matthew crashed around his study, moving the papers from the desk to the chair and back again, not making any progress with his search for the inventory he was looking for. For the last few hours he'd been unable to concentrate, worried as he was about Priscilla lying quietly upstairs in her sickbed. The doctor had visited in the early afternoon and declared she was a little stronger, but the fever still had a grip on her. The medical man had prescribed a concoction to bring down her temperature and told them bluntly that either the fever would break or it wouldn't. Now it was just a waiting game.

He wished he could take the illness for his niece, to suffer it in her place. Anything would be better than the torture of not knowing what would happen to her. She looked so young lying in her bed, the sheets tucked up to her chin. Young and helpless.

Forcing himself to sit down, he passed a hand across his brow and inhaled deeply. He wasn't used to having anyone else to worry about. For so many years it had just been him, no one else to fear for or consider. Now he had these two vulnerable girls dependent on him and he wasn't sure he was up to the challenge of looking after them. It felt so hard, watching Priscilla suffer and not being able to do anything to help her.

Matthew was pulled from his thoughts by a sharp rap on the door. Despite all his worries he smiled. Selina even knocked on the door like a governess, sharp and to the point.

'Come in,' he called.

She slipped into the room, closing the door quietly behind her as if she didn't want anyone to know she was there. Immediately his body felt on edge, as if it wanted to leap forward and take her into his arms, to take comfort from her.

'Priscilla seems a little better,' she said, hovering near the door. He waited for her to move closer, but as the seconds ticked on and she didn't move he decided to go to her instead.

'She's woken up?'

'For short spells. She seems very fatigued, but her chest isn't rattling as much and her cough is a little improved, and when she woke she was more lucid, more her normal self.' He could see the strain on Selina's face and knew she was suffering along with Priscilla. Even though she'd only been part of the household for a short while she already cared deeply for the girls.

And for you. Quickly he silenced the voice in his head. He knew Selina desired him, but sometimes he thought he caught a flash of something more in her eyes, despite her dislike for men of his class, her distrust of anyone who could be in a position to hurt her.

'That is a relief. I have not worried like this for a long time.'

She gave him a curious look, half-question, half-smile.

'You haven't had people to worry about?'

'No, not since…' He trailed off, aghast he'd been

about to mention Elizabeth's name to Selina. She certainly didn't need to know that bit of his past. 'Not since I left home,' he finished.

'I know you said you travelled around a lot, but there must have been someone you cared for. A friend? A colleague?'

'No.'

He saw the confusion in her eyes and realised it must be a strange notion for someone as caring as she. Selina had always had someone to care for, her parents, her friends, even in the last few years the children she looked after.

'I've lived a fairly nomadic life,' he said in explanation.

For the first time he realised how few bonds he'd made over the last decade. It was a mode of defence, a way to protect himself. After agreeing to marry Elizabeth against his better judgement and the difficulty and sadness that had followed he hadn't wanted anyone dependent on him. Even friendship had been too risky.

Selina had been the first one to get through his guard for a very long time. Selina and the two girls she looked after so well.

'Theodosia is petrified of losing her sister,' Selina said.

'I'm not surprised.'

'She's sitting with Priscilla now, quietly playing at the foot of her bed.' Selina paused, then turned to him with a deep vulnerability in her eyes. 'Do you think Priscilla will recover?'

Without thinking through the consequences he gathered her in his arms and pulled her body close to his. Selina dipped her head so it rested on his shoulder and he could feel her breathing deeply into his chest. Gently he stroked her hair, letting his fingers trail though the silky tendrils before they reached her well-pinned bun.

'I don't know,' he murmured. There was no point in lying to her, it wasn't just blind reassurance Selina was looking for, but comfort, someone to share her worry with. 'She's a strong little lady and she has a lot of people looking after her. I think in a day or two we might see her regain some of her strength.'

Selina nodded, her head still buried in his shoulder, and he had to resist the urge to lift up her chin and kiss her. Now wasn't the right moment, no matter how much he wanted to.

After another minute she stepped back, smoothing down the wrinkles in her dress where she had been pressed against him.

'I'm sorry,' she said.

'Don't apologise.'

'I shouldn't have…' She made a vague gesture in his direction.

'I think we need to discuss what happened in Whitby,' he said quietly. 'But perhaps now isn't the time.'

'When?'

'Tonight. After dinner. When you are happy the girls are settled in bed.'

Selina seemed to consider this for a moment and he had to suppress a smile. It was her nature to consider things from all angles before agreeing.

'Tonight,' she said.

Selina walked down the stairs, trying to make as little noise as possible. It was only nine, hardly late, but the house was quiet, the servants taking advantage of the early dinner served a few hours before and the lack of demands from their master to retire upstairs for the night.

Hesitating before she knocked, Selina wondered if she should have thought of what she would say to Lord West-croft before making her way downstairs, but she knew however much time she spent preparing it would matter little. She just needed to stick to her principles.

'Come in.'

Head high, back straight, shoulders down.

She stepped into the room, barely illuminated by the two candles burning on the large wooden desk.

'Have the girls settled?'

'They're both sleeping soundly.' She'd sat with them for half an hour after they'd fallen asleep just to check neither would stir and also to put off this moment. Already Selina felt her resolve crumbling.

'Good. Would you like to sit down?'

'No.' It came out as an abrupt refusal, a testament to how nervous she was feeling.

'No?' Even in the candlelight she could see the amused smile on Lord Westcroft's face.

'I thought we might go for a walk about the gardens. It is a pleasant evening and the rain has finally stopped.'

It was November, an overcast and grey day and now a cloudy and cold night, hardly pleasant in anyone's estimation, but Selina knew she would be safer outside. Safer from her own weaknesses.

He looked at her curiously for a moment and then agreed. 'I shall fetch my coat. No point in waking the servants to get it.'

Selina watched as he walked from the room. Already she could feel a nervous fluttering in her stomach.

'Courage,' she murmured to herself, then turned and followed him out to the hall, picking up her cloak from the little alcove tucked away next to the door.

'Shall we go out the back?' he asked, brandishing a

set of keys he must have taken from one of the hooks downstairs.

Selina followed him out through the library to the glass doors at the back that opened out on to the terrace. He unlocked the door, allowing her to slip through ahead of him, before turning to lock it again.

It was dark outside, with the clouds covering the moon and the stars, and for a moment Selina couldn't see more than a couple of feet in front of her. The house behind them provided no illumination, but slowly her eyes began to adjust to the darkness and she could make out the familiar shapes of statues dotted along the terrace and the bushes in the garden beyond.

Lord Westcroft offered her his arm, waiting for her to tuck her hand into his elbow before starting off at a sedate pace towards the stone steps that led down into the formal garden. They kept to the path, winding their way among the flowerbeds, avoiding the worst of the mud.

'How are you?' He spoke quietly, waiting until they were well enough away from the house so as not to disturb anyone inside.

'I feel drained,' she said after a moment. 'Worn. Worried.'

'About Priscilla?'

She nodded.

'You feel things keenly, don't you?'

'I do.' She sighed and glanced up at the man beside her. She thought he felt things keenly, too, but was a little better at hiding it.

They walked on in silence for a few more minutes, neither wanting to be the first to broach the subject of Whitby.

'I've been thinking,' Lord Westcroft said eventually, 'about your brother. And your father. I don't believe it.'

Selina stopped walking in surprise. 'You don't believe me?'

'I believe you. Of course I believe you. I don't believe what your brother told you. I want to see this will. I want to question this solicitor. Even if you are illegitimate, I don't see why a devoted father in life would provide nothing for you after death.'

Selina had questioned the same thing over and over again. Her father had *seemed* to love her very much, he'd doted on her, given her much praise and attention, but then again he'd loved her mother and still not given her the protection of marriage.

'It doesn't make sense,' he continued. 'I understand the title and estate would have to pass to your brother, but not the money, not your possessions. A very generous allowance could have been bequeathed, something to set you up for life.'

'Perhaps he didn't care,' Selina said softly. *That* hurt most of all, the idea he might not have loved her the way she thought he had.

'You know if a person cares or not.'

Selina squeezed her eyes shut and remembered the indulgent smile on her father's face as he patiently taught her Latin and the look of pride as Selina had won a debate over the dinner table against two Cambridge dons. She remembered his quiet indulgence as he'd helped her make her debut into society, delayed a year by her mother's death, and the tears they had shed together for the woman they had both loved.

'He did love me,' she said quietly.

'Then he would have provided for you.'

Selina felt a spark of hope. When her father had died and her brother appeared with the solicitor she'd been overcome by grief. She'd accepted what had been said, accepted the word of the solicitor, but she had never actually seen the will.

'Could he have really orchestrated a solicitor to deceive me out of my inheritance?'

'I don't know the man, but surely it would be possible. Money exchanged, bribes passed. You were a young woman alone without much knowledge of the world with no relatives to look out for you. Who was going to protest when he manoeuvred you out of the way?'

Selina felt the beginnings of anger start to course through her body. It wouldn't be out of character for her brother. She knew he could be cruel and vindictive, but this was beyond anything she could have imagined.

'It should be simple enough to find out. To trace the solicitor who was involved, talk to whoever drew up and witnessed the will. Would you like me to make some enquiries?'

Selina's thoughts were still whirring round the possibilities. She'd been grief-stricken, in a daze for so long after her father's death, that only now did she feel as though she could start questioning the events that went on around it.

'Yes,' she said decisively, now determined to understand the truth in all of this. 'Please do.'

'Although I'm loath to discover anything that might mean we lose you,' he said quietly.

We lose you, not just him. It was a stark reminder that she was most valuable to him as governess to the girls.

'If there is anything to discover, it will take years to unravel,' she said with a sad smile. 'I don't think there's any chance of me running off anywhere any time soon.'

'Good.'

They had reached the edge of the formal gardens and Selina had been about to suggest they turn back when

Lord Westcroft stopped and led her over to a little stone bench situated to look out over the parkland and the moors beyond. The view, stunning in the daytime, was nothing more than a series of dark shapes rolling out in front of them, but as always when Selina looked out over the moors she felt a sense of vastness, a realisation of how small she was in the world, how alone.

'Whitby,' Lord Westcroft said decisively. 'We need to discuss what happened.'

'Must we?' She knew that was the whole point of this stroll into the night, but she dreaded having to confront her feelings, especially when she wasn't quite sure herself what they were.

'I wish to make a proposition.'

'Lord Westcroft...' she said, knowing it wouldn't be a proposal she could accept and not wanting to strain things between them further.

'Matthew,' he corrected her.

'I can't call you that.'

'It's my name.'

'It's too familiar.'

'Don't you think we have reached the stage of familiarity?'

She remembered the kisses, the shameless way she'd allowed her nightdress to fall from her shoulders and his lips to dart over her skin.

'I think of you as Selina,' he continued. 'Always Selina.'

'I can't.'

'Go on, say it just once. Once and I'll be happy.'

She hesitated again and then closed her eyes, 'Matthew,' she said.

'Once wasn't so hard, was it?'

She looked at him, knowing that now his name had

crossed her lips it would be easy for it to do so again. No doubt what he had planned all along.

'I cannot stop thinking of that night in Whitby,' he said, his voice low.

'Nor I.' The admission slipped out before Selina could stop it. That night had plagued her thoughts from the moment she woke until she went to bed at night and then she dreamed endlessly of what could be between them. She'd had no respite, waking or asleep, until her body was tight with desire and her mind begging for one more moment of indiscretion.

'Good.' Even in the darkness Selina knew he was smiling. 'I know your views on affairs, liaisons, whatever you wish to call them. I know how your father's treatment of your mother has coloured your view on passion outside marriage.'

'You make my views sound strange, but not many women of any class think an affair is acceptable.'

'You'd be surprised,' Lord Westcroft murmured. 'I understand your reluctance to enter into anything, your need to deny what we both want.'

Selina didn't bother protesting. It was what they both wanted, but you couldn't always be ruled by desire, common sense had to prevail, especially for a woman on her own in the world.

'I understand you fear losing your position and your reputation, you fear not having the means to provide for yourself. My proposition would solve that.'

Selina felt a surge of hope. He had never hinted at wanting to settle down before, but maybe...

'I would give you a property, settle on you a sum of money that would see you spend your days in comfort if you were to move on from the position of governess here. I hope you would still wish to teach the girls, but if you ever felt that our relationship was too strained, then you could move on without any repercussions.' He paused, looking at her intently as if trying to gauge her reaction. 'And we could have the relationship we both desire.'

'I would be your mistress?' Selina asked, her voice emotionless.

'Mistress, lover, whatever you want to call it.' He gripped her hand in his own. 'The important thing is we would be able to be together. To enjoy one another.'

'And when you got fed up of me…?'

'That wouldn't happen, but if we did decide to go our separate ways you would have a secure future.'

Selina tried to suppress the anger that was coursing through her. Perhaps he didn't understand what he was asking of her, perhaps he didn't realise quite how much he was asking her to give up.

'So there would be an exchange of goods for…' she closed her eyes as she struggled to find the right word '…intimacy. I would be your whore.'

'No. Never.'

Selina rounded on him, 'That is exactly what you are proposing.'

'I merely want to remove the obstacles to us being together.'

'I was raised the daughter of a viscount,' she said, her voice sharp and cultured and filled with the cold clipped tones of the aristocracy. 'I was taught from a very young age that a woman's most precious possession is her reputation. It is how we are judged, how our worth is decided.' She stood, taking a few steps away from the bench so he wouldn't see the glistening of the tears on her cheeks. 'I may have found myself in much altered circumstances, but I'm still the same person, with the same values.'

She felt Matthew's presence behind her, the soft touch

of his hands on her arms. Gently, slowly, he pressed her to turn and face him.

'You're crying,' he said, reaching up with his thumb to wipe away the tears on her cheeks.

Selina closed her eyes, trying to conquer the feelings of disappointment and sadness raging inside her. When she'd heard the word proposition she'd felt an undeniable surge of hope. Hope that the man she was realising she cared for deeply felt the same way about her. Hope that he might be about to suggest settling down together, marriage. It seemed ludicrous now, given the solution he had put forward, but it had been her hope all the same.

'I'm sorry,' he said quietly, his eyes seeking out hers in the darkness. 'I never wanted to upset you.'

'I think we're just not compatible,' Selina said, the anger quickly seeping out of her. It was unfair to be annoyed with him, he'd never promised her anything, never hinted that he might want something more than a passionate affair, short lived and sweet, but with a very definite end date.

'I don't know if I can let you go,' he murmured into her hair as she sank into him.

'We want different things. When I give myself to someone, body and heart, I want it to be for ever,' she whispered. 'And you are not ready to settle. It just isn't meant to be.'

'I can't settle,' he said, a note of sadness in his voice. 'I can't marry and have someone dependent on me. I can't be relied on to make the right decisions.'

Selina frowned. Normally he was so confident, so sure of himself. He was a successful man, and he had travelled all over the world, building his shipping business from nothing, with no support from his family.

'Of course you can,' she said.

He looked at her, a sad smile on his face. 'No, I can't. Not when it comes to other people's welfare.'

'Did something happen to you?'

'Nothing you want to know about.'

She took his hand, knowing the gesture was too intimate given the limits she'd just imposed on their relationship.

'You've helped me these last weeks. Helped me to realise what happened after my father's death wasn't right, that I at least need to think about fighting it. I know a governess isn't the usual confidante for an earl, but let me help you.'

Matthew looked at her for a long moment, his eyes searching her face in the darkness. He was holding something back, keeping it bottled inside, and Selina realised this was what had sparked his reluctance to build a bond with the girls initially, this was what kept pushing him to run away back to India.

The cold was seeping through her cloak and she shivered as she waited for his answer.

'Let's go back inside,' he said. 'You're cold.'

'And then you'll tell me?'

He remained silent, gripping her hand in his as they hurried back towards the house.

'I've told you a little about my childhood,' he said, adding a few more logs to the fire from the basket that sat beside it. They were in the library, his favourite room of the house, and he had spent a few minutes lighting and building the fire to warm them after their walk in the cold November night. 'It was far from happy, especially after my mother died. My father disliked me, his interest was only in Henry as the heir. He was cruel and he liked to pit me and my brother against each other.'

'I can't imagine a childhood like that,' Selina said softly. Matthew couldn't imagine the childhood she'd described, surrounded by love and kindness.

'As second son I was little use to my father, but soon after I turned eighteen he made a series of bad investments. The estate was falling into ruin and he needed money for its upkeep. He came up with the plan to marry me off to some young woman with a large dowry.'

Matthew had been aghast when he'd first heard the proposition. He was eighteen, just about to go to university, with his whole life ahead of him. The last thing he'd wanted was a wife.

'I was unenthusiastic about the plan, but I think I had always had this desire to please my father, to do something he would be proud of.'

'You agreed?'

'I said I would consider it. My father found a candidate. A young woman named Elizabeth from the next county over. I was told her family were rich and would provide a large dowry with ongoing financial support.' He grimaced, that had been all the information his father had been interested in.

'Did you meet her?'

'My father was strangely reluctant to let me meet her before the wedding. I pushed and pushed and pushed, telling him I would not go through with it unless I could meet her, to check we were not completely mismatched, before our nuptials.'

Selina was watching him with wide-eyed horror, reflecting his feelings all those years ago.

'Finally he agreed, but before the meeting he sent my brother in to talk to me. Henry told me that Elizabeth was a sweet girl, pretty in her own way, but that her mind was not the brightest. In some matters she acted younger than her years.'

Selina's eyes widened.

'I met with her and she was sweet, although petrified of new people. After the meeting I refused to marry her. I didn't think it would be fair on either of us. She was vulnerable, in need of looking after, childlike in her manner. In my mind she needed a companion, not a husband, someone who would be gentle and patient with her.'

'What happened?'

'My father raged and raged, telling me I was disobedient, I was a disgrace. He threatened to cut me off, threatened not to let me near the family home or my brother ever again.' Matthew shook his head. It had been heartbreaking, having it proved once and for all how little his opinion, his feelings mattered to his father. 'Then Henry came and took me to a meeting with Elizabeth's father and my own. They told me if I didn't marry Elizabeth, then she would marry my father instead.'

He saw the shock in Selina's eyes.

'I know,' he said, shaking his head in disgust even now. 'The worst thing is I contemplated leaving her to it, leaving her to the cruelty I'd experienced over the years.'

'What did you do?' Selina's voice was no more than a whisper.

'I married her.'

'You're married?'

'Not any longer. I married her, a marriage in name only, and found a companion to stay with her.'

It had been a difficult time. He'd been eighteen, an adult, but still a child in so many ways. He'd been forced to navigate the cruelties of the world alone, then suddenly he had someone else to care for.

'She was unhappy, terribly so. Confused by being cast

away from her family, although by all accounts they had never been overly kind to her. Six months into the marriage she died.'

'What an awful situation.'

'It was,' Matthew said grimly. 'For a while after I hated myself, hated being so weak I allowed my father and her father to manipulate me.'

'It wasn't weakness, it was kindness, trying to save that poor girl from a much worse fate.'

'I should have stood up to them, insisted that I would not marry her, persuaded her father not to subject her to the brutality she would experience if she married my father.'

'You were eighteen.'

'When I agreed to marry her I took responsibility for her. She was unhappy and I wasn't able to give her the love or care she needed to make her happy.'

'And now you think you are not capable of it,' Selina said, realisation dawning in her eyes.

'I'm better off alone,' he said gruffly, 'with no one relying on me. I proved back then that my judgement was poor, that I could be manipulated.'

'You can't go through life not making any meaningful connections because of what happened over ten years ago.'

'I'm not fit to look after those girls,' he said, feeling his words catch in his throat. It was his biggest fear, that somehow he would make the wrong decision, that he would let an outside party influence him as he had all those years ago and Priscilla and Theodosia would be harmed because of it.

'Of course you are.' She slipped off her chair, kneeling at his feet, taking both his hands in her own. 'You did your best by that young woman, you married her to save her from your father and you tried to look after her, as well as an eighteen-year-old boy can. That shows the capacity in your heart for love.'

'But love isn't always enough.'

'It is a good start. No one knows how to care for another human when they first start out. A mother learns how to interpret every cry of her newborn baby day by day, a father how to stop his son's tears only by trying one thing and then another. As long as the love is there, the willingness to spend the time learning, then that is enough. That is all anyone has.'

He closed his eyes, gripping on to Selina's hands as if she were anchoring him to the earth.

'I'm better off alone,' he said gruffly. 'Alone I can't hurt anyone.'

'And alone you can't help anyone.'

Gently he pulled on her hands, tugging her up until she tumbled into his lap. Again he closed his eyes, burying his face in her neck. He wished he could believe her, wished he could have that faith in himself again. When he'd married Elizabeth it had felt so wrong, but he hadn't known what else to do. He *had* been trying to protect her, but he'd failed her. His actions had been influenced too much by the father he was scared of and the deep panic he'd felt when he realised he didn't know what to do.

'Is that why you went away?'

'Yes. I realised I needed to become my own man, away from my father and my brother. I needed to build a life I could be proud of and I needed to do it alone.'

'And you have. You're a very successful man.'

It was true, although always inside him there was a feeling that something was missing, that he needed to work harder, strive more, to find out what that was.

'In some ways,' he said. He inhaled deeply, catching

Selina's scent, that mixture of lavender and honey that made him want to bury himself in her completely and never come up for air.

'Do you think…' Selina said quietly, hesitating for a moment before continuing '…that what could be missing are relationships? Friendships, love, caring for other people. We all need those in our lives to make it complete.'

He knew she was right, but somehow couldn't bring himself to admit it. He'd felt happier, more complete, than he ever had done before these last few weeks at Manresa House. He might fear his ability to protect his nieces, but ever since he'd allowed himself to grow closer to them he'd felt more fulfilled.

And then there was Selina. He knew what he felt for her was more than lust, more than desire. He treasured their moments together, enjoyed when she challenged him, found pleasure in her sharp mind and deep conversation. For the first time in his life he was beginning to feel as though he belonged somewhere and he knew much of that was down to the woman in front of him.

Her question required no answer as they both already knew the truth of it.

In a movement so fluid he could not stop it Selina slid from his lap, standing and facing him with a sad little smile on her face.

'Don't run back to India just yet,' she said as she took a step away. 'You need the girls just as much as they need you.'

And you, he almost called after her as she turned and walked out of the door. He needed her, too.

Chapter Seventeen

Heaping another blanket in her arms, Selina glanced at the mirror hanging in the hallway briefly before turning away in disgust. She looked an absolute state, her skin was pale, her eyes rimmed by dark circles, her hair as usual trying to escape its neat little bun. Outwardly she was blaming her horrific appearance on the worry caused by Priscilla's illness, but the young girl had rallied the last couple of days and was now well down the road to recovery. In truth, Selina couldn't stop thinking about Matthew, about his proposition to make her his mistress, his revelation of why he refused to let anyone close and the damage his father and brother had done to him when they'd pressed him into a marriage he didn't want.

Now she understood much of what drove him. She understood his reluctance to let anyone close, his misguided idea that he could not be trusted to care for other people. She might understand it a little better, but that didn't make it any less frustrating.

'Are you ready yet, Miss Salinger?' Theodosia asked, pulling Selina away from her thoughts and away from the mirror.

'I've just got to ask one of the footmen to take a chair outside for Priscilla.'

It was a beautiful day, crisp and clear with a sky so blue it looked as if it had been painted on the horizon. Priscilla had insisted she needed to get out of the house, saying her head would explode if she didn't get a breath of fresh air.

'I'll get everything set up,' Theodosia shouted as she ran off, nearly colliding with Mrs Fellows.

'In my day the first thing children were taught were manners,' the surly housekeeper muttered.

Selina ignored her, having found over the past weeks it wasn't worth the effort of arguing with the head of the servants.

With one last grimace as she looked in the mirror Selina headed outside after Theodosia. Priscilla was already making her way out of the library doors at the back of the house on to the terrace on the arm of Thomas, one of the young footmen.

'Would you bring her a chair out from inside?'

'I'm not dying,' Priscilla said, but there was a note of affection in her voice.

Selina waited until Thomas had brought a comfortable armchair outside from the library, then settled Priscilla into it and began to pile the blankets on top of her.

'Ten minutes, no more, then we'll get you back inside,' Selina said, resisting the urge to lean over and kiss Priscilla on the head. There was less prickliness from the older of the sisters now, even a little affection, but Selina knew they still had a long way to go to build a robust trust between them.

'Go and help my sister before she injures herself.'

Down on the lawn the grass was still white with the

frost and it crunched underfoot as Selina made her way across it to where Theodosia was jumping up and down with excitement. They'd set up the target again and found the bow and arrows, and Theodosia was eager to try her hand at archery.

'Just remember, if your uncle comes out shouting and making a fuss we ignore him,' Selina reminded her. 'Don't let anything distract you. Ensure there is nothing between you and the target when you loose an arrow, then shoot.'

'I'm going to practise every single day until I'm as good a shot as you, Miss Salinger.'

Selina smiled indulgently. Theodosia's excitement was infectious and she found some of the worries from the last few days slipping from her shoulders.

Carefully she reminded Theodosia how to hold the bow, how to notch the arrow, how to lift the bow and aim at her target. She had her arms wrapped around the little girl, supporting much of the bow's weight, but she let Theodosia aim by herself, let her decide when she was ready to loose the arrow.

It flew through the air a few feet, landing just short of the target.

'Well done,' Selina said. 'Your first shot and nearly at the target.'

'Let's try again.'

Selina glanced up to where Priscilla was sitting on the terrace, giving the little girl a wave. She waved back, then gave a shooing gesture with her hand as if telling Selina to stop worrying.

Again they notched the arrow together, lifted the bow and, when Theodosia was ready, she drew back the bow-string and loosed the arrow. This one sailed through the air beautifully and thunked into the very bottom of the target.

'I did it,' she shouted, doing a little dance. 'I did it. I did it.'

They shot again and again, some of the arrows missing and a few hitting, but even the misses didn't do anything to dull Theodosia's enthusiasm.

'One more and then we must take your sister inside.'

Theodosia lifted the bow with help and shot, the arrow sailing beautifully through the air and landing on one of the blue circles.

'Well done, my darling,' Selina said, making sure the bow was placed carefully on the ground before embracing the little girl.

'I thought I would wait until you'd finished to approach.' Matthew's voice came from behind them.

'Did you see me shooting?' Theodosia skipped over to her uncle. 'I hit the target five times. It won't be long before I'm an expert like Miss Salinger.'

'Indeed. You were very impressive.'

Selina glanced at him, making sure she didn't catch his eye. Ever since the night when he'd made his proposition to her and then revealed the painful details of his past she had barely seen him. In a way it had been a relief. She didn't know how to act around him, or what their relationship could be. She knew they couldn't go back to a formal employer and employee arrangement, they knew each other too well, had shared too much for that. Equally she still felt the same about becoming his mistress. Her social standing in life might not have been what it was a few years ago when she'd been the toast of Cambridge society, but that didn't mean she had lost her moral values as well.

Still, she knew whenever she was near him it was becoming harder and harder to resist, harder to deny what her body wanted so badly.

'Can you shoot, Uncle?' Theodosia turned her little face up to him as she spoke.

'I have done before. When I was a boy your father and I used to spend hours practising shooting at the target. There wasn't much call for it in the navy or more recent years. I may be a little rusty.'

'Do you think Miss Salinger would win a competition between you?' Theodosia asked sweetly. Selina's eyes narrowed as she regarded the little girl. If she didn't know Theodosia was only seven she would think she was trying to push them together, trying to matchmake.

Matthew looked at Selina, his eyes seeming to penetrate through her body to her soul.

'I don't know about that,' he murmured.

'Why don't you try?'

Before either Selina or Matthew could protest Theodosia had skipped off to join her sister on the terrace, her head bent as she whispered something to her sister.

'Ever get the feeling you're being set up?' Matthew murmured.

'You can walk away.'

'Not with my honour intact.'

'It isn't likely to be intact when I shoot three perfect arrows,' Selina said.

'Ah, but I plan on using underhand methods,' Matthew said with a grin. 'I can be very distracting when I wish.'

Selina didn't reply, she was trying to stop herself thinking of all the ways he could distract her and failing miserably.

'You're thinking of how I might distract you.'

'In itself a distraction,' Selina muttered. 'You go first.'

She watched as he picked up the bow, weighing it in

his hands. He plucked the bowstring, testing the tautness, then selected an arrow from the quiver on the ground. All the movements were smooth with no hesitation and Selina realised that it might have been a while since he'd picked up a bow and arrow, but that didn't mean he wasn't just as good as her.

In a fluid motion he notched the arrow, took aim and let it loose, watching critically as it flew towards the target. It hit a little off centre, but not bad for a first attempt.

'Your turn,' he said, handing her the bow, his fingers brushing against hers and sending a jolt though her body. She wasted no time in preparing her shot, letting the arrow fly just seconds later. It hit the target a little further from the centre than his arrow.

'First point to me,' he murmured. 'Did we agree what the prize was?'

Selina remembered the last competition they'd played against each other, the kiss on the beach and the intimacy it had led to later that evening.

'Perhaps just for the satisfaction of winning,' she said as she handed the bow over.

'Where would be the fun in that?'

'What do you suggest?'

'Dinner. Tonight. After the girls have gone to bed.'

She looked at him for a long moment, trying to work out exactly what he wanted from her. After their discussion he knew she wouldn't be his mistress. Why bring them closer together when it could only be difficult for the both of them?

'Why?'

'I enjoy your company.' That was hard to argue against.

'If you win, we have dinner—what about if I win?'

'Dinner?'

Selina found herself smiling. 'Hardly a wager if the prize is the same no matter who wins.'

'You can choose something else.'

She shook her head. 'Dinner it is. And the satisfaction of knowing I've beaten you.' He shot another arrow, this one landing at the edge of the target, and Selina's arrow hit right in the centre.

'One apiece,' he murmured in her ear, standing just a little too close. 'It is all to play for.'

The last arrow he took his time over, adjusting his stance a couple of times, drawing the string to gauge the tautness, before notching an arrow. Selina coughed just as he shot and he spun to face her.

'Sabotage.' He grinned, his eyes dancing with mirth.

'Hardly. I have a tickle in my throat.'

They both turned back to face the target where his arrow was still quivering from the impact. It lay in the very centre of the bullseye, a perfect shot.

'It looks as though we will be having dinner,' Selina said as she prepared and loosed her final arrow.

'Good shot,' Matthew murmured as it flew through the air and embedded itself in the canvas just next to his. 'I call that a draw.'

'I don't know…' Selina stalked over to the targets '…I think mine might be a little more central.'

'Nonsense,' Matthew said, coming up close behind her.

'We have our independent adjudicators,' she said, inclining her head in the direction of Priscilla and Theodosia.

'They would swear blue was red for you.'

'Perhaps,' Selina admitted. Theodosia was her staunchest supporter, Priscilla less so, but slowly the elder of the sisters was beginning to let down her guard.

'Who won, girls?' Matthew called over, grinning as they consulted one another seriously for a few seconds.

'Miss Salinger,' they chorused.

Matthew raised an eyebrow. 'Dinner, tonight. And you get to gloat.'

Chapter Eighteen

The dining room at Manresa House had been rarely used since Matthew had returned and taken up residence. He'd dined here once on the first night Miss Salinger had arrived, a brief, brisk meal he'd been so eager to get through to hand over the responsibility of the girls to the capable governess. That had been almost two months ago and Matthew hadn't eaten dinner in the formal dining room since. It seemed far too grand for him to eat in alone with its long mahogany table with space for sixteen, far too reminiscent of the days when his father had insisted he and his brother present themselves for inspection whenever he entertained, to be poked at and ridiculed by him and his drunken friends.

Happier memories, he thought to himself. Manresa House was a dreary old pile, but he was beginning to see with a little time and a little care and attention it could be made more welcoming and the painful memories supplanted by far more pleasant ones.

Carefully he adjusted his cravat, smoothing the silk between his fingers. It had been a long time since he'd properly dressed for dinner, too. In India there was the odd formal occasion, dinners with the important local

men when Matthew worked his hardest to charm and daz-
zle in the hope they would supply whatever commodity
he was hoping to acquire. Then he dressed exquisitely,
almost flamboyantly, playing the part of the English aris-
tocrat, the part they wanted him to play. Here, he was
wearing a dark evening jacket and light blue waistcoat
and matching cravat, silk and expensive, formal but un-
derstated.

As he waited Matthew prowled around the room, adjusting a vase here and a picture there, his nervous energy mounting with every moment that passed.

'Good evening,' Selina said as she stepped into the
dining room. She looked exquisite tonight, with her hair
swept back elegantly and her eyes sparkling in the candlelight. She was still wearing one of her plain grey dresses,
the uniform of a governess, and he realised she didn't
have anything else in her wardrobe. For an instant he allowed himself to imagine her draped in silk, something
revealing and risqué, brightly coloured and luxurious, the
opposite of the practical clothes she wore out of necessity.

'Good evening.' He crossed the room, taking her hand
and bringing it to his lips. The skin was soft and warm,
with the faint scent of honey, and he lingered for just
a moment longer over her, drawing away and catching
her eye.

'I don't know why I keep doing this to myself,' she
murmured, biting her lip.

'Doing what?'

'Putting myself in your path.'

'You're worried one day your resolve will weaken and
you'll throw yourself at me?' he asked with a smile.

Although it was meant as a joke he could see he'd got
to the heart of the matter. Selina might have resolved
not to become his mistress, but that resolve was only

paper-thin and anything could upset it. He wondered for a moment if he should grasp the opportunity, take her in his arms and kiss her, push them towards the inevitable without any further delay, but the confusion in her eyes was enough to stop him.

'No seduction tonight,' he promised, wondering even as the words left his mouth if he already regretted them. 'Just companionship, friendship and good food.'

He led her to the table, pulling out her chair and making sure she was settled before taking the seat at right angles to her. They were close, close enough for him to lean over and take her hand, to caress the back with his fingers. Already the promise of no seduction was weighing heavily on him.

'I have this urge to kiss you,' Matthew said quietly. 'Talk to me, distract me, so I don't break my word thirty seconds in to our evening.'

She smiled at that, the uncertainty from moments before gone from her eyes.

'Something distracting…' she mused. 'I could tell you about the time I got trapped on the roof in just my nightgown…' she paused for effect '…and it started to rain.'

Matthew groaned, the image as clear and vibrant in his mind as if he'd been there right beside her.

'*That* is hardly going to make me want to kiss you less, but I'm going to have to hear it anyway.'

'Are you sure? Alternatively I could tell you about the time I got caught in a storm and had to beg far too small clothes from a stable boy to make my walk home in.'

'I think you're a cruel woman.'

'Or the time I went for a refreshing paddle in the pond on a friend's country estate and had to abandon my underclothes in the water as I got caught in the pondweed.'

'I really hope all these stories are true,' he said, leaning back in his chair and closing his eyes.

'I wouldn't lie to you.'

'Go on,' he said. 'You can't leave me to my own imagination. I want details. Vivid details.'

'The episode on the roof happened just six months ago. Before I came to you I worked for a Lord and Lady Gilchrist, teaching their little boy before he went off to school.'

'I'm struggling to imagine what led you to be on the roof in just your nightgown.'

Selina grimaced. 'For the first few months I worked for them I was treated as a servant, summoned to report my progress with Edward, but not seen or spoken to outside that meeting. I walked in the shadows.'

A hard change from the life she must have been used to. As a beautiful young debutante she would have always been the centre of attention, showered with compliments and never truly alone.

'I didn't really mind. I was still adjusting from my change in circumstances and still grieving my father. I liked to keep to myself. One evening Lord Gilchrist called me to his study, on the pretence of finding out how his son was faring with his Latin in preparation for school.'

Matthew felt the anger rise up inside him. He knew what was coming next, the older man taking advantage of the younger woman. A man in power trying to intimidate a woman alone, in his employ.

'He started getting rather over-familiar and, when I was less than accommodating, he suggested I should do as he desired or I would be out of a job.' She sighed. 'It was so clichéd, the employer and the governess.'

Selina sounded vaguely amused and wearied by it

rather than annoyed and Matthew found some of the tension seeping from him. Lord Gilchrist couldn't have got what he wanted going by Selina's reaction.

'He started trying to corner me in various locations around the house, whenever he thought no one was looking. Of course he wasn't anywhere near as discreet as he thought he was being and one day Lady Gilchrist took me to one side. I thought she was going to throw me out immediately, accuse me of trying to seduce her husband.'

'She didn't?'

'No, she was very reasonable, told me her husband was a randy old goat and she would appreciate it if I would submit to him, and that she would raise my salary accordingly.'

Matthew couldn't help but laugh, although he was shocked. 'Probably glad to get the old man out of her bedroom and interested in someone else.'

'I refused, politely, of course, but I found myself having to go to more and more ingenious lengths to avoid both of their machinations.'

'And the rooftop in the rain?'

Selina smiled at the memory of it. 'Not one of my finest hours. I kept my bedroom door firmly locked and one of the maids who had previously been on the receiving end of Lord Gilchrist's attentions showed me how to wedge a chair underneath the handle for added security. When I was in there I could at least relax a little.' She paused, looking at Matthew for a moment and moving her fingers on the table so they were just touching his. He felt a jolt pass through him and knew, no matter what he'd promised, he wouldn't be able to stop pursuing Selina, not until she was his entirely. 'One night Edward was restless in the nursery. I went through to his bedroom and sat with him a while. His tossing and turning must have woken his father and I heard the old man coming up the stairs. My bedroom was back along the hall, too far away to safely get back to it and lock the door. I had two options: to stay where I was and risk being pawed at in the nursery, or climb out the window and hide on the roof until Lord Gilchrist had lost interest.'

'You chose the roof?'

'It wasn't a hard decision.'

Matthew had a perfect image of Selina dressed in her floor-length cotton nightdress swinging her legs out of the window and scrambling up on the roof.

'I stayed very quiet and very still and my plan would have worked perfectly if Lord Gilchrist hadn't decided to close his son's bedroom window before leaving the room.'

'He trapped you?'

'He didn't know I was out there, but, yes, he trapped me. It was only about midnight, a balmy summer's night luckily, but a couple of hours later it started to rain. There was nowhere to shelter, no way of getting down and, to top it off, the roof started to get very slippery as it became wet. I had to cling on to a miniature stone turret for about four hours, shivering in my sodden nightdress.'

'You paint quite the picture,' Matthew murmured. He had a very vivid image of the scene. In it Selina was wearing something scanty and see-through and was draped across the roof in a rather enticing manner. 'How did you escape?'

'One of the maids caught sight of me in the morning as she started cleaning. She had to summon one of the footmen to help me inside.'

'Lucky man.'

'It wasn't one of my finest moments.'

'Please tell me you left the Gilchrists' employ very soon after.'

'Only when their son left for school.' She looked at him straight in the eye. 'Governess jobs aren't that easy to come by, especially when you have a rather vague past like me. I can hardly tell potential employers who I really am, I doubt anyone would want the illegitimate daughter of Lord Northrop bringing any hint of scandal into their house.'

'Then they are fools,' Matthew said, sitting back as the first course was brought into the dining room by two footmen. Only when they were alone again did he continue. 'How did you get your first job with no references and no formalised education?'

'You would be surprised how little people check on what you tell them. I made some references to a school for girls in Cambridge I used to help out at occasionally, and people just assumed I'd first been educated there and then stayed on as a teacher.'

For a moment they fell silent, then Selina's eyes flicked up to his.

'Now I've told you one of my most embarrassing moments it's only fair you reciprocate.'

'I could tell you about the time I got trapped in the family crypt and was so convinced the skeletons of the dead were about to rise I was a babbling wreck for weeks after. Or the time I had a very narrow escape from the bedchamber of an Indian noblewoman who had a reputation for suffocating the men she lured to her bed.'

'I'm intrigued,' Selina said, her eyes lighting up. 'You have to tell me more.'

'It was during a visit to the very southern tip of India. I had just started looking into the spice trade and was on a trip around the region, scouting for opportunities to acquire whatever they had available. On these trips I often spent much of the time wooing the local royalty or nobles, setting up good relationships for future deals.' He paused. Just talking of India conjured up the sights, the smells, and he felt the familiar yearning for the heat and the thrill of succeeding in setting up another successful trade. 'Much of the land was owned by one very influential landowner who I spent much time with. He was genial and had a keen intelligence—a man who liked to have long dinners discussing the state of the world.'

'Strange to think that no matter where people reside in their world, what country they are born in, we are basically all the same. The same needs and desires, the same interests.'

'You're right, human nature is the same in London as it is in the most remotest area of Tamil.'

'Tell me more about this man and his wife.'

'He confided to me one evening that he was content in life apart from one thing. His wife had a voracious sexual appetite and he wasn't able to satisfy her. He suggested it would be a great favour to him if I visited her.'

'Had you met her?'

'No, the dinners were always just me and him. I didn't want to get involved. I wanted to build a long-term trade relationship with him and knew, no matter what he said, if I did what he asked he would always carry some resentment for me.'

'So what happened?'

'The next night he invited me to walk about his gardens and the walk just happened to end up in his wife's bedchamber. He patted me on the back and walked away, locking the door behind him.'

'He locked you in there with her?'

'He did. We weren't alone, there were half-a-dozen female attendants buzzing around excitedly. One was quite young, new to service and looking absolutely petrified.

I was led to a seat and plied with wine and delicacies, all the time wondering how to make my escape without offending my host.'

Matthew shook his head ruefully at the memory of it. He'd felt an exhilaration at the time, the thrill of a problem to be solved. That memory seemed so far removed from his life here and he expected to feel more nostalgic, more eager to jump aboard the nearest ship and set sail for the country that had been more of a home than England these past few years. Instead he felt a peculiar contentment he'd never expected to feel about living in England, in Manresa House, with a life of simple domesticity.

'While I was being fussed around the young serving girl came up and whispered in my ear. She told me quite firmly I needed to get out, right away. I could see by her expression she was deadly serious, but she had no time to tell me anything more. Just then the nobleman's wife appeared, dressed in layers of brightly coloured silk designed to tempt and tease. She was quite large, with long dark hair and eyes that seemed to pin you to the spot.'

Selina was leaning forward in her chair, utterly engrossed in his story, and he had to suppress the urge to take her fully by the hand. He'd promised no seduction tonight and the only way he would be able to keep that promise was if he kept his distance.

'I've never been a superstitious man, never believed in the occult, but right then I had some sort of premonition. I knew if I stayed it would turn out badly for me. The door had been locked, but the windows were only shuttered, opening from the inside. I bowed, begged the nobleman's wife for forgiveness, then threw myself out of one of the windows. Luckily it was on the ground floor and I was able to pick myself up and beat a hasty retreat.'

'Did you go back? Finish your trade deal?'

Matthew shook his head. 'I made some subtle enquiries. It seemed the nobleman's wife had a reputation as a predator. She would get her husband to lure men into her bedchamber, have her way with them and then strangle them at the climax of their union.'

'Surely someone would have put a stop to that?' Selina said, her eyes wide with shock.

'They were the most powerful landowners in the entire region, no one dared challenge them. I realised that the nobleman knew exactly what was going to happen when he locked that bedroom door and the wonderful relationship I thought we had was actually all a ruse. He'd sent me in to his wife as a way of ridding himself of a troublesome foreigner wanting his resources.' Matthew smiled ruefully. 'I kept well away after that.'

'I wonder if the rumours about her were true?' Selina mused. 'History can be very cruel to women who don't conform to stereotype.'

He shrugged. 'I wasn't about to stay around to find out.'

His eyes met hers for a moment and he felt a warm glow in his chest, a contentment he hadn't felt for a very long time. There was something wonderful about sharing these little bits of his life with someone. For so long he'd blocked himself off from any deeper human interaction, not even allowing his comrades in the navy to get to know who he really was. It felt good to open up to someone, to trust someone.

'Do you know, I've never told anyone else that story,' he said quietly.

'Why not?' Selina looked puzzled. It wasn't particularly personal or damaging to him.

'I've never had anyone else to tell it to.'

He held her gaze for a long moment, wondering when

she had crept under his skin and into his heart. There was desire coursing round his body whenever she was near, but there was more than that. He cared for her, cared about what happened to her, how she felt. Cared for her happiness. Cared what she thought of him and cared that she did think of him, often.

For so long he'd been so careful about protecting himself from any connection, scared that he wasn't worthy, scared of anyone having any hold over him, but somehow Selina had managed to slip through all his defences and slip into his heart.

He could tell she was just about to say something and by the sentiment that glistened in her eyes he suspected it was something rather emotional, but at that moment the footmen entered the room and whisked away the dinner plates, placing a perfectly formed tray of marzipan fruits between them.

The moment was lost, he saw that as soon as they were alone again, and Selina's eyes were now shuttered and wary.

'When do you plan to return to India?' Throughout the entire time he'd known her this subject had been the most difficult to discuss. First she had worried about the girls losing another person from their lives, but now he suspected she felt as he did—that he would miss her terribly as well.

'I don't know,' he said, his fingers tracing patterns around the marzipan fruits. 'I had planned to leave next month, to sail before Christmas.' Ever since he'd left India he'd felt this urge to get back, to return to safety where no one *really* knew him, where no one had any expectations of him.

'You had planned?' Selina challenged him softly a spark of hope in her eyes. 'What do you plan now?'

'I find myself more and more reluctant to leave.' It was the truth, finally admitted. He couldn't imagine sailing away, leaving Selina and his nieces behind. Not knowing how they fared for months on end, not being part of their daily lives.

Selina looked down at the table as if not able to bring herself to look him in the eye.

'Don't go,' she said quietly. 'None of us wants you to.'

Eventually he would have to. It was where his business was based, his livelihood. Everything he'd built up from nothing, everything he was proud of. Eventually…but not yet. He'd left a very capable man in charge of keeping things going, a man with vision and ambition. From the reports he'd received since returning to England everything was going well so far, although being so far away the news lagged months behind. Still, it was a flourishing business that was in steady hands—a few more months in England surely wouldn't hurt.

'I never thought of staying,' he said after a long pause. 'Not for more than a few months.'

'Sometimes life goes in a completely opposite direction to what you expect.'

Matthew nodded, leaning back in his chair. He could stay for Christmas at least, see in the New Year. Perhaps wait for the spring and better sailing conditions to set off.

'Perhaps I could,' he murmured, feeling a relief spread through him at the idea. He'd felt so panicked at the thought of leaving, but he'd been so set on that path it had seemed impossible to even think of anything else. Now he'd broached the subject in his own mind he would need some time to adjust, some time to get used to the idea of staying a little longer, but already it felt as though a great weight had been lifted from him.

'Never in my life would I have thought I'd want to stay

longer here at Manresa House,' he said, looking round the oppressive decor.

'A house is only made a home by the people in it.'

'Wise words, Selina.'

'And you could always do a little redecorating.' She looked around the dining room critically.

'Could anything make a dark house on the moors homely?'

'Some fresh wallpaper and new curtains and the place will be unrecognisable.'

For the first time ever Matthew had the urge to make the house into a home, to put his own heart into it and supplant those who had come before.

'Perhaps…' he said, lost in the idea of a home. Something he hadn't had for a very long time.

Next to him he vaguely noticed Selina getting to her feet. She stepped closer to him and bent down, kissing him gently on the cheek.

'Goodnight, Matthew,' she said, then disappeared before he could open his mouth to protest.

Chapter Nineteen

Selina awoke with a smile on her face. Priscilla had completely recovered from her fever, the sun was once again shining across the moors and she'd slept better than she had done in months. She wasn't sure if it was the fresh country air or finally feeling settled and content, but the sleepless nights were fast becoming a thing of the past.

As she slid out of bed she acknowledged the main reason for the smile on her face. Last night at dinner Matthew had admitted he didn't want to leave, at least not yet. As he'd said the words she'd longed to hear, that he would stay a little longer in England, Selina had felt like jumping from her chair and flinging her arms around him. She'd managed to control herself, to remain dignified, but the smile from last night was still there on her face this morning.

You've fallen for him, the little voice in her head said and Selina knew she couldn't deny it. She had fallen for him, utterly, completely. Despite the fact he was a gentleman, despite the fact Selina had thought she would never trust a man of his class again, she'd fallen head over heels in love with him.

And now he was staying, at least for a little longer.

She knew she couldn't get her hopes up. She had to remain realistic. Matthew was staying for the sake of his nieces, for the chance to build a relationship with them. Never had he hinted that he wanted anything more from her than the affair he had proposed a few days ago. Although last night there had been a wistfulness about him, a hopefulness that Selina had only ever glimpsed before.

Before she started to dress she looked at herself critically in the small mirror hanging on her wall. She looked plainer than she had when she'd been a debutante with a full dance card and plenty of admirers, plain and sensible. Hardly what an earl would be looking for in a wife. Matthew could have the pick of the eligible young women both in Yorkshire and London. He was a young, handsome earl, with a thriving business and, if the rumours among the servants were to be believed, a fortune to rival the wealthiest in the country. Once his presence in the country was known the ambitious parents of every single young woman would be knocking the door down of Manresa House to try to ally their family with his.

'He could have anyone,' Selina murmured, sweeping her hair back. It was a sobering thought. One day he probably would decide to marry, to settle down with a woman from a reputable family. A mother figure for the girls, a woman who would not want Selina in her household. Or perhaps she wouldn't see the plain governess as a threat at all.

Shaking herself, she resolved to think of happier things. For now she was just grateful he wasn't going to be disappearing any time soon. The girls would get longer with their uncle and she would be able to spend more time with the man she couldn't stop thinking about. The man she loved.

'Enough,' she said quietly. There was to be no more thoughts of love.

Selina quickly dressed, pulling on one of the grey woollen dresses and wishing for a moment that she had something more elegant to wear. The grey wool was practical and kept the chill of the North York Moors from her skin, but she longed for the silks and satins from her debutante days.

'Good morning,' Lord Westcroft said, startling her as she left her room heading for the nursery. Selina wasn't easily caught off guard, but she yelped in surprise.

'What are you doing here?' she asked, hearing the accusatory tone in her voice. It *was* his house, but he really couldn't have any good reason to be loitering up here.

'I've come to see Priscilla and Theodosia,' he said.

'This early in the morning?'

'I assumed they would be up. I was always up early as a child.'

'Priscilla may be. She's often reading when I go in to hurry them along in the mornings, but Theodosia would sleep until noon if I let her.'

'Curious, although I suppose it makes sense. She has to recuperate from expending all that energy at some point.'

He walked next to her along the corridor, their arms brushing every couple of steps, making it hard for Selina to focus on anything but the man beside her.

The girls shared a bedroom just off the nursery itself, a little way along the corridor from the schoolroom. Matthew leaned against the wall as Selina knocked at the door and peeked inside. As she had predicted, Priscilla was sitting curled up in one of the comfortable armchairs placed in front of the window, reading her book. Theodosia was still snuggled under her sheets, just a mass of tangled blonde hair on the pillow framing rosy cheeks.

Crossing the room, she greeted Priscilla first, dropping a kiss on the top of her head. Then she went over to the bed where Theodosia was still sleeping and perched on the edge.

'Time to wake up, sleepy head,' she said, gently peeling the sheets back and giving Theodosia a little rub on her shoulders. The girl opened one bleary eye and promptly turned over, muttering something into her pillow. 'The day is wasting away—you don't want to miss the sunshine.'

Reluctantly Theodosia turned back over and after a few seconds sat up and wriggled into Selina's lap.

'What are we doing today?' The little girl's eyes were still closed, her body still heavy with sleep.

'Our normal lessons and perhaps a walk about the gardens as it's such a beautiful day.'

'I have a suggestion,' Matthew said, stepping further into the room. Selina had hoped he was here to tell the girls he would be staying in England longer, that way it would be hard for him to change his mind, but it seemed he was thinking of something else today. 'Do you remember in Whitby we were all a little disappointed we couldn't have ice creams? Well, I thought today would be the perfect day to try out the recipe I brought back.'

Theodosia's eyes shot open and she jumped from the bed. Selina didn't think she'd ever seen the little girl move so fast.

'Can we? It's going to be amazing. Can we make ten different flavours and eat them all for breakfast?'

Matthew chuckled as Theodosia took him by the hand and led him over to her bed, pushing him to sit down next to Selina and climbing on to his lap as she continued talking. 'We could make ice creams every single day and eat them for breakfast, lunch and dinner.'

'I think we might get sick of ice cream if we did that,' Selina said.

'Never. Never, never, never, never, never.'

'Let's have a normal breakfast,' Matthew said soothingly. 'Then I've given Cook the morning off so we should have the kitchen to ourselves. One of the footmen is bringing up some ice from the ice house—he assures me there is some left over from summer—and we can get started once it arrives.'

'Thank you,' Theodosia said, flinging her arms around her uncle.

Eyeing the clean surfaces and neatly tidied utensils, Selina wondered what state the kitchen was going to be in once they'd finished. Theodosia was already bouncing around and even Priscilla seemed excited by the prospect of making ice cream.

'Right,' Matthew said, smoothing out the recipe in front of him. 'First we need that large bowl and a lot of cream.'

Selina began rummaging through the supplies in the pantry, bringing out the jug of cream, a couple of eggs, sugar and salt. The ice block sat slowly dripping in the sink and she saw Theodosia eye it with concern.

'Don't fear,' Matthew said, catching his niece's glance as well, 'we'll have the ice cream made and eaten long before that great lump of ice melts.'

Selina stood back, watching as Matthew instructed the girls on how to measure out the right quantity of cream into the bowl and add the eggs. Already the three of them were sticky, with egg yolk on their fingers and splatters of cream on their clothes.

'Next the sugar and some flavouring. What flavour should we make?'

'Strawberry,' Priscilla said quickly. 'That's my favourite.'

Theodosia considered for a moment, then nodded in agreement.

'It isn't really the season for strawberries,' Selina said, wondering whether the girls would be satisfied with something a little less summery.

'We could try using strawberry jam,' Priscilla said, eyeing the jars of preserves on the high shelf in the pantry.

'I don't know if it will mix in, but why don't we try it? If it is strawberry you want, then it's strawberry we'll have.'

Selina watched as they scooped a blob of strawberry jam into the mixture and Theodosia swirled it round, her face alight with happiness.

'When do we add the ice?'

'I'll have to chip smaller pieces off,' Matthew said, taking out a knife from the block and testing the sharpness with a finger. 'I'll chip, you girls can add it to the bowl. Miss Salinger, you're in charge of stirring and adding the salt.'

They all watched as he began to chip off small pieces of ice from the large block, passing the slippery shards to the girls so they could throw them into the bowl. Selina quickly measured out the right quantity of salt, adding it little by little as the bowl filled up with ice. She stirred vigorously, watching in amazement as the mixture turned creamy and pink.

When the right amount of ice had been added they all looked in the bowl, amazed that it at least looked more or less the right consistency.

'Now for the test,' Matthew declared, crossing to the other side of the kitchen and taking four spoons from the drawer where they were kept.

Theodosia dived straight in, taking a big scoop, and Priscilla followed suit. Selina took her own spoonful, darting out her tongue to test it before slipping the spoon into her mouth. It was cold and creamy and unbelievably sweet. There were still small pieces of ice mixed in with the cream mixture, making it less smooth than the ice cream she'd had before, and the jam was perhaps a little too sweet for a flavouring, but she was surprised at how well it had turned out.

'It's heavenly,' Theodosia declared and dug her spoon in for another scoop.'

Matthew pulled chairs up for them all and they sat, dipping their spoons into the bowl and savouring the ice cream.

'It tastes better when you make it yourself,' Matthew declared. Theodosia was leaning in to him, a large grin on her face, and Selina could see the happiness behind his smile. The man who had initially not wanted to get too emotionally involved with his nieces had been completely overcome with love for them. It was a heart-warming sight.

'That was amazing,' Priscilla declared as she took a last scrape of the fast melting ice cream from the bowl.

'Can we make some more?'

'Perhaps next week. Let's all think of what flavour we'd like and we can order something in from Whitby if need be.'

Selina sat back, knowing in a few minutes she would have to take the children back upstairs to start their lessons, but just allowing herself to enjoy the moment. Here, at Manresa House, she felt something she hadn't felt for a very long time. She felt as though she belonged.

'Uncle, may I talk to you?' Priscilla asked quietly, licking the last of the stickiness from her fingers.

'Of course. Shall we go to my study?'

Selina frowned, wondering what was worrying the little girl, but ushered Theodosia from her chair and took her hand to lead her upstairs.

Matthew sat down facing Priscilla, taking in her serious face and troubled expression.

'Is something worrying you?' he asked gently.

'Yes.'

'Why don't you tell me what it is?'

Priscilla shifted in her seat and seemed to be thinking of how to begin.

'I'm worried you're going to mess things up,' she said eventually.

Matthew knew the surprise was showing on his face. He hadn't been expecting that.

'How might I mess things up?' he asked.

Priscilla sighed. 'People often seem to, don't they? When they're happy, and others around them are happy, they go and do things that makes everyone stop being happy.'

It was quite a profound observation from a nine-year-old.

'I like Miss Salinger,' Priscilla said and Matthew blinked at the direction of the conversation. 'I tried not to—in my experience governesses can be cold and indifferent and often don't stay that long—but Miss Salinger is different.' She paused as if checking he were following her line of thought. 'Miss Salinger *cares*. She's kind and interesting and she sat by my bed every night when I was ill.'

'She is a treasure of a governess,' he murmured.

'Quite. And I don't want her to leave,' Priscilla said.

'Why do you think she will leave?'

Matthew had to suppress a smile as the little girl rolled her eyes at him. 'Weren't you listening to me? Because you'll mess things up.'

'How do you think I'll mess things up?'

'Miss Salinger is in love with you,' Priscilla said, speaking slowly as if talking to a particularly dumb sheep. 'At some point you'll probably break her heart and then she will leave.'

'She's not in love with me,' he said instinctively, but as Priscilla looked at him with her large blue eyes he recalled every look, every touch, every kindness Selina had ever given him.

'She is. And you're in love with her, but you're too silly to admit it.'

Matthew opened his mouth, but no words would come out. Priscilla had barely spoken more than four sentences at a time to him before now, always quiet, always watching. Yet here she was telling him his own feelings as if she were the most confident child in the world.

'You should marry her,' Priscilla said with an emphatic nod. 'And then she'll stay. That way it doesn't matter if you need to go back to India, we can all come with you.'

'I don't think…' Matthew said, but was silenced by another roll of the eyes from Priscilla.

'You love her, she loves you. *We* love her. If you don't marry her, then you're a fool.'

'A fool,' he murmured quietly, then quickly rallied. 'I seem to remember you saying a few weeks ago that *you* would never marry.'

Priscilla sighed. 'It is completely different for me, Uncle. I am a woman, a wealthy woman. If I marry, all my money will go to my husband, who can then tell me what to do. Why would I want to marry?'

'Surely that is the same for Miss Salinger.'

'She's not wealthy. And she loves you.' Priscilla blinked a couple of times, then looked him directly in the eye. 'Don't be a fool, Uncle.'

She stood and stalked out of the room, closing the door firmly behind her, leaving Matthew completely in shock. He wouldn't have been able to follow her even if he wanted to, his body seemed to have grown roots and anchored him to the spot.

'She doesn't love me,' he muttered to himself, but immediately he knew it was a lie. Selina did love him— now Priscilla had voiced the words it was hard to deny it.

He rocked back in his chair, pushing it away from his desk and balancing on just the two back legs. The question he really needed to consider was how did he feel about Selina. He cared for her, enjoyed time spent in her company, desired her as he'd never desired another woman before. He thought of her smile, her laugh, the little pensive expression she got when trying to work something out. The idea of losing her, of never seeing her again, made him feel sick.

'I love her,' he said, shaking his head with disbelief.

Standing quickly, he crossed to the window, looking out over the formal gardens. Priscilla was right. Manresa House would be a cold shell without Selina's presence, the girls miserable and he…well, he would still be lonely and shut off from the world.

For a moment he felt a panic rising inside him. He'd never planned for anything like this, never thought he would let someone close to him. Now Selina was there in his heart he didn't know what to do. He felt all the familiar doubts bubbling up, the thought he would let her down, that somehow he wasn't worthy.

'Enough,' he said firmly. He'd allowed the past to rule him for far too long. He was a different man from the eighteen-year-old lad who'd been bullied by his father into a marriage he hadn't wanted. This decision was all his own.

He was going to marry her.

Matthew almost stalked out of the room to find her right away, but he held himself back. This would be Selina's one and only proposal, if all went to plan. That meant he had to do it right, make it something they would always remember. A little time and a little planning, that was what he needed, even if part of him wanted to run to the schoolroom and secure her promise immediately.

Chapter Twenty

Selina frowned. The girls were up to something. For the past day they hadn't stopped whispering and throwing glances in her direction. She knew it wouldn't be a prank, they were far too well behaved for anything mischievous, but she couldn't work out what they were planning.

'I'm dying in here,' Theodosia suddenly declared, dramatically putting her hand to her forehead and flopping back in her chair.

Selina had to suppress a smile.

'We're only on page two,' she said, gesturing to the slim volume of poetry on the desk between the two girls.

'I think Theodosia needs a break. Some fresh air,' Priscilla said quickly.

'It's rather cold out and windy,' Selina said, eyeing the leaves blowing across the garden in the wind out of the window.

'What is it you always say? A little wind never hurt anyone.'

'I suppose we could go for a brisk walk about the gardens.'

The girls eyed each other and Selina knew whatever they were planning was about to come to fruition.

'Can we go to the folly? It's a clear day, we might see the sea.'

Deciding to go along with whatever the girls were planning, Selina nodded and then set about finding their coats. Within ten minutes they were outside, Theodosia and Priscilla walking quickly ahead, looking back every few minutes to check Selina was following.

It took half an hour to reach the folly, half an hour of cold, whipping wind and toes that felt as though they might fall off. It wasn't the most pleasant of days to be doing a long walk, but Selina couldn't deny her mind felt refreshed and sharper.

The girls had stopped outside the door to the tower and were watching her approach with impatience.

'You go up first, Miss Salinger,' Theodosia said. 'We'll follow.'

Allowing herself to be swept along, Selina began the climb, wondering what she would find at the top. She was halfway up when she realised the girls weren't following, not yet at least, and she paused, considering whether she should continue upwards or climb down. After a moment she carried on to the top, knowing she would be able to see them from the edge of the tower.

'Good afternoon,' Matthew said as she emerged out of the narrow door. He took her hand and placed a kiss on its back, just below the knuckles. Whatever Selina had been expecting it wasn't this. Matthew was dressed in a simple dark brown jacket and light brown breeches with a brilliant white shirt underneath. He looked dashing in the late afternoon light and Selina felt her heart squeeze in her chest.

'What's happening?' she asked, trying to find a reason the girls would have lured her here to meet with Matthew.

'I have something very important to ask you, and I thought I would do it at the most picturesque spot on the estate.' He grimaced. 'I had hoped it wouldn't be quite so windy.'

'Something to ask me?'

'I've come to a realisation, a very important one. I've realised that I can't bear to think of my life without you. If I imagine a future without you it looks grey and dull.'

She felt a surge of hope and knew her eyes had widened in surprise.

'I know I've been a fool, suggesting you become my mistress. I think I was so traumatised by my marriage to Elizabeth, so ashamed of how I'd gone along with something I'd known was wrong, I didn't think I deserved happiness, but you've given it to me anyway.' He smiled at her, gripping her hand tighter in his own. 'I don't want you as my mistress. I want you to be my wife.'

Selina felt herself stumble and gripped hold of the stone parapet for support.

'Marry me, Selina. I promise I will do everything I can to make you happy.'

She wanted to throw her arms around him, to kiss him until they both forgot everything but the taste of the other, but something held her back. There was a little voice of caution telling her not to rush in.

'What about India?'

'We'll work it out. Perhaps we will all go for a short while, just so I can appoint someone to run the business in my absence. We will find a way to make it work.' He smiled at her reassuringly. 'I know you are cautious, after what happened with your father, but I promise I will take care of you. You may not trust many people, but I think you trust me.'

Selina realised it was true—after just a few short months she did trust him.

'You haven't given me an answer,' he said softly.

She would be a fool to say no. She loved him, had dreamed of this.

'Yes,' she said, flinging her arms around his neck. For a long moment they kissed, their lips coming together as his arms wrapped around her waist.

'Have you asked yet?' Theodosia's voice came from the doorway.

Selina and Matthew pulled apart, but she noticed he kept a hand resting lightly on her waist.

'I have.'

'And what did she say?'

'I hardly think they'd be kissing if she'd said no,' Priscilla observed from behind her sister.

'Have you given her the ring?'

Matthew dug into a pocket and produced a sparkling ruby surrounded by diamonds set on a delicate gold band. 'A betrothal gift.'

In a daze Selina held out her hand for him to slip it on, looking down at the beautiful piece of jewellery. When they'd set out from Manresa House half an hour earlier she'd had no inkling this was going to happen and she felt as though her head was spinning and the rest of her couldn't keep up.

'Lady Westcroft,' Matthew murmured in her ear. 'It has quite a ring to it.'

It would take a little getting used to. In the space of two years she'd gone from debutante to governess and now to future wife of an earl. Future wife of the man she loved.

'I know you're not going to be our mama, because Uncle Matthew isn't our father, but it'll be almost like having a mother again,' Theodosia whispered to Selina, squeezing her hand. 'I'm so pleased you're going to stay.'

Selina dropped a kiss on her unruly blonde hair. 'I'll always be here, no matter what.'

Priscilla squeezed out through the doorway on to the top of the tower and in an unprecedented show of affection she threw her arms around Selina's waist and buried her face in the fabric of her dress.

A gust of wind hit the tower, making all four of them totter backwards towards the door.

'Let's get home,' Matthew said. 'When I pictured the proposal it was a little less grey and windy.'

'It was perfect,' Selina said, but quickly ushered the children back through the door to the stairs. It was cold and it wouldn't be long before it got dark, hardly the place to linger.

Matthew tipped his head back and caught Selina's eye. They had celebrated their engagement in the library at the girls' insistence with steaming cups of hot chocolate and three different kinds of cake. It was dark outside now and both girls were curled up on the sofa, sleeping soundly.

'Let's get the children to bed,' Matthew said, 'and then I can kiss my future wife like I've been wanting to all afternoon.'

Quickly he scooped first Priscilla and then Theodosia up, making the climb up to their bedroom with their heads nuzzled in to his shoulder and their breathing deep and regular. He almost ran back down the stairs when he was sure both girls were settled in their beds.

Selina was standing by the fire, the flickering light illuminating her in a warm glow that Matthew found mesmerising. He crossed the room in a few short strides and pulled her into his arms.

'I haven't been able to think about anything but kissing you,' he murmured and his lips came to meet hers. She was sweet on his tongue, sweet and warm, and he felt the desire swell up inside him like an unstoppable force. 'I don't know how I ever thought I could be without you.'

Selina let her head drop back as his lips traced a path down her jaw and on to the smooth skin of her neck. A soft moan escaped her lips and he knew he wanted to elicit that moan over and over again in a thousand different ways.

He ran his hands down the length of her back, feeling her arch towards him. Her body was warm through her clothes and he longed to feel the heat of her skin against his.

'Matthew,' she said, her eyes coming to meet his, 'soon we will be married.'

He blinked, then suddenly understood the emphasis she put on the words and had to hold himself back to stop his hands ripping the clothes from her body. She might have just suggested they could pre-empt their marriage vows by a few weeks, but he still had to remember it would be her first time.

'Shall we go upstairs?' he asked, not knowing what he would do if she said no.

Selina placed her hand in his and together they hurried for the stairs, almost tripping more than once in their rush to reach the bedroom. Matthew pushed open the door, ushered Selina through and then kicked it closed behind him, pausing only long enough to click the lock into place to ensure they were undisturbed for the entire night.

He turned and for a moment he was rooted to the spot. Selina had pulled the pins from her hair and let it cascade loose over her shoulders. As he watched she began fiddling with the fastenings at the back of her dress, her eyes never leaving his.

With two steps he was by her side.

'You don't know how many times I've imagined this,' he said, his voice ragged.

'Me, too.'

Suddenly he had an image of Selina tossing and turning in her bed, hot with desire for him.

Matthew gently turned her around, reaching for the fastenings of her sensible wool dress and fumbling with the intricate design.

'From this moment on I'm banning you from wearing grey,' he said, almost letting out a yelp of celebration as the first fastening came loose.

'I only own grey dresses. Suitable attire for a governess.'

'I shall buy you new dresses, every colour of the rainbow.'

'And until they arrive?'

Matthew grinned at the thought of Selina walking around completely naked. 'You shall have to stay in bed,' he murmured, catching her earlobe between his teeth and feeling her shudder beneath him. 'And I'm a gentleman, so of course I'd keep you company.'

'Of course. It wouldn't be gentlemanly to leave me by myself.'

He trailed his lips along the back of her neck, lacing his fingers through her hair to move it to one side before returning his attention to the fastenings of her dress. The last one came free and he almost shouted with triumph, but instead satisfied himself with pushing the thick material from her shoulder to expose the creamy white skin underneath.

Selina turned to face him, shrugging the loose material from her shoulders and allowing it to fall to the ground. She was still clad in her chemise and petticoats, but these were much thinner, leaving her body much more accessible.

'You're beautiful,' he said as she stepped closer, pressing her body against his. Matthew could feel the curve of her waist and the flare of her hips and he had the urge to lay her back on the bed and explore every hidden inch of her with his hands.

Selina kissed him again, her hands roaming over his body, pulling at his clothes. She managed to loosen his shirt and with a swift movement Matthew pulled it off over his head, letting out a low groan as her hands danced over his chest. Never had he wanted anyone the way he wanted Selina. He felt her grip the waistband of his trousers and begin to tug downwards and at the same moment he lifted her chemise over her head. She wiggled out of her petticoats and finally she was standing naked in front of him.

Matthew paused, wanting to store this picture of her for ever. His eyes roamed over her, revelling in her soft curves and creamy white skin, drawn to the rosy buds of her nipples and then lower to the soft curls between her legs.

'You're perfect,' he said, then gathered her up in his arms and toppled her on to the bed.

Instinctively her arms encircled his back, pulling him closer so his body brushed against hers. They kissed, all the time his hands tracing a path over her body, revelling in the smoothness of her skin and the instinctive way she writhed and moved underneath him.

'Are you sure you want this?' he asked, not knowing what he would do if she said no.

'Yes.' Selina had broken away only long enough to utter the one word and then she returned to kissing him.

Gently Matthew allowed his hands to drop a little lower, caressing the taut muscles of her abdomen and then ever so slowly dipping into the soft curls below. His body screamed for him to bury himself inside her, but he knew he needed to make this wonderful for her and, as this was her first time, that meant taking everything slowly.

He felt her stiffen as his fingers found her folds, then let out a moan as he slowly began tracing backwards and forward, dipping and caressing and making her hips thrust up involuntarily again and again.

Underneath him he felt her breaths become shallow and her skin flush with warmth and then she tensed for a long ten seconds, her head dropping back and her mouth opening, any sound silenced by the deep kiss he gave her as she climaxed.

Once she had caught her breath Matthew felt her hands guide him on top of her, her hips pressing up into him. He pushed inside her, almost shouting out in pleasure at the sensation, forcing himself to take things slowly. Gently he pressed forward, stopping when he was fully inside her and only beginning to thrust when her hips shifted underneath him. Again and again they came together, until Selina moaned loudly again and tensed, sending Matthew over the edge into his own climax.

For twenty seconds he didn't move, unable to do any-thing but hold himself above her. He felt as though his body were floating in the air above the bed and only slowly did he come back to earth. Gently he rolled off her, scooping her up into his arms and manoeuvring himself behind her so they lay cradled together.

'I could get used to that,' Selina said quietly. 'We should do it again. Lots.'

'I'm very happy to donate my body.' He kissed the nape of her neck. 'Very happy.'

Selina snuggled back into him and Matthew wondered at how incredibly contented he felt right now. Here he was, lying with the woman he loved naked in his arms, ready to settle down, ready to face the demons of his past and accept he did deserve a little bit of happiness.

'Matthew,' Selina said, her voice heavy and her body already slipping into sleep. 'I love you.'

He felt his heart squeeze. Never had he expected he would hear those words. For so long he'd kept everyone at a distance, but now he was just beginning to realise how much he'd missed having someone to care about and someone who cared for him.

Chapter Twenty-One

'I am going to ride every single day for at least three hours,' Theodosia said. 'And then when I'm the best horsewoman in Yorkshire it would be silly for me not to have my own horse.'

'Silly indeed,' Matthew murmured, trying to suppress a smile and failing terribly. Luckily Theodosia only had eyes for the docile grey mare she was sitting on, holding the reins as if they were made of porcelain.

'I'm going to have a beautiful black horse, completely black, but with a white diamond on its forehead,' she continued and Matthew knew he would soon be scouring the country to find a horse that matched that exact description. Quickly he glanced at Priscilla, but she seemed to be relaxing into the outing now.

He'd suggested he take the girls out on the horses the evening before, after remembering the comment Theodosia had made about wanting to learn to ride. On close questioning he had learned they had ridden a handful of times before, but not consistently. His brother had never been keen on riding or any of its associated leisure pursuits and evidently neither had their mother. It meant both girls knew the very basics of how to sit and urge the horse forward, but anything more was out of their experience.

Theodosia had reacted with excitement as he'd expected. Priscilla's reaction had been a little more reserved and, when she had first been assisted on to the back of her beautiful bay mare, she had looked stiff and scared. Slowly Matthew had coaxed her into relaxing a little and now the horses were walking slowly down the drive away from the house with Priscilla looking as if she were in control.

It was the first time he'd been alone with the girls since Selina's arrival at Manresa House. Back then the idea of spending an afternoon in charge of the two children would have filled him with dread, but over the last few weeks his confidence had grown and his mindset changed.

'Shall we pick up the pace?' He showed them how to shift their position in the saddle almost imperceptibly to allow for a gentle trot. Theodosia squealed quietly in excitement as her horse eased itself forward, but even the excitable little girl seemed to know to keep her voice under control around the animals.

'How are you doing, Priscilla?' he asked, looking at his elder niece's serious expression. She'd been nervous around the horses when they'd first gone into the stables to see the mares they would be riding, but slowly he had seen her shoulders relax and her demeanour soften. She'd vaulted up easily on to Nightshade's back and had found her seat and gripped the reins as if she'd been riding her whole life.

'Very well, thank you,' she said, her eyes fixed ahead on the horizon.

He suppressed a smile. Already she was growing up. Although she was only nine years old often he saw her as a young lady rather than the child she really was. He supposed it was partly losing both parents at such a young age and having Theodosia to look after, but also just her personality. Whereas Theodosia would always be loud and exuberant, Priscilla would be serious and quiet. Still, he was hoping he could give her a few more years of childhood before she really had to grow up. A few more years of laughter and carefree days. A few more years of not having to worry about the world.

They had travelled a fair distance from the house now and he wondered how long to continue the ride before turning back. They were both enjoying it, but he remembered from his own childhood learning to ride could be tiring. The effort of staying in the saddle in exactly the right position meant you used muscles you didn't normally engage and he could remember many days of waddling round with sore legs after a gruelling riding lesson.

'Ten more minutes and we'll head back,' he said, smiling indulgently as Theodosia patted her horse on the neck and started whispering something in its ear.

'Uncle,' Priscilla said, manoeuvring Nightshade over so she was trotting beside him, 'when will you and Miss Salinger get married?'

It had been a question they had both been deliberating for the past few days. There seemed no reason to dally, no reason they shouldn't become husband and wife as soon as possible. Neither of them had family to notify. It would be an intimate affair, just them and the two girls and a couple of witnesses. Matthew had suggested they speak to the vicar and have the banns read as soon as possible, and Selina had readily agreed.

'A few weeks, as soon as we can organise it.'

'And then…?'

'What do you mean?' He saw the flicker of concern

on her face and wondered what Priscilla was worrying about. She worried a lot, quietly and secretly, but sometimes he could see flashes of it in her expressions and her actions.

'Will you return to India?'

He sighed. He'd been meaning to talk to the girls about this.

'I think I'm going to have to,' he said, watching Priscilla's expression. 'I have my business over there, a lot invested in it. I need to at the very least go over for a few months to hand the reins over more permanently to someone else.'

She nodded as if she understood.

'Miss Salinger and I wanted to discuss this with you girls. We thought you might like to make the voyage with us. It would be a long time at sea and then perhaps six months in India before the trip home.' He watched her face to try to gauge her reaction.

'You wouldn't leave us behind?'

'No, definitely not. Not if you wanted to come with us.' He smiled at her softly. 'If you both really did not wish to go, then Miss Salinger would stay here with you—we would never leave you alone.'

The idea of having to leave Selina behind for what would probably be nearly two years almost ripped him in two, but they had both agreed the girls couldn't lose them both at the same time. Hopefully Priscilla and Theodosia would want to join them on the trip, but if not he knew Selina would have to stay, even if they both would suffer every minute they were apart.

'What do you think?' he prompted her softly. It was so hard to fathom what was going on behind her blue eyes.

'We'd get to see the world, to see India. Of course we'd rather that than staying here.'

He smiled, wanting to lean over and hug his niece, but knowing the movement could unbalance her.

'Good.'

Matthew was about to call ahead to tell Theodosia the plan when he noticed she had got a little further away that she should have.

'I'm going to ride up and get your sister,' he said. 'Wait here, I'll be back soon.'

Urging his horse into a canter, he made up the ground quickly, slowing a few paces before he got level with his younger niece to ensure he did not surprise her horse.

'Time to go back, Theodosia,' he said, showing her how to pull on the reins gently to guide the horse round to face the other way. As they started back he saw Priscilla up ahead turn her horse around and slowly begin to head in the opposite direction.

'Wait for me, Priscilla,' Theodosia called, never liking to be left behind. She urged her horse forward, pressing her heels in just a little too hard and making the mare spring into a canter. Matthew called out, speeding to catch her up, all the time having visions of her slipping from the saddle and falling to the floor.

'Pull on the reins,' he shouted. 'Nice and firmly, but no sudden movements.'

He didn't know if Theodosia had heard him, but there was no slowing of her horse. Quickly he caught up with her and saw in her surprise at the change of speed she'd dropped her hold on the reins and was now fumbling to pick them up. He placed them into her hands and watched as she pulled firmly on them, immediately slowing to a much more sedate pace.

'Well done,' he said, trying not to let on how his heart was hammering away in his chest. 'You handled that well.'

'Thank you,' she said, looking over at him and giving him a beaming smile. Matthew looked back, checking Priscilla was not in any trouble. His eyes widened as he saw her hurtling towards them at high speed, her hair flying loose behind her and a mask of panic on her face. Before he could react Priscilla's horse had raced passed them and in doing so Priscilla's leg had caught Theodosia's. Theodosia was wrenched from the saddle and thrown to the ground with such force Matthew heard a sickening crack and saw her little body bounce and shudder at the impact. In an instant he'd dismounted and was crouching down by her side, praying that she would open her eyes and give him one of her beautiful smiles.

There was nothing, no reaction, no movement, and he felt his whole body tense as he picked up his hand and rested it on her chest, petrified he wouldn't feel the steady thump of her heart. Matthew felt the relief seep through him as he detected her heartbeat and saw the steady rise and fall of her chest with her breathing. Still there was no response to his touch and when he gently opened her eyelid he saw only the whites.

He knew there wasn't much he could do for her out here, so he quickly scooped her up into his arms and laid her gently over the front of his horse. Vaulting up behind her, he picked her up and cradled her as he urged his horse forward, all the time aware he also needed to check Priscilla was unharmed.

Matthew rode as fast as he dared, his mind filled with terrible thoughts and a huge sense of guilt. Theodosia was his responsibility and now she was hurt. Hugging her to him, he almost cried out with relief as he spotted Priscilla, now dismounted and leading her horse at a much more sedate pace. She looked unharmed.

'What's happened to Thea?' There was panic lacing her voice and a raw fear in her eyes.

'She fell. I need to get her back to the house.'

Priscilla nodded, her eyes roaming over Theodosia's limp body.

'I'll send out someone to come and accompany you home,' he said. He hated leaving her here like this, but he knew the most important thing was getting Theodosia back to the house. Priscilla was in the grounds, she would be safe, and one of the grooms would be with her in a matter of minutes.

Spurring his horse on, he made the mistake of looking back at Priscilla's drawn face. She'd lost nearly everyone dear to her and now Theodosia was seriously hurt, too. It was exactly the same look he'd seen on Theodosia's face when Priscilla had been lying in bed delirious with fever and it was a stark reminder of how close the two little girls were, how they relied on one another for love and comfort.

'Help me,' Matthew commanded as he reached the stable yard at the back of the house. Two of the grooms immediately came to his side, lifting down Theodosia while he dismounted. 'Priscilla is out near the dead oak tree, take a horse and go get her as quickly as you can. Brooks, ride for Dr Barrington, ask him to come immediately.'

Gently he took Theodosia back into his arms and headed for the house.

'What's happened?' Selina asked as soon as he walked through the front door. She was by his side immediately, stroking Theodosia's head with concern.

'She fell from her horse,' he said stiffly. It was his fault, his responsibility, and he couldn't bring himself to look Selina in the eye.

'Has she said anything?'

'Nothing. She was knocked unconscious by the fall and hasn't woken. I'll take her up to her bed.'

Selina nodded, following closely behind. Together they manoeuvred the little girl into her bed, with Selina pulling back the sheets before he set her down. When she was lying with her head on the pillow he stepped back, willing Theodosia to open her eyes and feeling his dread deepen when she stayed completely still.

'I've sent for the doctor,' he said, watching all the time for any little sign of movement.

'Thea, darling, open your eyes for me. We're terribly worried.' There was no response, not even a flicker of an eyelid. 'Squeeze my hand if you can, my angel,' Selina said, taking the little girl's limp hand in her own.

Matthew took a step back and then another. It felt as though the walls of the room were moving slowly inwards, slowly coming to crush him. His shirt felt tight at his throat and the muscles of his neck seemed to thicken, making it hard for him to breathe.

'Thea, darling, we're right here with you,' Selina said.

With an effort he pushed away the panic. Right now Theodosia needed him. Later there would be time for recriminations and self-blame, but now he needed to focus on doing whatever he could to help his niece recover.

Slowly he came back across the room to the bed, sitting down beside Selina and reaching out to smooth Theodosia's blonde curls from her forehead. Carefully he ran his fingers across her scalp, probing softly until he found what he was looking for: a large lump, growing by the second, in the hair just below her right temple.

'What happened?' There were tears in her eyes as she turned to him.

'Theodosia lost control so I went after her and helped

her slow down, but then Priscilla's horse was frightened and raced away. Theodosia's leg was caught and it unbalanced her and she tumbled to the ground.' As he spoke he realised how inadequate his supervision had been. Both girls had been inexperienced riders and he should have taken a groom with him to help in a situation such as this.

He looked again at her deadly still form in the bed, having to watch carefully to check for the rise and fall of her chest that showed she was still breathing.

'She'll wake up soon,' Selina said with more conviction than he was sure she felt. 'She has to.'

'Thea,' Priscilla shouted, running into the room. 'Is she awake?'

Matthew felt his heart squeeze as the little girl flung herself towards her unconscious sister, kissing her pale cheeks and lacing their fingers together in a firm grip.

'Wake up, Thea,' Priscilla begged, the tears flowing freely down her cheeks. 'Please wake up.'

Selina made space for Priscilla beside her, allowing the little girl to be cradled in her arms while still holding on tightly to Theodosia.

'The doctor is on his way,' Selina reassured her.

'I'm sorry, Thea. It's all my fault.' Priscilla spoke so quietly Matthew barely heard her and it took a moment for the words to register.

When they did he stood and moved around so he was in front of Priscilla, then knelt down before her. 'It is *not* your fault,' he said firmly. 'Don't ever think that.'

'I lost control of my horse.'

'It was my fault,' Matthew admitted. 'Neither of you was experienced enough to go out with just me. I lost control of the situation. You did absolutely nothing wrong.'

'But I…'

'Absolutely nothing wrong,' he reiterated, waiting for Priscilla to nod before he rose.

They sat in silence for a long time, the minutes ticking past, all mesmerised by the rise and fall of Theodosia's chest, no one daring to look away in case the movement stopped.

Selina glanced at Matthew's drawn face and wished she could reach out and embrace him. Theodosia was being checked over by the doctor, a sombre man whose expressions did not give anything away. Matthew looked full of guilt and pain and every moment that passed without Theodosia waking up he was withdrawing further and further into himself.

'Nothing is broken, nothing is outwardly wrong,' Dr Barrington said eventually, straightening up and turning to address Matthew. 'Most of the time with injuries to the head such as this the patient just wakes up.'

'Most of the time?'

Doctor Barrington shrugged. 'Sometimes they don't...' he held up his hands '...but in this case there are no worrying signs, no seizures, no abnormal movements, no differences in her pupils.'

'When will she wake up?' Selina asked, refusing to believe Theodosia wouldn't come back to them.

'It could be a matter of hours or it could be days. Unfortunately all we can do is wait.'

'There is nothing you can do? Nothing we can do?'

'No.' The doctor picked up his bag and walked towards the door. 'If nothing changes, I will come back tomorrow and see her again. If you have any concerns in the meantime, send someone for me.'

'Thank you,' Matthew said, his voice flat.

Once the doctor had left Selina crossed the room to Matthew and took one of his hands in her own.

'She will wake up,' she said, 'She's so strong.'

He nodded, but Selina could see the doubt and self-recrimination in his eyes.

'I'll bring up some chairs so we can sit with her. I don't want her waking up alone.'

Matthew was only gone for a few minutes before he returned with a couple of footmen in tow, each carrying one of the comfortable armchairs from the library. Priscilla was lying down on the bed next to her sister, stroking her hair and arms, murmuring words that were too quiet for them to hear. Selina marvelled at the bond between the two girls. For a long time they'd only had each other and now she knew nothing would induce Priscilla to move away from her little sister's side.

They sat, each lost in their own thoughts as the light outside faded and the evening drew in. Mrs Fellows appeared to bring them first some tea and then a selection of sandwiches, but the food lay untouched on the tray. Even the sour old housekeeper looked worried and popped into the little bedroom more than was strictly necessary, Selina suspected, to check if anything had changed.

'Get some rest,' Matthew said softly as the evening crept into night. Priscilla had fallen asleep an hour ago, still cradling her little sister, and Selina's eyes had begun to droop as even the candles weren't enough to save the room from darkness. 'I'll sit up with her.'

'I'm not going anywhere,' Selina said. She glanced across at the man she loved and reached out for his hand. 'This isn't your fault,' she said softly.

'It is. I shouldn't have pushed them so hard, shouldn't have expected so much of them. They were inexperienced, but I thought I could handle both of them and now Theodosia is paying the price.'

'It was an unfortunate accident, nothing more. There was no malice, no neglect, it could have happened to anyone.'

'But it didn't.'

Selina knew what he was thinking, she could see it written across his face. It had been the first time he'd taken the girls out alone and Theodosia had been seriously injured. He was doubting his ability to care for them, doubting his suitability as their guardian.

She was about to say something more when there was a little sigh from the bed and immediately both of their heads snapped around. Theodosia was shifting a little, her eyes still closed and the same peaceful expression on her face, but she had rolled over on to her side and curled up as she always did when she was sleeping.

'Thea,' Selina said softly, rising and going to her side. 'Wake up, Thea.'

She almost shouted with relief as the little girl's eyes flickered open and focused on her for a second before closing again.

'She's awake,' Selina said, pulling Matthew over so he could see for himself.

'Thea, open your eyes for me.'

The little girl frowned, wriggling on to her back and screwing up her nose. 'Don't want to,' she muttered.

Selina kissed her on her forehead and cheeks, making her squirm even more. Matthew let out a huge exhalation and Selina saw a little of the tension seep from his shoulders.

'My head hurts,' Theodosia said as she allowed her eyes to open.

'You had an accident,' Selina explained. 'You fell from

your horse and hit your head. I'm sure it'll feel better in the morning.'

Theodosia nodded sleepily and snuggled in to her sister's warm body, promptly closing her eyes and falling back asleep.

Selina turned to Matthew and buried herself in his arms, breathing deeply, feeling her body begin to shake. While Theodosia had been unconscious she had held all of the worry in a tight ball inside her. Now that worry was spilling out. She felt the tears of relief flood her eyes and spill on to her cheeks and wrapped her arms tighter around Matthew as he placed a kiss on her head and began to murmur reassuringly to her.

'She's fine,' she managed to splutter through her tears. 'She's absolutely fine.'

A headache was unpleasant, but was hardly the worst that could have happened and Selina had spent the last few hours imagining the worst.

Matthew nodded, his body still stiff, and Selina knew he would find it hard to forgive himself even now Theodosia had woken up. He'd withdrawn into himself a little, his eyes had become shuttered, any sentences he was forced to say more abrupt than usual.

'Go and rest,' he said insistently when Selina took a step back. 'She's going to need us to look after her these next few days. I'll sit with her for now, you can take over when you're rested.'

His words made sense, but Selina didn't want to leave him alone. She knew he would be sitting here in the dark, mulling over all the ways he had failed his nieces.

Already he had turned away, sitting back in the armchair and focusing his eyes on Theodosia's sleeping form.

Selina hesitated and then slipped out the door. Tomorrow he would see Theodosia was back to normal and there was no lasting damage. Perhaps then he could begin to forgive himself.

Chapter Twenty-Two

Matthew prowled around his study picking up sheets of paper and books of invoices and flicking through them, but not seeing the figures on the pages. He hadn't been able to concentrate on anything for days, not since Theodosia's accident. She had bounced back to her normal self quickly once she'd woken up. For a day she'd complained of headaches, but after that it had been almost as if the accident hadn't happened. At least to the little girl. In Matthew's mind it was happening over and over again.

He knew he was being distant with Selina and the girls, knew he was pushing them away when he needed them the most, but he couldn't seem to help himself. He was caught up in a cycle of self-recrimination and self-doubt. He felt like a failure, the only time he'd looked after the girls on his own and Theodosia had got badly hurt. All the fears and worries from his younger life were resurfacing and once again he was beginning to doubt if he was fit to be entrusted with the care of other people. Perhaps his decision-making abilities were innately flawed.

In frustration he threw down the papers he was carrying. He needed to get outside, get away and have time to think this over.

India, the little voice in his head taunted him. India, where everything was simple, where the only person he had to look after was himself, and no one else got hurt if he failed.

Glancing over his shoulder at the book of maps he had carried with him throughout the long voyage, he hesitated, then retraced his steps and picked them up from the desk. It couldn't hurt to take them with him. Perhaps they would help him decide what he wanted to do with his life, whether he should stay here and try to be a better guardian, to take on responsibility for Selina as well as the girls, or whether to run back to where he felt safe and successful.

Quietly he slipped out the door and padded along the corridor, making his way out to the stables before anyone could see what he was doing. Right now he needed to be alone, to have space to think. Selina would tell him none of this was his fault, but he couldn't accept that. He needed to think long and hard and decide if Selina and the girls would be better off without him.

'The master has gone out,' Mrs Fellows said, her face sour as usual, her eyes flitting over Selina in a disapproving manner.

'Where has he gone?' Since their engagement they had made a habit of having dinner together every evening after the children were in bed. Often the meal was cut short by a stray kiss that led to Matthew tumbling her upstairs to the bedroom and a night spent in each other's arms.

'Out. He didn't deign to tell me he wouldn't be here for dinner.'

Selina frowned. He hadn't told her either.

'Are you sure he's gone?'

'Yes. His horse has gone from the stables and Tom said he left in a hurry earlier this afternoon, carrying a bundle with him.'

Selina felt her heart sink in her chest as if it were made of the heaviest metal.

'He didn't say to Tom where he was going?'

'Ask him yourself.'

Selina stood, smoothing down her dress and trying to cover the absolute panic that was welling up inside her. He'd gone, suddenly and without any message. If it had been an emergency, he would have at least told one of the grooms or stable boys as they were getting his horse ready, he wouldn't ever leave without giving at least a brief message to be passed on.

Unless…she pushed the thought from her mind. He had been hit hard by Theodosia's accident, blaming himself for the tumble she'd taken and the period of unconsciousness afterwards. Selina knew it had dredged up the old feelings of inadequacy, of not doing the right thing for the people he was responsible for, and she'd seen him withdraw into himself.

It didn't seem to matter that Theodosia was back to her normal self, bouncing around and creating havoc everywhere she went. Selina had tried to broach the subject with him a few times, but he'd smiled and told her nothing was the matter. Stubborn man. He was too used to doing everything by himself, coping with everything by himself, he didn't see that talking and sharing could make one see a problem in a different light.

'Tom,' Selina called, spotting the young stable boy as she entered the yard. It was dark and she suspected he was soon heading to bed in his little nook above the stables.

'Yes, miss?'

'I understand you got Lord Westcroft's horse ready for him earlier today.'

'Yes, miss.'

'Did he say anything about where he was going? Or when he would be back?'

'No, miss.'

'Mrs Fellows said he was carrying something with him?'

'A book, miss, all tatty and heavy.'

Selina felt her heart sink. It was his book of maps, the maps he'd carefully hand drawn over the years he'd spent in India. Maps of the country he loved so much, the country where he'd finally been able to be happy in himself.

There wasn't any reason to take them if he was just going for a ride about the countryside or a few drinks in the local tavern.

'He's gone,' she whispered, earning her a puzzled look from Tom. She gave him a weak smile and quickly headed back to the house. Inside she made her way directly to his study, almost raising her hand to knock on the door before she remembered he wasn't there.

There was a noticeable gap on the desk where the tattered book of maps normally sat, a gap that made Selina let out a little cry. Her legs felt weak underneath her and somehow she managed to make it to one of the comfortable armchairs.

She sat there for a moment, still in shock, before the tears started to stream down her cheeks.

'You fool,' she muttered to herself. 'You absolute fool.'

For so long she'd guarded herself against letting anyone close. After the betrayal of her father, after finding out how he had never bothered to marry her mother, she'd said time and time again she would never trust a gentleman, not even one who seemed kind and caring like her father. Then she had fallen for Matthew and pushed away all her doubts, allowing herself to trust and hope, and look where that had got her.

Selina closed her eyes and sobbed, feeling as though her heart was pulling apart in her chest. Every little sound, every little creak of the old house made her look up, hating the hope that flared inside her that Matthew might have made a mistake, that he might have just spent too long in the tavern.

'Enough,' she said eventually. It was completely dark and still outside the window now and the candle she'd brought in with her had burned down to nothing. It was time to go to bed, alone for the first time in weeks, and in the morning she would have to start rebuilding her life for a second time.

Selina awoke with a pounding headache and wished she could just roll over in bed and bury her head under the pillow. Instead she took a few deep breaths and stood up, moving around her room as if she were wading through honey, but eventually managing to get dressed.

Despite the late hour she had turned in Selina had barely slept, spending most of the night tossing and turning until the bedsheets had become so tangled she'd thrown them on to the floor in frustration. Now she felt numb, as if separated from her body and looking down on the world from a distance.

She couldn't pretend that part of her had hoped Matthew would sneak into her bed in the middle of the night, that she'd been wrong in her assumption that he'd left.

The empty space when she had awoken had made the ache in her chest throb and pulse even more.

'What are we doing today?' Theodosia asked, bouncing around the room already, making Selina feel a little nauseous as she tried to follow the rapid movement.

'Are you unwell, Miss Salinger?' Priscilla came closer and peered at Selina's face. 'You look terrible.'

'I do feel a little poorly,' Selina admitted, passing a hand across her forehead. 'Perhaps this morning you girls could choose a book each to read quietly. I'm sure in an hour I'll feel better.' She was sure of no such thing. In an hour Matthew would have still abandoned them and broken her heart.

Priscilla looked as though she were going to say something, but thought better of it, dragging her sister over to the well-stocked bookshelf in the corner of their room and choosing books for both of them.

Selina sat on the window seat, looking out at the gloomy morning. There was a thin fog covering the ground, floating wispily among the flowerbeds. In the sky the sun was pale and weak, hardly breaking through the clouds and bestowing only a little light on the garden below. As she looked out she felt her life slipping away from her, felt that horrible helplessness she had after her father had died and her half-brother had thrown her out.

'No,' she said, louder than she had planned to.

'Is something wrong, Miss Salinger?' Priscilla looked up from her book as she spoke.

'I think I need to do something, girls,' she said, surprising herself with her words. She paused, wondering if it was a foolish notion and then pushed away the doubts. Matthew had left and once again she was at the mercy of a man's whims. That was going to go on no longer. 'I need to travel to Cambridgeshire, to see my brother.'

The idea of confronting her brother, of seeing him again, made her feel giddy, but she knew she could avoid it no longer. She closed her eyes, then nodded resolutely. When she had left London she had heard her brother had moved temporarily to the house in Cambridge while Northrop Hall was undergoing repairs after damage to the roof. It would be hard seeing William living in the home she had loved so much, the home she had hoped would one day be hers, but that couldn't be helped.

'Now?' Theodosia asked.

'Yes. Well, as soon as possible.' If she left it too long, she might lose her nerve.

'What about Lord Westcroft?' Priscilla's eyes were sharp and probing and Selina shifted under her gaze.

'He's gone.' There was no point hiding it from the girls, they would find out at some point their guardian had left. This way they could begin adjusting to his abandonment.

'Gone?'

'I think he's gone back to India,' Selina said, a little more softly.

'Without saying goodbye?'

'He was upset by your accident, I think he blamed himself and somehow told himself we would be better off without him.'

'Are you sure he's gone?'

'He's not here, he took his maps with him, I can't see where else he would be.'

'But he never told you.'

She shook her head, trying to hold back the tears that were threatening to spill.

'He'll be back,' Theodosia said with a conviction Selina envied.

Priscilla nodded, thoughtfully, then turned back to Selina. 'But that shouldn't stop us from going to confront your horrible toad of a brother.'

'You won't be doing any confronting, young lady,' Selina said, having to repress a smile at the thought of William being given Priscilla's hard stare.

'We'll have to come with you, you can hardly leave us here by ourselves.'

It was true. In her fire and anger she hadn't thought what she was going to do with the girls while she stormed into her brother's house and demanded to see her father's will.

'No…' Theodosia's eyes widened theatrically '…you can't leave us behind.'

'I wouldn't leave you behind. Perhaps I should just write to him instead,' Selina said, knowing any letter would probably be thrown in the fire unopened. Then she shook her head resolutely. Matthew had gone, leaving the girls in her care without any instruction or farewell. She *would* take them to Cambridge and she would confront her brother. It was time to take control of her life and if that meant bringing the two little girls along with her then that was what she would do.

'Go to your bedrooms and start to pack a bag,' she instructed. 'We'll be gone for a week, maybe two at the most. I'll come in to help you shortly.'

Selina stood, looking out over the gardens, and wondered if she was making a mistake. Perhaps Matthew would change his mind, perhaps he would decide India wasn't the answer to all his problems. Perhaps, but she couldn't rely on it, she couldn't rely on him. Now she was going to make her own future.

Chapter Twenty-Three

Matthew walked up the drive, leading his horse by the reins. His head was thumping, the consequence of far too much alcohol the night before. It was now twenty-four hours since he'd left Manresa House, twenty-four hours during which he'd drunk copious amounts of alcohol, but also done a lot of thinking. For the first hour in the tavern he'd pored over the maps of India, tracing the familiar lines and invoking all the good memories. He'd regaled the other patrons with tales of tigers and poisonous snakes and the perils of the Indian Ocean, talking into the night, reminiscing.

As dawn had broken he'd still not slept, but a wonderful clarity had stolen over him as the sun had begun to rise in the sky. India had been wonderful, it had been the place he had made his fortune, but more than that it was the place he had learnt to respect himself again. There he had been a success, he'd built something to be proud of, but that didn't mean he should go running back there now.

That would be cowardly. Now he had people he cared about, people he loved. He could never leave Selina behind, the very idea of never seeing her face again made him feel sick to the stomach. And then there were the girls. Again he saw Theodosia's little body bounce as she hit the ground after falling from the back of her horse, he heard the sickening crack and felt the desperate panic that followed.

'You'll never be better if you don't try,' he had murmured to himself.

Suddenly it had all seemed so clear. It was hard caring for someone, hard taking responsibility for them, but it would be even harder to leave them behind.

'I love them,' he'd said, loud enough to draw the landlord in from the small kitchen behind the bar. 'I love them, all three of them.'

'Do you need any assistance, my lord?' the landlord had asked, surveying him critically.

'No. I need to get home.'

Matthew had just left without a word. Selina would be worried. The girls would even notice his absence. He needed to get back to Manresa House.

He'd stood, his head spinning as soon as he'd levered himself to his feet. Instantly he was cursing the alcohol he'd drunk the night before and quickly he had to sit back down.

'I've a comfy bed upstairs, my lord. A few hours' sleep and you'll feel much better.'

He had taken the offer of the bed from the landlord this morning and slept for eight hours straight. When he'd awoken the day was already mostly gone and he'd felt a dread inside him at the thought he'd left Selina on her own and worrying for so long.

He'd ridden most of the way back to Manresa House, the residual headache from his excesses the night before not getting the better of him until he'd reached the wrought-iron gates at the front of the property. There he had dismounted and now he was walking slowly towards the house.

Matthew expected Selina to come running from the door. Perhaps angry, perhaps relieved, but definitely there.

The house was dark, the front door remained closed and when he tried the handle it refused to turn, staying resolutely locked. He hammered on the door, listening for the shuffling footsteps of Mrs Fellows and having to restrain himself from calling out to hurry her along.

'Where's Selina?' he asked before the door was even half-open.

'Gone.' Mrs Fellows looked surprised to see him and took a moment to look him up and down before she remembered who she was speaking to. 'Gone this afternoon, my lord.'

'Gone? Where?'

'To Cambridge.'

'And the girls?'

'She took them with her.'

Matthew had to reach out a hand to steady himself, feeling the rough stone exterior beneath his fingers.

'She said you'd gone to India, my lord, seemed quite convinced of it.'

He closed his eyes, hardly able to restrain the shout of frustration that wanted to break forth from deep inside. He should have anticipated this. Matthew could imagine Selina finding his study in darkness, with no note but just his damned book of maps missing, and jumping to all the wrong conclusions. He knew she found it difficult to trust anyone after what had happened with her father and her brother, he should have anticipated this would happen.

'Cambridge,' he repeated weakly.

'Come inside, my lord. I'll get you something to

eat from the kitchen.' They were the kindest words he thought Mrs Fellows had ever spoken to him and even her expression had softened a little.

Not knowing what else to do, Matthew allowed himself to be led inside. There was a fire burning low in the drawing room and as he slumped into one of the chairs a maid scuttled in to build it up.

Cambridge. Although he would much rather her here in his arms with him, he had to admire her grit. Selina thought she'd been abandoned by the man she loved and instead of wallowing in self-pity she'd decided to take control of her own life and confront her brother over the dubious conditions of her father's will.

Quickly he stood, feeling his head spin for a moment, and cursed again the alcohol he'd imbibed the night before.

'I need to catch them,' he declared to the empty room. On horseback, riding fast, he could catch a carriage that had left a few hours earlier within a day or two at most. Selina would be back in his arms and the girls under his care.

If she'll have you, the voice in his head said. Matthew sank back down into the chair. Surely when she realised he hadn't run away to India, hadn't abandoned her and the girls at the first sign of trouble, then she would forgive him.

'Cook is preparing you a light supper, my lord,' Mrs Fellows said as she stalked into the room.

'I need to go after Miss Salinger and the girls. Tell Roberts I will need a fresh horse and a comfortable saddle.'

'I wouldn't presume to tell you what to do, my lord,' Mrs Fellows said stiffly, in a tone that said she was about to do exactly that, 'but it is dark outside and the roads are treacherous at this time of year. You will hardly be any use to anyone with a broken neck.'

He opened his mouth to protest, but deep down he knew Mrs Fellows was right.

'Damn,' he cursed, pressing his lips together to stop any further profanities escaping.

'I'll tell Roberts to have the horse ready for you at first light.'

'Thank you.'

He leaned back in the chair, wondering if he would still be able to catch up with Selina and the girls before they reached Cambridge. He would give anything to be holding Selina in his arms, kissing her, carrying her upstairs to their bed.

Tomorrow, he promised himself. Tomorrow he would ride at such a pace it would be as if he were flying towards Selina. Tomorrow he would hold her tight in his arms and never let her go again.

Chapter Twenty-Four

Selina felt her heart lift as she looked out of the carriage windows and saw the familiar spires of Cambridge. Nerves had threatened to overcome her throughout the journey, but now she was back in the city where she'd been born and raised she felt a strange calm come over her.

'These buildings on your right are the colleges,' Selina said, marvelling at the beautiful buildings. When she'd lived here they had become part of the scenery, little noticed, but after a period away she could appreciate their elegance anew. 'This is St John's and the next one is Trinity College, founded by Henry VIII.'

Both girls had their noses pressed up against the windows of the carriage, taking in the bustling little city filled with scholars and townspeople.

'What's that one?' Theodosia pointed to the grand façade of King's College chapel.

'The chapel at King's College,' Selina said.

'It's beautiful here, and big, much bigger than Whitby. Why would you ever want to leave?'

'She didn't, remember, Thea,' Priscilla said, shaking her head at her sister.

They had just reached King's Parade and soon would be crossing into Trumpington Street and the house where Selina had spent her childhood. Inside her chest her heart begun to flutter and she knew she needed to get herself under control before she confronted her brother. Not for the first time in the last three days she wished she had Matthew there beside her, with a soft word in her ear and a reassuring squeeze of her hand, and she would be ready to storm into her brother's house and demand to know the truth.

Quickly she pushed the idea away. It would do no good to dwell on what she'd lost, instead she had to keep moving forward, otherwise she suspected her heart would break entirely and her body cease to function.

'Can we go somewhere else first?' she called out of the window to the coachman.

'Where would you like to go, miss?' He was an affable man with a thick Yorkshire accent that Selina found difficult to interpret, but kind eyes and a loud and unabashed laugh.

'There's a little church in Trumpington I'd like to go to first,' Selina said, picturing the old stone building. 'If you carry on down this road out of the city you'll come to the village of Trumpington.'

'Right you are, miss.'

Selina sat back on her seat and smiled at the girls as they gave her enquiring looks.

'The church where my mother always said they got married,' she explained. 'I went there after my father died and the vicar denied any knowledge of the marriage, he even said he'd checked the register.'

'Do you believe him?' Priscilla asked.

'He's a man of God, surely he wouldn't lie...'

They all settled in for the ride out of the city. The street soon became much quieter and it wasn't long before there were more green spaces between the buildings.

After twenty minutes they entered the village of Trumpington and immediately the square tower was visible. The carriage stopped in front of the church and for a moment Selina didn't move.

'Would you like to wait here, girls?'

'No.'

'Definitely not,' they said at the same time.

She shrugged, hopping down from the carriage and turning back to help the girls alight. The walk up the path reminded her of the same walk she'd done nearly two years ago after her brother had revealed her parents had never married. Then she'd still been in the first stages of grief, tense with shock and filled with the sensation of loss.

As they approached the church Selina saw the tall, thin figure dressed in black she'd spoken to before emerging from a side door. His walk was loping and his shoulders hunched as if he were trying to make himself smaller somehow.

'Good afternoon,' Selina called out, watching the vicar's face as he turned in surprise. His expression went from mild puzzlement to overt guilt and he even recoiled a few steps as he remembered who she was. 'I was hoping I might have a few moments of your time.'

He glanced back over his shoulder as if considering whether he could vault the low wall around the churchyard and make his escape up the High Street, but seemed to think better of it.

'You'd better come into the vicarage,' he said with a resigned murmur.

Selina followed him through the little gate at the side

of the churchyard into the vicarage garden and up the path to the front door. He opened it and motioned for Selina and the girls to go inside before him, then led them through to a comfortable but small room with a couple of armchairs.

'You remember me,' Selina prompted him when she sat down.

'You're Lord Northrop's daughter.'

'Forgive me, I've forgotten your name.'

'Father Whittle,' he supplied with a watery smile. 'I had wondered if you would come back and see me again.'

An older woman bustled into the room, bringing a tray of tea and setting it down on a little table. She smiled warmly at Selina and turned to the girls.

'I've got some biscuits fresh out of the oven if you would like to come and test them for me.'

Theodosia was on her feet immediately, but Priscilla gave Selina a questioning look.

'Go and try them,' Selina said quietly. 'I'll come and fetch you in just a moment.'

'Ever since your last visit I have been plagued with guilt,' he said quietly once the girls had disappeared into the kitchen. 'I wronged you and I had no way of putting it right.'

'Wronged me? In what way?' She felt a flare of hope, but tried to keep it under control. He might mean something else entirely.

Father Whittle sighed and passed a hand through his thick grey hair.

'I was approached by the new Lord Northrop a few days before your visit,' he said, not able to look Selina in the eye. 'He knew some…troubling things about my past and he threatened to reveal them. I would have lost my position here, my livelihood, my home.'

She forced herself to nod, kept her lips pressed to-gether so she wouldn't rush him. She needed to hear the story in full in his words, only then would she be able to decide what the truth was.

'He said he would keep quiet, even become my patron in the future, if I did one little favour for him.' Father Whittle looked up and caught her eye, his expression be-seeching. 'I knew it was wrong, knew I should say no to him, but I was selfish and thought only of myself.'

'What did he ask you to do?' Her voice was flat, de-void of sympathy for this man who had helped to ruin her life as she knew it.

'He wanted me to deny I had married your parents and to destroy the evidence of their union.'

'So when I came to see you…?'

'I did as he asked, I told you I had not performed the ceremony all those years ago.'

'And the marriage record? Did you destroy it?'

He looked at her for a moment, then shook her head. 'Lord Northrop asked me to and I told him I had, but I couldn't bring myself to destroy that permanent record. I hid the book instead.'

'May I see it?'

Slowly he rose, his first couple of steps stiff and hesi-tant, and Selina wondered if he would return when he left the room without a backward glance. Two minutes later he did reappear with a heavy leather-bound book in his arms.

'All of the marriages from 1790 to 1800,' he said. Se-lina's parents would have been married in 1790 or 1791 at the latest, right at the beginning of this particular re-cord book. Hesitantly he passed over the book and with her heart thumping in her chest Selina opened it.

The entries were in neat black ink, rows of names

of the couples who had married in this church in date order. Halfway down the second page Selina stopped, tears welling in her eyes.

Alexander Harrow, Viscount Northrop, and Amelia Salinger
1st July 1790

'They *were* married,' Selina whispered. She thought of every unkind word, every curse she'd made against her father and burst into tears. 'I'm sorry, Papa,' she whispered. 'I should never have doubted you.' It had been so hard being suddenly alone in the world, but perhaps she should have fought a little harder against her brother's lies.

'I have regretted my decision to lie to you every single day,' Father Whittle said softly. 'I wanted to write, to tell you what I had done, but no one I asked knew where you had gone.'

'You truly regret what you did?'

'I do.'

'Then come with me when I confront my brother. I will need you to show my brother his web of lies has been uncovered.' The vicar blanched, but eventually nodded, wringing his hands at the thought of tangling with Selina's brother. 'We'll go now. I've waited for almost two years, two years of hardship and misery. I will not wait any longer.'

She stood, only pausing to check he was following on behind, and swept out of the door. In the hall she called out to the girls and they came hurrying out of the kitchen with a little parcel of biscuits.

As they returned to the carriage both Priscilla and Theodosia were looking at Selina expectantly. It was lovely having them so concerned about her happiness and she felt a pang of deep sadness that Matthew wasn't here to share the end of the journey with them. Then the sadness was replaced by anger. He *could* be here, if he'd only shared exactly what had been going on in his mind. Then they could have worked through it together.

Now was not the time to get all maudlin about Matthew. She had a viscount to confront and she needed her mind on the task in hand.

'Take us back to Trumpington Street,' she said to the coachman.

'Perhaps you should wait outside,' Selina said as she eyed the house that had once been her safe haven. Now it looked a little sinister in the early evening light.

'No,' Priscilla said firmly. 'We're coming in.'

'I could wait outside,' Father Whittle said, giving her a nervous smile.

'No, you're definitely coming in.' Selina scrutinised Priscilla and Theodosia, wondering what best to do with them. She didn't like the idea of leaving them unattended in the carriage, but the confrontation inside the house might become heated and that wasn't the best environment for the children either. She had to hope some of the old servants were still in position, a friendly face to whisk the children off downstairs while she discussed the matter with her brother.

Selina stepped down from the carriage, ensuring everyone was following her before she opened the black wrought-iron gate and started up the path to the house.

'Selina,' a voice called out behind her, a voice that made her forget to breathe for almost half a minute.

Unable to trust her ears, she slowly turned around

and blinked a few times at the figure approaching in the semi-darkness.

'Matthew?' she whispered.

He didn't reply, just walked up to her and swept her into his arms.

'I thought you'd left,' she said. 'You had left. You disappeared.'

He grimaced. 'I was a fool, Selina, forgive me for not telling you where I was going. I felt as though I were collapsing under the guilt and the weight of responsibility after Theodosia's accident. I needed some time to myself.' He pulled away a little and surveyed her, stroking his fingers down her cheek. 'I went to the Wheel and Compass and drank rather too much, I had to sleep it off the next day.'

Selina's eyes widened, trying to piece together everything that had happened with his words.

'You never meant to go to India? But you took your maps.'

'To reminisce.' He shrugged. 'I don't think I can honestly say it never crossed my mind to run away and hop on a ship back to India. I'm sorry, my love. But as I thought more about it, I realised what I have here is much more important than anything I could ever have over there.' He looked at her earnestly and Selina felt herself swaying towards him. He was hard to resist with his honesty and the concern in his eyes.

'You disappeared,' she said. 'And you considered going. Next time how do I know the lure of India won't win out?'

He moved in so they were only inches apart. 'I promise you,' he said, his voice low and earnest, 'and I will not break my vow to you. I will never leave you. We will face everything together.'

For a long moment she studied him. Her body and her heart were crying out for her to believe him, but her mind just needed a few more seconds.

'I think my heart broke when I thought you'd left.'

Matthew raised a hand and placed it on her cloak over where her heart was thumping away in her chest.

'Then I will spend the rest of my life doing everything I can to mend it.'

Selina nodded, closing her eyes for a moment as she felt overcome by relief.

'I'm sorry, too,' she said quietly. 'For not trusting in you, for thinking the worst.'

'I understand why you did. Although it was a bit of a shock to get back from the tavern to find my fiancée and nieces had all disappeared.'

'Forgive me?' She knew now what a mistake she'd made and couldn't imagine how Matthew had felt coming home to find that she and the girls had disappeared. 'I was too quick to doubt you.'

Matthew leaned in. 'Perhaps we can spend the rest of our lives making it up to one another,' he said, his words tickling her ear.

Selina was about to reply when Theodosia launched herself at Matthew. 'I knew you'd come after us,' she said as she was swung up into his arms. 'I told Miss Salinger you wouldn't leave.'

'Never,' he said, planting a kiss on the top of her head.

Priscilla stepped forward, 'I thought you'd come, too, but much, *much* quicker.'

Matthew grinned. 'I had every intention of catching up with you before you even left Yorkshire, but I was plagued with bad luck. My horse lost a shoe and then everywhere I went there was a shortage of fast mounts to take me on the next leg of my journey.'

'Well, I think it's perfect,' Theodosia declared. 'You're here just in time to see Miss Salinger shout at her brother.'

Matthew turned to her. 'Shout? Well, I am looking forward to this.'

'Not shout,' Selina corrected them, 'but I am planning on having harsh words with him. He lied about my parents' marital status,' she explained quietly, 'and I think he lied about the will.'

'I'm right here with you, my love,' he said, slipping his hand into hers.

Head high, back straight, shoulders down.

She knocked on the door, almost breaking out into a wide smile as Mrs Shelby, the motherly housekeeper, opened the door. The older woman's face lit up at the sight of Selina and she rushed out on to the step to embrace her.

'Excuse me, my dear, I'm just so happy to see you. We've been so worried about you. All this time and we had no idea if you were even alive.'

Selina held Mrs Shelby to her again, feeling transported back to her childhood at the familiar scent and embrace.

'I'm very well, Mrs Shelby, although I've missed everyone here sorely.'

'I'm so glad you're safe, I've prayed for you every night since you left, thought about you every day.'

'Is my brother home, Mrs Shelby? I need to speak to him with some urgency.'

'He is. He's having dinner. If you wait in the drawing room, I'll let him know you're here.'

Selina stepped inside her old home, feeling all the memories come flooding back. The mirror where her mother would adjust her bonnet every time she left the house, the stairs where Selina would sit and wait for her father to finish working in his study so he could teach her Greek or Latin or tell her about the brave and daring Greek heroes. And the drawing room where she and her mother had sat together, talking about everything and nothing as Selina had grown into a young woman.

'Could you perhaps take the children downstairs?' Selina asked before Mrs Shelby disappeared. 'I don't want them to hear what I have to say.' She turned to Father Whittle. 'You go, too. I'll call for you when you're needed.'

'Of course, my dear. Why don't you follow me, girls, I'll see if we have any dessert left over.'

Matthew and Selina were left alone in the drawing room and immediately they moved so they were standing side by side. Selina held on to his hand, drawing strength from the man she loved. She wasn't sure if she would have been able to go through with this without Matthew there by her side. It showed her how much they needed one another.

'Selina.' Her brother's flat, nasally voice came through the door before him.

'William.'

'This is a surprise.' William stopped as he entered the room and saw Matthew standing there beside her. 'I don't think we have been introduced.'

'Westcroft,' Matthew said shortly, not offering his hand to the other man.

Selina saw her brother stiffen. A man like William didn't like to be outranked, it meant he couldn't use the air of superiority so easily.

'What can I do for you, Sister?' Selina noted he didn't enquire as to how she'd been these past two years since he'd thrown her out without a penny.

'I want to see Father's will,' Selina said.

'Whatever for?' He was good, Selina had to give him that, but there was a slight flicker before the smooth response.

'Father loved me, he would have provided for me.'

'I told you at the time, *I* was his heir, *I* inherited the title, the estate, the money. He wasn't even married to your…mother.' He almost spat out the last word.

'Yes, he was,' Selina said serenely.

'No, he wasn't. You went to the church…you spoke to the vicar. He told you the sordid truth. You're a bastard, a nobody.'

Beside her she felt Matthew bristle and had to quickly fling out a hand to warn him to stay back before he punched her brother in the face. Not that William didn't deserve it, he deserved that and so much more, but finally Selina was going to be the one to stand up to him.

'Father Whittle,' she shouted, probably much louder than she needed to.

Selina watched her brother's face, saw the expression turn from confusion to disbelief to outright panic as the elderly vicar came into the room.

'You,' he spat out, looking as though he wanted to throw the clergyman out of the window.

'I went to talk to Father Whittle before I came to call on you,' Selina said, taking a step towards her brother's stocky form. 'He told me of his regret in allowing himself to be blackmailed by you into denying my parents' marriage. A marriage that did go ahead.'

'You worthless little…' William swore, turning on the vicar.

Father Whittle took a step back, bumping into a small table and having to reach out and steady himself.

'It does make one wonder,' Matthew said quietly, 'if you lied about that, what else did you lie about?'

'I have no idea what you're talking about,' William blustered.

'I should imagine it was rather easy. Your sister was grieving, in no position to dispute anything you said. All you needed was a crooked solicitor to lie about the will and you could be rid of Selina and the money I have no doubt her father bequeathed her would now be in your pocket.'

'That is slander.'

'I wish to see Father's will,' Selina said. 'I know his signature, I helped him with his correspondence for years. Show me the will and if all is in order I will leave you alone and be out of your life for ever.'

'I don't have it here. It was eighteen months ago. It will be with the solicitors, *if* they kept a copy.'

'I was thinking about that,' Matthew said. 'Who made your father's will? He must have had his own solicitor.'

'Mr Humphries. He passed away a little before Father.' Selina eyed her brother. 'But he had a son, also a solicitor, I'm sure he will be pleased to help us get to the bottom of this.'

'There is nothing to get to the bottom of,' William said, drawing himself up. 'I am the son and heir, you are nothing, an afterthought with the daughter of a housekeeper.'

'Lord Northrop,' Matthew said, his voice cold and hard and authoritative, 'I think you are one of the worst kinds of people. A cheat, a crook, the sort of man who would turn out his vulnerable sister and pocket the money that was rightfully hers.' He held up a hand to stop William from interrupting and Selina was surprised to see her brother close his mouth and remain silent. 'I've been making enquiries about you. I know of your political aspirations, your desire to climb higher through the ranks of society. And I know how much someone like you values your reputation.'

Selina watched as her brother weighed up Matthew's words, as if deciding whether to listen a little longer or throw them out there and then.

'I am willing to offer you a deal. Show us the will, the genuine will, and hand over what is rightfully Selina's and all this will remain private. Not a word will get out to those you seek to cultivate as your patrons.' William gave Matthew a long, hard look. 'Continue to deny your deception and I will pursue you with all the might of my power and influence and money. No one in England will be ignorant of the sort of man you are.'

William stood completely still for ten seconds, his eyes flicking between Selina and Matthew, his expression unreadable. Eventually he spoke. 'I will see you at Mowbry's solicitors tomorrow at ten.'

Selina felt like shouting with joy. They hadn't seen the actual will yet, but she knew it would contain some provision for her, and more than that she knew that everything she had thought about her father when he had been alive, about his love for her and his love for her mother, had been true.

Matthew offered her his arm and together they walked out of the drawing room, trailed closely by Father Whittle. Outside in the hall Mrs Shelby was waiting for them and quickly bustled downstairs to fetch the children.

'Did you win?' Theodosia asked as she came into the hallway.

'I rather think we did,' Selina said, taking the little girl's hand.

'Good.' Priscilla was close behind her. 'I don't like bullies.'

'Come.' Matthew gathered them all together and ushered them out into the street. 'I'd rather not stay here for any longer than we have to.'

Selina followed Matthew out on to the street, feeling dazed with shock. They had just spent the last half an hour with a shifty solicitor and her brother, going through her father's will. There had been the expected initial bluster, where the solicitor had pretended to have misplaced his copy, quickly remedied when Matthew had reiterated his threat to make William's shady deeds public. Finally the solicitor had brought out a pristine copy of her father's will, complete with genuine signature.

'It seems you are now a lady of means,' Matthew said with a triumphant smile. 'Probably one of the most eligible of the Season.'

'Perhaps I was too hasty in agreeing to marry you,' she said, unable to keep the smile from her lips.

'Ah, but you did agree and a woman of good moral character such as yourself would never go back on such a promise.'

'Very true. It would seem I am stuck with you.'

He stopped for a moment, spinning her to face him.

'Congratulations,' he said, 'on finally getting the truth from your brother.'

'I couldn't have done it without you.'

'You could. I just sped things along.'

It was true—without Matthew she would have one day found out what her father's will had contained, but Matthew and his influence had hastened that moment probably by a couple of months.

'You now have a house to retreat to when I become too much to bear,' he said.

'Thank goodness for that.' Not that Selina ever thought she would want to spend a night away from her husband to be. Still, it would be nice to spend time in the house she had called her home until the death of her father. In his will he'd been scrupulously fair, splitting the property and money quite equally between his two children. William had inherited Northrop Hall where he'd spent much of his childhood and Selina the house in Cambridge where she'd spent much of hers. William had inherited the money, but Selina had been granted a very generous allowance, meaning she could live in comfort for the rest of her life. It was fair, just as her father had always been.

'I'm very glad I met you,' Selina said, looking up into his dark eyes and feeling the familiar warmth spread through her body. 'Do you know, I considered turning round and running back to London when I first set eyes on Manresa House. I'm very glad I didn't.'

'I'm very glad you didn't, too.'

Drawing her in closer, Matthew kissed her, running his hands down the length of her back. Selina felt the rest of the world slipping away as Matthew filled all her thoughts.

'Ew, they're kissing again,' Theodosia said.

'They're *always* kissing,' Priscilla said with a resigned air, shaking her head as if she had to put up with more than a nine-year-old should.

'Always kissing,' Matthew murmured in her ear. '*That* sounds like a good idea.'

Selina took his arm, smiling as Theodosia grasped hold of her free hand. Priscilla slipped her hand into the crook of Matthew's other elbow and together they walked down the street. Her perfect little family she'd found in the most unlikely of places.

Epilogue

Matthew closed his eyes and spent a moment revelling in the warm sun and the spray of sea on his face. They were making good progress, after a week spent barely moving as the wind dropped and the ship bobbed without travelling more than a mile in a twenty-four-hour period. Soon they would catch their first glimpse of India and already he could feel the anticipation building.

'Can you see anything yet?' Selina asked as she emerged from below decks with Theodosia and Priscilla in tow. She was holding two letters in her hand, the correspondence she'd promised to write her friends Violet and Felicity on the voyage after a tearful farewell just before she had boarded the ship. There would be no opportunity to post them before India and Selina had asked the Captain of their ship to take them back on the return voyage.

'Not yet. Keep watching the horizon, I think you'll see the first outline of the shore very soon.'

He watched indulgently as Priscilla and Theodosia jostled for the best position, settling themselves up against the rail and squinting into the distance. As the wind whipped their hair backwards he was reminded of his brother looking wistfully out to sea as they stood on the beach at Whitby as children. These last few months he'd noticed more and more of his brother in the two little girls he loved so much. They reminded him of the boy he'd looked up to, the boy who had been his ally throughout a difficult childhood. For so many years he'd forgotten that boy, all his memories overshadowed by the betrayal over Elizabeth and Henry's part in that, but slowly he was coming to accept that Henry had only been young himself at that time and had lived with constant pressure from their father. Matthew smiled to himself—his older brother couldn't have been that terrible if he'd helped to raise two such wonderful little girls.

'How are you feeling?' he asked Selina, stepping down and coming round behind her, wrapping his arms around her middle.

It was his favourite position at the moment, allowing his arms to cup her stretched belly, his hands pressing against her skin. Every so often he would be rewarded with a little kick from the baby nearly fully grown inside.

'I'm looking forward to feeling solid ground underneath my feet,' Selina admitted. She'd suffered the first half of the voyage with terrible sickness. At first they had assumed it was from the motion of the ship, but as time passed and everyone else found their sea legs Selina had confided in him that she thought something more might be contributing to her nausea. Sure enough her tummy had begun to swell and now by their calculations she was almost eight months pregnant.

'Solid ground and a proper bed,' he said. 'And a meal cooked with fresh ingredients.'

'Vegetables.' Selina sighed. 'I don't know how you lived aboard ships when you were in the navy. I can cope with one voyage, but only because I know it will end.'

Right now his time in the navy seemed a distant memory—everything before Selina seemed a distant memory. He couldn't imagine what he had done with his days before they were filled with the laughter and arguments of his nieces and the soothing words and sweet nature of his wife.

It would be strange returning to India with his family in tow, but they had all decided it was necessary. Matthew needed to spend a little time sorting out his business, finding the right people to hand over responsibility to and organise things so he could run it from England going forward. There had been no question of leaving Selina and the girls behind, so together they had planned the trip, deciding that there was no better time. They would likely be gone from England for two years, with the length of the voyages and the need to spend some time travelling round to tie things up. Priscilla was ten, so even if they were away a little longer than anticipated they would still be back in England in plenty of time for her to begin learning how to deport herself as a debutante.

'I'm glad we didn't turn back,' Selina said, allowing herself to sink into his arms.

'Me, too.' When they had discovered Selina was pregnant he had offered to find them all a passage back to England so Selina could give birth at home. She had waved away the suggestion, telling him thousands of women gave birth in India every day. He'd acquiesced, having learnt that when Selina set her mind to something it wasn't easily changed.

'There,' Priscilla shouted, pointing into the horizon. 'I can see land.'

Matthew and Selina turned to the rail, both looking out over the sparkling blue water. Five seconds passed and then ten before Matthew could focus on the very faint outline of the coast of India.

'I see it,' he said, giving Priscilla a one-armed hug. 'Good spot.'

'I see it, too,' Theodosia shouted, jumping with excitement. 'I can see India.'

Silently Matthew gathered the girls and Selina to him and together they watched as the faint line on the horizon grew and became clearer, taking the shape of the country he loved so much. Now he would get to share it with them, to experience it with the people he loved the most.

'When I walked up to Manresa House for the first time in the cold October rain this wasn't where I pictured myself ending up,' Selina said quietly. 'I might not have been able to imagine how my life would unfold, but I'm very pleased with how it has.'

He kissed her, ignoring the over-dramatic sighs from Priscilla and Theodosia, pulling her into his arms and holding her tight to him.

'I love you,' he whispered in her ear. 'Never forget that.'

'I love you, too. More, in fact.'

'That's not possible.'

'Don't you doubt it. I've travelled across half the world for you. Queasiness and all.'

'That is commitment,' he murmured. 'But don't forget you also shot me in the foot with an arrow.'

Selina pulled away slightly, her face taking on what he thought of as her governess expression.

'That was entirely your fault,' she said, pausing for a moment with a little smile on her face, 'although I can't pretend the memory of it doesn't make me chuckle every now and then.'

'Heartless,' Matthew said. 'I wonder why I love you so.'

'Do you?'

He kissed her softly. 'Never. You're my saviour, my heart, my anchor.'

'That's a lot to live up to.'

'Good job you're the most talented woman I know.'

Selina turned back to the rail, allowing her body to relax into his arms. She studied the ever-growing shoreline while he studied her profile.

'I love you,' he murmured into her hair, before planting a kiss on her temple. Around them the sailors were calling out, busy preparing the ship for its arrival, but Matthew hardly noticed any of it. Instead all he could think of was Selina and his little family, and all the wonders he wanted to show them in the coming months.

He felt perfectly contented, perfectly relaxed...and then Theodosia started to lean out a little too far over the rail.

'Get back,' he called, pulling her by her dress as he felt her body begin to topple.

She tumbled to the deck and Matthew closed his eyes. Never would he be able to relax again. Despite himself he grinned. At least life wasn't dull with Selina and the girls to keep him on his toes.

* * * * *

If you enjoyed this book, be sure to check out the
Scandalous Australian Bachelors miniseries
by Laura Martin

Courting the Forbidden Debutante
Reunited with His Long-Lost Cinderella
Her Rags-to-Riches Christmas